A Wolf in the Woods

Also by Nancy Allen

The Code of the Hills

A Killing at the Creek

The Wages of Sin

A Wolf in the Woods

An Ozarks Mystery

NANCY ALLEN

WITNESS
IMPULSE
An Imprint of HarperCollins*Publishers*

This book is a work of fiction. References to real people, events, establishments, organizations, or locales are intended only to provide a sense of authenticity, and are used fictitiously. All other characters, and all incidents and dialogue, are drawn from the author's imagination and are not to be construed as real.

Digital Edition FEBRUARY 2018 ISBN: 978-0-06-243878-2

Print Edition ISBN: 978-0-06-243879-9

Cover photographs: © Morgan Somers / Shutterstock; © yfwong / Getty Images (trees)

FIRST EDITION

18 19 20 21 22 LSC 10 9 8 7 6 5 4 3 2 1

For Randy,
ever and always

Acknowledgments

TAKING THIS NOVEL from the seed of an idea to publication has been a joy, and it's a pleasure to recognize some of the folks who assisted in the journey. I want to thank my fabulous editor Nicole Fischer for her discerning eye as we crafted the story into its final form. My agent, Jill Marr of the Sandra Dijkstra Literary Agency, is an unwavering source of support. I'm indebted to my copy editor, Tracy Wilson, for her fine work. Showers of thanks go to my friend Cassie Priest for her outstanding editorial assistance. Professor Stanley Leasure generously shared examples of regional vernacular. And I couldn't have tackled the subject matter of this story without the wise counsel and legal expertise of Jill Patterson, John Appelquist and Susan Appelquist.

As always, I must thank the three people who mean more to me than words can express: my beloved husband Randy, my precious Ben, my darling Martha.

"Beware of the false prophets, who come to you in sheep's clothing, but inwardly are ravenous wolves."

Matthew 7:15

"Behold, I send you out as a sheep in the midst of wolves; so be shrewd as serpents and innocent as doves."

Matthew 10:16

"The better to eat you with, my dear."

Brothers Grimm, 1812

Prologue

A DARK-HAIRED MAN lounged behind a battered desk in a second-floor room at an EconoMo Motel that sat on the highway in fly-over country, Missouri. He pulled up Skype on his laptop and studied his own image on the computer screen, rubbing the tattoo that covered his neck. Behind him, the unmade bed was visible on the screen. A thin cotton sheet covered the form of a young girl.

He adjusted the angle to cut her from the shot. The bed disappeared, replaced by beige curtains at the window, hanging askew on the rod.

The place was a dump. He could afford better accommodations, without a doubt. It was business, and business was booming. His greatest challenge was procuring sufficient supply to meet the constant demand.

On the desktop, bottles were scattered near the computer. Alprazolam. Oxycodone. Rohypnol. Diazepam. Three value packs of Benadryl: cherry flavored. A plastic bottle of Aristocrat vodka sat beside a jumbo container of Hawaiian Punch.

As he pushed them aside, the bottle of roofies rolled off the desktop and onto the dirty carpet. He caught it just before it rolled under the dresser.

A ding notified him: his Skype appointment was ready. Right on time. He liked the girls to be punctual.

He hit the button on the mouse and fixed a smile on his face. "Lola! How you doing, baby!"

A giggling girl with a mane of curly blond hair greeted him onscreen. "Tony, you're so funny. I'm not Lola, I've told you a zillion times."

"But you look like a Lola. If you want to make it in the modeling trade, you'll have to project glamour. Drama." He stretched his arms over his head, displaying muscled biceps covered in ink, and locked his hands behind his neck.

"Cool." Her eyes shone.

"Leave that country girl persona behind in Podunk. Where are you from again?"

"Barton. Barton, Missouri. Where's Podunk?"

He laughed, running his hand over his thick hair. "Podunk is where you're sitting right now. What you're itching to ditch. How's life?"

Desiree shrugged, pulling a face.

"They still giving you shit at school, baby?"

She rolled her head back onto her neck. "All. The. Time."

"And how's living at home?"

"Lame."

"Wish you could leave it all behind?"

"Totally."

The girl turned her head; he heard a whisper from someone off-screen. Sharply, he asked, "Are you alone?"

A second head appeared over Lola's shoulder. He saw a mixed-race girl. She was taller than Lola, but he pegged her at the same age: an adolescent, around fourteen.

And she was a diamond in the rough—a black diamond. Unblemished skin, full lips, high cheekbones. Lola said, "You asked if I had any friends who wanted to meet you."

He smiled, tapping his hand on the counter. "Who's this?"

The tall girl looked at her friend, then into the computer. "I'm Taylor Johnson."

"And you're interested in modeling?"

She blinked. A nervous twitch. He shot a grin, to reassure her. "You've got the bone structure for it."

The tall girl pinched her lips together. "Maybe. I think so."

"We'll need to conduct some auditions by video, maybe an interview, before you can qualify for a live shoot at the agency."

She looked skittish. He wouldn't get anything from her today.

"Let's just get acquainted, okay?" He was about to launch into his patter: find out her story, gain her trust.

But a moan sounded from the bed behind him. The girl was coming around. He glanced over, fearful that she might raise a ruckus that could scare off his new prospects.

Tony picked up his phone. "Aw shit. Call's coming in from one of our clients. I gotta take it." He winked and shut off Skype just in time.

In a weak voice, the girl said, "Tony. Help me. Please, take off the cuffs."

He sighed. Picking up a dirty plastic cup, he poured a measure of vodka and Benadryl, and topped it off with the red punch.

The girl spoke again, in a pleading tone. "Don't make me do it, Tony. It hurts."

He stirred the drink with his finger and walked toward the

bed. “Mandy, Mandy. You look like you could use a magic drink, baby. This will fix you right up.”

The girl tried to sit up as he extended the red plastic cup. Tony stared down at her, shaking his head. “What’s that saying? ‘The customer is always right.’ You know what you got to do.”

The girl began to thrash against the mattress. But she was handcuffed to the metal bed frame.

Chapter 1

Seated at the counsel table in the Associate Circuit Court of McCown County, Missouri, Elsie Arnold watched the judge toy with the file folder before him on the bench.

Judge Calvin ran a hand through his prematurely silver hair. "I'm binding him over, ladies. But it's a close call."

Elsie heard her co-counsel, Assistant Prosecutor Breeon Johnson, exhale with relief. Elsie wanted to echo it. The judge was right; the preliminary hearing on the felony assault was not an open and shut case. Their victim was a homeless man who had been inebriated at the time of the attack; and though his injuries were grievous, his testimony was spotty. Seemed like he'd forgotten more than he could recall.

After the judge left the bench, Elsie twisted in her seat to check the clock at the back of the courtroom. "That ran long."

Breeon nodded. "We're working overtime, girl."

Elsie snorted. For a county prosecutor, the idea of overtime was a fiction. As salaried public servants, they routinely worked long hours with no additional compensation.

The women exited the courtroom and walked the worn marble stairway down to the second floor of the century-old county building. Their footsteps echoed in the empty rotunda. The McCown County Courthouse, an imposing stone structure, had graced the center of the town square of Barton, Missouri, for over a century. While other county seats in southwest Missouri had opted to build new structures, to accommodate twenty-first century demands of security and technology, McCown County voters stubbornly clung to the old facility.

"Five thirty, and it's a ghost town," Elsie said.

"Not quite. My baby is waiting for me in my office."

At the bottom of the stairway, they exchanged a look. Elsie didn't need to speak the obvious: Breeon's daughter would be highly impatient with the delay.

But who could blame her? Taylor was a fourteen-year-old kid. Hanging around the empty courthouse was a snooze. Breeon, a single mother who hailed from St. Louis, Missouri, tried to keep regular hours. While Bree was a dedicated prosecutor, her devotion to duty was bested by her devotion to her teenage daughter.

Elsie, on the other hand, was a local product: a Barton, Missouri, native. Still single, at the age of thirty-two. And still enjoying her extended adolescence.

As they entered the McCown County Prosecutor's Office, Breeon made a beeline for her office. "Tay-Tay! I'm done, hon."

Elsie poked her head into the open doorway of Breeon's office. Taylor sat behind Breeon's desk. Her hand was on the computer mouse.

With a sulky face, she said, "Finally. I've been bored af."

"Uh-uh." Bree's voice was sharp. "I don't like that *af* talk. Don't use it when you're around me, do you hear?"

Elsie's eyes darted to the wall. The *af* abbreviation was a common sight in her texts. And her tweets. So much speedier than actually spelling out the words.

"Baby, have you been on my computer?"

"Yeah. Just for something to do."

"Taylor, it's the county's computer. We're not supposed to be on it for personal use."

Taylor spun in her mother's office chair and stretched her coltish legs across the tiled floor. "I was just doing some homework. Looking stuff up."

"Well, remember to stay off it from now on. We don't want Madeleine mad at us."

Madeleine Thompson, who held the title of Prosecuting Attorney of McCown County had been known to get her nose out of joint for smaller offenses, Elsie thought.

To lighten the mood, Elsie said, "Taylor, your mom says your birthday is coming up. Just around the corner. I can hardly believe you're almost fifteen years old."

Taylor's eyes lit up. "Mom, I know what I want for my birthday."

Breeon was digging in her briefcase, sorting through files. "You already told me. Those rain boots in purple." Bree glanced at Elsie. "Do you know what Hunter rain boots cost? It's a crime."

Elsie shrugged. When she was a teenager, rain boots weren't even a thing—not in Barton, Missouri. On rainy days, she'd walked around town with wet shoes on her feet.

Taylor spoke again, with a challenge in her tone. "Yeah, well, I changed my mind. I want headshots."

Breeon zipped her bag. "What?" she asked, incredulous.

"Headshots. By a photographer. A real one."

Curious, Elsie stepped through the office doorway and dropped into a chair facing Bree's desk. "What do you want pictures for? You don't need your senior portrait till after your junior year in high school."

"Is this for the yearbook?" Breeon asked.

Taylor's eyes dropped.

"Not the yearbook. For modeling."

Elsie and Bree both burst into laughter; but when a cloud crossed Taylor's face, Elsie tried to choke it back.

Taylor's face was stormy. "You think I'm too ugly to be a model?"

Breeon stepped over her daughter's outstretched feet and ran a gentle hand over the girl's hair. "Oh honey. You're beautiful. And smart, and talented, and strong."

"So why can't I do modeling?"

"Baby, we're in the Ozark hills of Missouri. Even if I wanted you to be a model—you can't be one here. There's no modeling industry around here."

A glance out of the window behind Breeon's desk provided the truth to her claim. Tree-covered hills rose up in the distance, behind the town square where the courthouse sat. Barton, Missouri, the county seat of Barton County, Missouri, was a tiny town in the hill country of the Ozarks.

A bare whisper escaped Taylor's downturned head. "Maybe there is."

Elsie said, "Why would you want to be a model? They don't get to eat."

Taylor rolled her eyes.

Undeterred, Elsie continued: "They have to starve. And their career is over before they hit thirty. And they don't get to use their brains; they are human clothes hangers."

Without acknowledging Elsie, Taylor bent to pick up her backpack. "I wanna go home, Mom. We have a game tonight. Coach doesn't like it when I'm late."

"Sure thing." Breeon shot Elsie a pleading look over Taylor's head. "Can you lock up, Elsie? Taylor needs to be at the gym by six thirty to warm up, and I have to fix something for her to eat."

Taylor spoke up, with a look of anticipation. "Are we going to the grocery store? I want to get the new *Cosmo*."

"No, we're not. But I got you something better." Bree rummaged on her desk, pulling up a manila envelope. "It came in the office mail. I wanted to surprise you."

Taylor tore open the package. A paperback book fell out onto the desktop. She picked it up with a listless hand. "What's this?"

"Alice Walker. My favorite of her novels. You're such an advanced reader, I think you're ready for it." She kissed Taylor on the forehead, then turned to Elsie. "So you'll lock up?"

"No problem. Hey—I'll probably see you all over at the school gym tonight."

Taylor's face turned in Elsie's direction. "You're coming to see me play?"

"Well, I'll be there for the ninth-grade boys' game. I'm meeting Ashlock, since his kid's on the team." With an effort, Elsie kept her voice upbeat. She would much prefer to meet Detective Bob Ashlock, her current flame, in a darkened barroom after work. "But I'll try to get there early, so I can see your team, too."

Breeon said, "That'd be great. Right, Taylor?"

Elsie stepped over to Breeon's desk to pick up the felony hard file they'd handled in Judge Calvin's court while Breeon packed up her briefcase. Taylor bolted out of the office, with her mother following. Breeon's voice called out as their steps retreated down the hallway. "See you later, Elsie."

Elsie flipped through the file and set it down. Giving the desk a final glance, she saw that Bree's computer was still turned on.

Their boss, Madeleine, had recently sent an office wide email, instructing the employees to log off and shut down the computers at night. It was her new "green" policy.

Elsie leaned over the desk and clicked the mouse, preparing to log off Bree's computer. Images popped up on the screen. Elsie leaned in to examine it.

It looked like a link for a modeling agency, pitching glamorous jobs for girls from twelve to twenty-five. Elsie shook her head. "Taylor, Taylor," she murmured.

Idly, she skimmed through the text on the screen. It promised that the agency could make a young woman's dream of fame and fortune come true, through an international modeling career. Elsie clicked the mouse to expose the bottom of the page, pausing to study a selfie of the agent in charge. It depicted a dark-haired man with a tattoo on his neck. He wore a smarmy grin.

A chill went through her; she grimaced. It set off a buzz in Elsie's radar. The man in the picture was not the type of individual that a mother would want sniffing around her teenage daughter.

She turned off the computer and got ready to depart. Before she turned off Breeon's office light, she glanced down at the trashcan near the door.

At the top of the garbage was the brand new Alice Walker

paperback novel. Elsie reached into the wastebasket to rescue it; but it had fallen on the remains of Breeon's lunch. Mustard and ketchup smeared the cover. Elsie dropped it back into the can and headed for the women's room to wash a streak of ketchup dripping from her fingers.

Chapter 2

THAT EVENING, ELSIE pulled open the doorway of the Barton Middle School gymnasium and stepped inside. The old facility was steamy, and smelled of sweat and athletic shoes. The walls were lined with trophy cases holding dusty prizes. Elsie didn't bother to look for any plaques bearing her name, though she had attended the school in her teenage years. Her medals were in a different hallway, by the speech and debate room.

A teacher with frowsy gray hair stood behind the counter with a roll of tickets. "Three dollars," she said, then peered over her bifocals. "Elsie Arnold!"

"Hey, Mrs. Simmons."

"I had you in eighth grade math. Or was it ninth grade?"

"Ninth, I think." Elsie pulled three one-dollar bills and set them on the counter.

"I always thought you'd end up in the law. You'd argue with anyone about anything." She gave Elsie a bright smile.

Elsie wasn't certain that the statement was a compliment. But it was probably true. "Have you seen Bob Ashlock come through?"

"Oh, he got here early. Detective Ashlock never misses a minute of his boy's games. So you and Detective Ashlock are still keeping company?"

"Yep," Elsie said with a tight smile, as she thought: *nosy old bag.*

"Well, I bet your folks are tickled. You're finally settling down with a nice man. You couldn't do better than Detective Ashlock."

When the teacher handed Elsie her ticket, Elsie took it without comment. In fact, Mrs. Simmons was correct; Elsie's parents were overjoyed that she and Ashlock were a couple. And it could certainly be argued that Elsie couldn't do better than Bob. A lifelong law enforcement officer, he was a local hero in the community for his stellar record of service. He was also really good in the sack.

As Elsie walked into the gymnasium, she entertained the fantasy of whispering some of Ashlock's finer skills into Mrs. Simmon's shocked ear; it restored Elsie's spirits and made her grin. While she scanned the bleachers for Ashlock, a ponytailed cheerleader bumped into her, nearly causing Elsie to drop the cup she held: a giant drink from Sonic.

She spied him, several rows up, facing center court. As she joined Ashlock on the bench, he looked pointedly at her cup.

"Did you pour a shot into that?"

Elsie frowned, wounded. "I only did that once. One time. Since then you act like I'm swilling at every game."

"Sorry." He pointed at the opposite side of the bleachers. "Bree's here. The ninth-grade girls just wrapped up."

"Did Taylor play?"

"Oh yeah. Damn, she's good."

"Shoot. I should've gotten here earlier. I wanted to see her on the court."

Elsie shifted on the hard seat, wondering whether she should run over and say hello. Across the gym, Breeon was beaming at her daughter, wrapping her in a hug. The other girls on the team clustered around Taylor, their faces animated.

Elsie set her purse at her feet and sucked on the red Sonic straw. No way was she going to crash that happy scene when she hadn't made it into the gym in time to witness the victory. As she watched Taylor's teammates buzz around her like bees in a hive, Elsie wondered why the girl would even entertain an interest in modeling. Seemed like Taylor had it all.

"Ash, why do you think girls all want go into modeling these days?"

He grinned at her, his eyes crinkling. "You thinking about moonlighting? As a model?"

"Oh please."

His hand grasped her knee and gave it a little squeeze. "I'd like to take some pictures of you. Can think of some nice poses. But I be damned if I'd let anyone else look at them."

His hand slid up her thigh. She grabbed it, pushing it down to a less sensitive spot. There would be no point in getting hot and bothered at the school gym.

"You know, if you wanted to, we could Snapchat."

"What's Snapchat?"

Elsie waved a hand, didn't bother to reply. She was thirty-two; Ashlock was almost ten years older. Snapchat was a young people's game.

He was watching the gymnasium floor, but Elsie persisted. "Why would a modeling agency reach out to a young girl in Southwest Missouri with no experience?"

On the gymnasium floor, the cheerleaders ran out waving

green and white pom-poms. Ashlock pointed at the boys' locker room. "They're heading out. Keep your eyes peeled for Burton."

When the players ran onto the gymnasium floor, bouncing balls and shooting baskets, Ashlock stood and whistled, a piercing sound that made Elsie want to cover her ears. She watched his son, Burton, aim at the basket. The ball slipped neatly though the net.

Elsie cheered; but when she and Ashlock settled back onto the bleachers, she had a thought. Ashlock had three children from a prior marriage: Burton, who lived with him, and two young daughters who lived with his ex-wife in the boot heel of Missouri. Elsie tugged at his arm.

"What about your girls? Do they ever talk about being models?"

He scoffed, his eyes still trained on the game. "My girls are playing with Barbie dolls."

She persisted. "What if one of your daughters was communicating with an agency?"

"Communicating? Communicating how?"

"Hell, I don't know. Online, or maybe through social media?"

His head jerked to face her. "Are you kidding? My babies aren't on social media. They're not messing around on the internet either. Good lord, Elsie. They're still in grade school."

Burton's team scored; Ashlock rose, repeating the ear-splitting whistle. But this time Elsie barely registered the assault on her hearing, as she debated whether to advise him that twenty-first century children knew how to search the internet as soon as they learned to spell.

When Ashlock sat, he asked, "Have you eaten dinner?"

She shook her head. He gave her knee a pat. “Good. The moms from Burton’s team are having a potluck in the cafeteria after the game. I signed us up for KP duty.”

Elsie sucked on her Sonic drink, wishing that she’d had the foresight to spike it after all.

Chapter 3

ELSIE MADE IT to the courthouse early the next morning, hoping to run Breeon down before the judges started the morning docket. She headed directly to Bree's office, but it was empty. A glance in the waste can showed that the garbage had been disposed of. Elsie was curious to know whether Breeon had spied the Alice Walker book in the trash. But she didn't want to be too nosy; and if Breeon hadn't seen the ketchup-spattered book, Elsie had no intention of snitching Taylor out.

She leaned into the reception area, where Stacie, the young receptionist, was behind her desk, unwrapping an Egg McMuffin.

"Have you seen Bree?"

Stacie looked up with a resentful face. "Well, that's nice. Good morning to you, too."

Elsie leaned against the door frame. "Sorry. Morning, Stacie. Have you seen Bree?"

Stacie bit into the breakfast sandwich and chewed before answering. Elsie kept a stoic face; if she sniped at the young woman, the information would be delayed even further.

She swallowed and said, "She headed down for coffee. With Madeleine."

As Elsie walked past the reception desk, she muttered, "Well, that's cozy." Historically, Elsie had a strained relationship with Madeleine Thompson, the woman who held the title of Prosecuting Attorney of McCown County, Missouri. Though Elsie had served as assistant prosecutor under Madeleine for over four years, they had never enjoyed a friendly vibe—despite Elsie's outstanding trial performance. In the past weeks, they had grown more civil; working as co-counsel on a recent murder case had been good for their professional connection.

But they still weren't chummy.

She walked down the stairway at a slow pace, hesitant to broach the topic of Taylor in front of an audience. When she reached the courthouse coffee shop, she was unsettled to see Breeon and Madeleine seated at a table together, laughing.

"Cup of coffee, Elsie?" Tom, the coffee shop proprietor, picked up the pot.

"Thanks. Black, please. For here."

Sipping the hot brew, she walked over to the Formica-topped table and paused. Breeon pushed a chair toward her. "You got here early this morning. Sit down, Elsie."

She sat beside Bree, facing Madeleine. Her boss gave her a tight smile, making a bare movement of her eyebrows. Due to Madeleine's addiction to Botox, her forehead didn't budge. "Breeon was bringing me up to date on the preliminary hearing you all handled yesterday."

Elsie blew a shrill whistle. "Bloodbath."

"So I heard," Madeleine said. She chuckled: a low sound in her throat, like a witch's cackle. "Some dude?"

Breeon broke into laughter, and Elsie joined her; but Elsie's laugh was hollow. It hadn't been funny at the time.

The prior afternoon, when she was conducting the direct examination of the assault victim, she stood before her witness and spoke clearly.

"And sir, please tell the court: who was it that shot you with the rifle on the date in question?"

He shrugged. "Some dude."

In fact, the "dude" who attempted to kill her witness was sitting right in front of him, at the defense counsel table.

Stunned by the nonresponsive answer—because Elsie had carefully prepped the witness prior to the hearing—she had repeated the question. That brought the defense attorney to his feet. While he raised his objection—"Asked and answered"—the state's witness spoke again.

"I dunno, man. Some dude."

The judge's shoulders were shaking, but it wasn't a comical moment for the prosecution. They would have lost, had the defense attorney not grown cocky. On cross-examination, he pointed at the witness and said, "So you have no idea who shot you with a firearm."

The man said. "Yeah, well, he's sitting right there. That dude."

With a wave of his hand, the witness indicated the defendant. Elsie literally wiped sweat from her brow. The defense attorney tried to argue. "But sir, didn't you just state under oath that you did not know who assaulted you?"

The witness scratched his head. "I don't know his name, man."

Recalling the scene the morning after, while Elsie nursed her coffee at the Formica-topped table in the coffee shop, she reflected that trial practice was rarely dull. Maddening, yes. But not boring.

Madeleine peered at Elsie over her bejeweled reading glasses. "I've told you before. A witness has to be properly prepared before he gets on the stand."

Elsie opened her mouth to mount a defense, but Breeon beat her to it. "We both worked with him, Madeleine. For thirty minutes or more. That guy's brain was fried long before he took a slug from that rifle. We should probably plea bargain."

That's just what I was about to say, Elsie thought, a touch sulky. To change the topic, she pasted on a smile and asked, "So Madeleine—how was the Missouri prosecutor's conference?"

"Oh my word. The accommodations were wretched." She pulled a napkin from the dispenser and wiped her hands, as if they were soiled.

Breeon leaned back in her seat and shot Madeleine a wink. "Did your husband go along? You all have a little second honeymoon?"

"Goodness, no. What would I have done to entertain him during the presentations?"

Madeleine's husband was the John Deere distributor for three counties. Elsie wasn't surprised that he'd opted out of the prosecutor's convention.

Breeon eyed Madeleine over the coffee cup she held aloft. "I figured the convention might give you some time together. A little getaway."

"Dennis isn't particularly interested in getaways." She paused, toying with an empty Sweet 'n Low packet, and added, "As a couple. He's tied down to his business. And hunting."

A moment of silence followed. Elsie glanced away, remembering the one time she'd seen Madeleine and her husband together at home. They sniped at each other. In front of company. Money didn't buy happiness, apparently.

Madeleine cleared her throat and said, "But they had an excellent session on search and seizure. I'll share the notes."

"That's great," Breeon said; while Elsie thought, *I've already read the cases. Don't need your goddamn notes.* But she kept her mouth shut.

"And a woman from the U.S. Attorney's Office in Kansas City gave a fascinating talk."

Elsie snorted. "What do the Feds have to say that helps us with criminal prosecution at the state level?"

Madeleine gave her a frosty stare. "Human trafficking. The Western District of Missouri has prosecuted more sex trafficking cases this year than anywhere in the nation."

Elsie's eyes widened at the revelation. Breeon set her cup down and said, "Madeleine, what's up with that? We can't be the hotbed of the sex trade for the whole country."

"Well, she said they're being very proactive. But sex trafficking is a problem in the heartland. I was appalled to hear it." She took a dainty sip from her coffee cup.

Elsie leaned forward, placing both elbows on the table as she focused on Madeleine. "Who are the victims?"

"Of sex trafficking? Both female and male, though more girls than boys."

"Age?" Elsie asked.

Madeleine spoke in a whisper. "It's shocking. Eleven to sixteen. And adults, too."

Breeon stirred her coffee with a spoon. "How do they target the victims?"

Madeleine frowned, thinking. "Runaways, of course. That's an old story. But the federal attorney said the new development has to do with outreach over the internet and through social media."

"Huh," Breeon said. "What kind of social media?"

"Oh, the websites that young girls like. That they tend to visit."

Elsie's forehead wrinkled. "Such as?"

"Those dating websites—what are they called? Is one something like Tenderheart? And the websites that advertise modeling careers for teenagers."

Elsie knocked her coffee with a jerky hand, causing it to spill onto the tabletop. "Modeling websites?"

"Yes—modeling websites. Do you need a napkin? You're making a mess."

"Which modeling websites?" Elsie felt a tremor go through her, as if someone was walking on her grave.

"How would I know? Some are undoubtedly legitimate. They're not all predators. But some, on the other hand. . . ." Madeleine stood, picking up a Dooney & Bourke briefcase. "I need to get up to my office. I'll have Stacie reproduce my search and seizure notes. Look for them in your inbox today."

"Will do," Breeon said. Elsie gave a bare nod of her head.

Madeleine said, "And we need to have a meeting in my office this week. The three of us, and Chuck."

Elsie looked up at her, curious. "What about?"

"Upcoming jury dockets. Judge Calvin has a panel assembling on Monday of next week."

Elsie laughed. Madeleine gave her a disapproving look, so she masked the laughter with a cough and said, "Well, that will be a short meeting. Calvin's an Associate Circuit Judge. He only tries misdemeanors before juries. Misdemeanors never go to the jury trial."

Madeleine glanced away. "Sometimes they do."

Bree broke in. "When do you want to meet, Madeleine? Afternoons are best for me."

"I'll let you know." Without another word, she was gone.

Breeon was drinking the dregs of her coffee. Elsie cleared her throat and said, "Bree, I need to tell you something."

Chapter 4

TAYLOR SPUN THE combination on her lock and gave it a jerk. Opening her locker, she pulled her ninth grade English book off the shelf and tucked it inside her green backpack.

A squeal down the hallway made her turn her head. Desiree was running toward her, waving frantically.

"Taylor," Desiree said. "O! M! G!"

Desiree's eyes were sparkling. Her frizzy blond hair was pulled away from her face with a pink headband decorated with sparkly magenta hearts.

When Desiree reached Taylor's locker, Taylor tapped the pink headband with a finger. "Girl, what are you wearing on your head?"

"It's lucky." Desiree's hand flew to her head, adjusting the pink plastic band. "I used to wear it to pageants. For luck."

Taylor rolled her eyes. Desiree did a pageant pivot and posed with her back to the green metal locker beside Taylor's.

"Don't you wanna hear?"

"Hear what? Hey, why weren't you at my game last night?"

"Mom was working; I didn't have a ride. But it's a good thing."

She leaned in and whispered in Taylor's ear. "A real good thing I stayed home. A lucky thing."

Three girls walked by. One of them, a tall girl with sky blue braces on her teeth, called out.

"Taylor! Come to the cafeteria with us. We've got time to get a Snapple."

Taylor glanced down at Desiree. Her friend gave her head a shake. The movement made the pink band slip down onto her forehead. She pushed it firmly back into place.

Taylor looked back at the trio, lingering nearby. "Later, okay? See you in a minute."

Desiree watched the girls go down the hall toward the school cafeteria. Once they were safely out of earshot, she turned back to Taylor.

"We have an appointment with Dede."

"Who's Dede?" Taylor said, pushing her locker shut and securing the lock.

"Dede is Tony's assistant. Like his number two person at the agency. And she's going to meet us."

Taylor's eyes widened. "How'd you make that happen? OMG."

"Tony texted me last night. Asking how I was doing, what was up. I told him I was hanging, at home alone, and he said, so let's talk. We got on Skype. He said he had somebody he wanted me to meet. Dede came on, too; she is soooo glam."

"But what about the appointment?"

"I was getting to that. They've looked over our applications, and they're ready for an interview. Tony said he wants to put us on a fast track. Doesn't that sound cool? It's exactly what he said: 'fast track.'"

Taylor looked doubtful. "You mean, me, too?"

"Yes! Both of us."

"You sure?"

"Positive. Dede said she said she wanted you to come with me."

Huddled against the lockers, Taylor spoke in a hushed voice. "Like, where? How we gonna meet her anywhere? We can't drive. You told them we were older."

Desiree did a little hop, bouncing on the balls of her feet with excitement. "I fixed that. I said we can't drive to see her because we don't have a car. So she is coming here." The timbre of her voice raised to a squeal. "To Barton."

Taylor shook her head in wonder. "I can't believe it."

"Well, it's true. She's meeting us at the Denny's by the highway for a modeling interview. We can ride our bikes to Denny's. It's not that far."

"When?"

"This week."

Taylor looked away. She lifted the metal lock where it hung and toyed with the dial. "You know I've got basketball practice."

A shade fell over Desiree's face, dampening the glow in her eyes. "Taylor, this is modeling. It's important. We're talking about a career."

When Taylor shrugged, Desiree persisted. "Basketball is a stupid game. You think you're going to be a basketball player when you grow up? They don't even have girl teams."

Taylor's jaw tensed. "Actually, they do."

"Well, I never heard of one." Desiree pulled a worn blue backpack off her shoulder. She unzipped the center pocket and pulled out a glossy magazine.

"The new *Cosmo*," she said, holding it out. Running a reverent finger down the cover, she said, "This could be us."

Taylor regarded the magazine with a hungry eye. "Can I have it during study hall?"

"Sure," said Desiree, tucking it back inside the backpack. "Because you're my BFF. Ever since that day you saw me crying in the bathroom at the start of the school year and helped me out."

Taylor shrugged off the praise. "It's what anyone would've done."

"Nuh-uh. All those other girls just walked right on by. You were the only one in the whole school who cared about my feelings."

Taylor bent down and whispered in Desiree's ear. "It's like I told you. You can't be worried about not making cheerleader. I mean, it's not really even a sport."

Desiree nodded, her face intent. "I get that now. Who cares about being a cheerleader? It's not a career. Not like modeling."

"Taylor!" The voice rang from the end of the hallway. Taylor peered around Desiree's shoulder. At the end of the hall, her teammate with the braces stood, holding up a bottle.

"I got you, Taylor!" the girl with braces called.

Taylor pushed away from the locker. "Des, I'm thirsty. Gonna go drink a Snapple."

Before she walked away, Desiree grabbed her elbow. "Anyone would think you've got everything. All the girls follow you around, all the time. I still can't believe that you feel like an outsider, too. Just like me."

"Well, it's not easy. Being practically the only black kid in the whole school."

"We'll show them all. Especially the snotty ones. When we have our pictures in magazines. So we're in, right? For the interview?"

Taylor blew her breath out in a slow exhale. "I don't know what my mom's going to think."

Desiree squeezed her arm. "My mom is totally psyched. She even wanted to tag along to the interview, but I said no way. I mean, we're supposed to be eighteen. This isn't a pageant, it's not Miss Missouri Petite."

When Taylor didn't reply, Desiree whispered, "If you think your mom won't like it, you can keep it a secret. Until we get the job, anyway. Then you'll be like: Surprise, Mom! I'm famous!"

"Taylor!" The girl with braces was frowning.

"I'm coming," Taylor called. "Des, I'm going to chug that tea before homeroom. Okay?"

Desiree released her arm. With an anxious face, she said, "Pinkie promise?"

"What?"

"The interview. I want you to go. I'll be too nervous by myself. I want us to do it together."

Taylor's eyebrows knit. At length, she said, "Okay. It's just Denny's, right?"

Relief washed over Desiree's face. "Right! Like I said, you don't even need to mention it to your mom. It's just Denny's, for god's sake."

Taylor gave her a nod. "'Kay."

"So you're in? You promise?"

Taylor lifted her chin and gave Desiree a mocking look. "I'll promise to go if you promise to leave that dumb headband at home."

Desiree's hand flew to the pink band. "It's lucky. Really."

"Stupidest thing I ever saw. So. Lame."

As Taylor headed down the hall toward the cafeteria, Desiree trotted behind. Pulling the headband out of her hair, she said, "Okay. I'll put it in my locker for now. But when we go to the Marvel Modeling interview, I'm gonna hide it in my purse."

"Gawd," Taylor moaned.

"It's lucky. One time when I wore it, I won the Grand Supreme."

Clutching the pink band, Desiree turned back and ran down the hall, stopping before her own locker; and Taylor joined her basketball teammates, who passed off the orange bottle. Taylor twisted off the lid and drank it with a thirsty gulp. As they walked to homeroom, her friends chattered about the ball game they'd played the night before. Taylor nodded, pretending to pay attention.

But all she could think was:

My mom isn't gonna like it.

Chapter 5

"YOU'RE KIDDING ME. Right?"

Elsie clutched the foam coffee cup, trying to frame the correct response to Bree's question. Her friend was gazing at her like she had a bug squashed on her forehead.

Bree's eyes flashed. "You think my daughter is up to something I don't know about."

"I didn't say that." Elsie drank a swallow of the lukewarm coffee, half wishing she'd never broached the topic.

Bree crossed her arms on her chest. "You're talking about Taylor? My daughter?"

Elsie sighed. "I could be so off base about this," she said, before Bree cut her off.

"Off base? Hell yeah. My baby doesn't have time to get into trouble. She's a straight A student—which you should know, she's in your mom's English class at middle school. She's the star of the girls' basketball team. They practice every day, play twice a week."

"I know that. Of course I do."

"And that's not all." Bree leaned in, giving Elsie the eye that defense attorneys in Southwest Missouri had learned to fear. "She's got a mother watching out for her."

Under her breath, Elsie hissed, "Jesus fucking Christ, Bree. I'm not the enemy."

The statement appeared to take Bree back a peg. She broke eye contact with Elsie, and looked out the window, where weak sunlight made shadows between the coffee shop and the county jail.

Elsie chose her words with care. "I'm probably overreacting. All the sex cases we see, and Madeleine talking about that stuff she heard at the conference. About sex trafficking, and kids Taylor's age."

Bree's expression was tight. With a stiff nod, she said, "You're just overreacting. I get that."

"But last night, when you told me to shut down your computer, I saw the page Taylor had been looking at."

Breeon turned to Elsie with a look of alarm. "And?"

"It was a modeling agency."

She watched Breeon's face, waiting for the impact. When Breeon broke into a smile and began to laugh, Elsie leaned back in the plastic chair, confounded.

"That's it? That's what's got your panties in a wad? Jesus." Bree exhaled, turning to pick up the purse beside her chair. "Good Lord, what a relief."

Elsie studied Breeon, copying her rueful smile. "You're not worried about that?"

"My baby fantasizing about modeling? No. It's a thing, something girls dream about. Like having their own reality show." She stood, looking relaxed. "I'll talk to her."

Elsie nodded. "Good."

Breeon gave her a look. "I bet you put your mama through worse than that back in the day. I'd bet a fortune on it."

Elsie swallowed. Because she couldn't deny it.

Her phone hummed; she picked it up. "Who's calling?" Bree asked.

Elsie looked at the caller information. "Speak of the devil. It's Marge Arnold."

Breeon squeezed Elsie's arm, her good humor restored. "Who's the devil? Not Marge; your mother is a saint." With that, she left the table and pushed through the screen door into the courthouse hallway.

Elsie answered the call. "Hey, Mom."

Her mother's voice roared into her ear like a megaphone. "Elsie? Hello? Are you there?"

"Yeah, Mom. It's me. What's up?"

Elsie walked up to the counter of the coffee shop and handed her empty cup to the proprietor. "I need one to go, Tom," she said.

Marge's voice rang; Elsie winced. "I just heard from your uncle Rod. He's coming for Thanksgiving."

With the full coffee back in hand, Elsie held the phone between her neck and shoulder as she secured a lid onto the cup. "Well, that's nice. He always jazzes things up."

Uncle Rod was a lot of fun at a family gathering. He and Elsie were drinking buddies.

"So I was wondering: will Bob Ashlock be able to join us? I know he trades holidays with his ex-wife. But we'd be so happy to have him. And his son, Burton. The little girls, too."

Elsie grimaced into the phone, glad her mother couldn't see it. Negotiating holidays, when your romantic partner was a cop with a crazy ex-wife and three kids, was a trying proposition.

"I'll ask him. I know he'll join us if he can."

"Well, good. Glad to hear that." Marge sounded only half-satisfied. "You know, your daddy and I would be thrilled if you decided to make Bob Ashlock a member of the family."

Shutting her eyes, Elsie said, "Seems like you've mentioned that a time or two."

Her mother's voice dropped to a whisper. "You're thirty-two, sweetheart. A fine age to have a baby. But you can't wait forever. Mother Nature won't let you."

Ooooohhhh gawd, Elsie thought. "Got to get to work."

"Yes, baby; I'd best let you go. My phone is about to go dead, I think."

Elsie shook her head. "Mom, I've told you. You need a new phone. Your old dinosaur won't hold a charge."

"This phone is perfectly satisfactory."

"Get an iPhone."

"I don't need one. All those apps—I wouldn't know what to do with them. I need to get off, honey. My homeroom will be coming in any minute."

Though Elsie was eager to end the call, a thought seized her. "Mom—you've got Bree's daughter in class, right? Taylor Johnson?"

"Yes I do. You know that."

"How's she getting along?"

Marge Arnold's voice grew guarded. "Are you asking me about her grades? Because, Elsie . . ."

"Mother—"

"Elsie, I can't reveal her grades to you, because of federal law."

"Jesus Christ."

"Hush," Marge whispered. "Don't you cuss on a school call. It's FERPA. I cannot reveal that information."

Elsie frowned into the phone. "Mother, please. I know she's a stellar student. I just wanted to know—is she okay?"

Marge paused for a beat. "What do you mean?"

Elsie glanced across the counter. She didn't think anyone was listening, but she moved into the hallway, just to be certain. "Has she changed recently? Her focus, her friends?"

There was a pause. Elsie waited.

Marge whispered, "Friends."

"Yeah. Her friends. Is anything up with that?"

Elsie heard Marge clear her throat; it meant she was thinking, Elsie knew from experience.

"Taylor always hangs out with the girls on her teams: the athletes."

"Yeah?"

"But in my class, I put them in alphabetical order. She's sitting next to Desiree Wickham."

Marge fell silent. Elsie urged her on.

"Is that a problem?"

Her mother sounded defensive. "Desiree's sweet. Pretty little thing. Just kind of—I don't know—flighty."

Elsie listened, waiting for her mother to render a judgment. Marge Arnold knew middle schoolers inside and out.

"Desiree is sweet, honestly. But her motivation—"

The words were cutoff; Elsie was receiving another call. From the Barton City Police Department.

It was Detective Ashlock.

"Mom, Ashlock's calling."

Her mother said, "Be sure to tell him about Thanksgiving." She hung up.

Elsie pushed the answer spot. Ashlock's voice warmed her ear.

"What you doing for supper tonight?"

She leaned against the door frame of the coffee shop entrance. "What you got in mind?"

"I've got to cook for Burton tonight, after practice. It's as easy to cook for three as two."

Tilting her head back against the wooden frame of the door, Elsie hit the metal hinge; she rubbed her scalp to ease the ache. In recent weeks, she was doing her level best to come to terms with Ashlock's new custody arrangement. But she missed the days when his free time was all hers. These days, their opportunities for sex grew more and more infrequent. And Elsie longed to scratch that itch.

She sighed silently, and then smiled into the phone. "Sounds great."

Chapter 6

THAT AFTERNOON, TONY jammed the plastic key into the slot on the EconoMo Motel door, Room 217. Nothing. No buzz, no green light.

He gave the doorknob a vicious twist, just for good measure. It wouldn't open.

He pulled the plastic rectangle from the slot and pushed it back inside. Then again. He was so focused on the key that he failed to note the dried blood coating his knuckles and embedded in his fingernails.

He could hear movement inside the room. Good; Dede was inside. He knocked on the door with the side of his fist.

Though Dede's voice was muffled by the door, he heard her respond to the knock. "Don't want to see anybody. Go away. I'm in bed."

He pounded on the door, wishing it was someone's face he was striking. Maybe Dede's. Sometimes his bottom bitch needed a reminder about their relative positions. Or better yet, he'd enjoy giving another pop to the little piece of trash he'd worked over in the Rancho Motel in Barton, Missouri.

The girl had needed to be taught a lesson. And he taught her one. Taught her good.

The door opened a crack. He pushed it wide, walked in, and slammed it behind him.

"Don't ever leave me waiting."

Dede took a step back. Tony walked to the bathroom for a cup. The sight of Dede's cosmetics; her curling iron and hairspray, scattered around the sink, pushed his foul temper several notches higher. With a sweep of his arm, he knocked the items to the floor. Face powder made a snowy pattern on the bathroom tile.

Dede peered into the doorway. "Damn it, Tony. That eye shadow was brand-new." She knelt down and picked up a plastic case of blue and green shades in a palette. "The mirror is broken."

Tony turned the tap and scrubbed his hands with the miniature bar of soap. The lather on his hands was rust-colored.

With a mournful face, she said, "I'm afraid to use it now. What if I get glass in my eye?"

The towels were scattered on the floor, piled beside the tub. He plucked up a damp bath towel and wiped his hands.

"Clean this shit up," he said. He picked up the cup and made his way to the desk. A few cubes floated in a puddle of water in the plastic ice bucket. He scooped them into the cup and filled it with vodka. Then he opened one of the prescription bottles, shook out two pills, popped them in his mouth, and chased them with the liquor.

Dede was standing in the doorway of the bathroom, her broken eye shadow in her hand. She eyed him with trepidation.

"Where's Mandy?"

"Fuck," he said. Tony walked to the unmade bed and sat. He

took another swallow before placing the cup on the scarred bedside table. "She's right where I left her. Trashy bitch."

He stretched out, leaned against the headboard, and pulled his cell phone from his pocket. He stared at the screen, frowning.

Dede took a tentative step in his direction. "I thought you'd bring her back when she was done."

"I guess I didn't." He didn't look up, just scoured texts on the phone. "You'll have to go get her." He glanced up. "Get out of that bathrobe. And do something about your hair."

Dede's hand ran over her hair, smoothing it away from her face. The auburn waves were frowsy, flattened by sleep.

"What's that on your shirt?"

He didn't answer. Cautiously, she sat on the corner of the bed.

"Is it blood?"

He looked up. "What do you think?"

She swallowed before answering. "I think it looks like blood. Kind of."

He shot Dede a look that should serve as a warning: *watch your mouth.*

Because he didn't feel bad about slapping Mandy into line. It was business. And he was a businessman.

In his line of work, Tony was the boss. The girls? They were inventory. And if the boss man couldn't control the inventory, the business would go to shit in a New York minute.

Tony hadn't been raised to understand the principles of running his own operation. His old man had always worked under somebody else's thumb. Never got to be in charge. That was why he came home at night with an itch to kick the household around. Tony's mother. The kids. Even the damn dog.

Tony hadn't learned how to make a buck from his old man; but he'd learned how to throw a punch. He'd had lots of opportunity to observe that, back in the shithole where he grew up, in Sweet Home Alabama.

Tony hated that song.

He studied the cell phone and commenced typing on the phone with his thumbs. Dede stepped over to her suitcase and pulled out some clothing. As she slipped a shirt over her head, she said, "What happened?"

"Mandy got out of line. That's all. I had to remind her who's in charge."

Dede pulled on a pair of jeans, and then dug in her purse for a hairbrush. Standing before the mirror on the dresser, she ran the brush through her hair, while keeping her eyes trained on Tony's reflection.

"What happened? If you don't mind me asking."

When Tony's eyes met hers in the mirror, he saw her flinch. He smiled.

"Mandy had an attitude problem. We've got a hot new client down there in hillbilly country. He was prepared to pay top dollar for the services he wanted. Top fucking dollar."

The hairbrush stopped moving, midstroke. "And?"

"And Mandy didn't feel like doing what he'd paid for. The dude texted me. Asked for a refund. Shit."

He returned his attention to the phone, with his thumbs moving at a furious pace. In an offhand voice, Dede spoke again.

"Will she be able to work?"

"Not for a while."

She fastened back her hair with a plastic barrette. "I'm pretty good with makeup."

"Yeah, I dunno. I kinda flipped out. Gave her a pretty good

smackdown. You'll need to pick up the slack. It'll give you something to do, other than sitting on your ass." He tossed the phone onto the mattress. "What you still standing around for? It's a forty-minute drive to Barton. Go get her before she starts wandering off."

He threw a hotel key at her. It fell onto the frayed carpet. The key read RANCHO.

Dede picked up the key and headed for the door. Before she opened it, Tony said. "We need more girls."

She paused, looking at him over her shoulder, but didn't reply.

He said, "We came all the way from Birmingham to stake out this territory. I've worked the internet connections, made contacts, built the clientele. We got prime location for highway traffic. I should be raking in a fortune. This ain't like the drug trade. You sell your stash and it's gone—done. But these girls. That pussy don't disappear. You can sell it over and over again."

Dede spoke. "I'm working on it. I'm gonna meet with the kids you hooked up—same town as your new client."

"Why aren't they lined up yet?"

She stared at the floor, grimacing.

"One of them is gung ho—the white chick. She's a piece of cake. But the other one, the pretty black girl; she's kind of jumpy. It won't be that easy to bring her into the stable."

Tony picked up the vodka and took a deep swallow. He sighed and tucked a flat pillow behind his head. His Elvis combo—booze and painkillers—was starting to work its magic. His muscles relaxed, his mood was lifting.

"Get that pretty black kid in here to meet me. She needs to see me in the flesh. I know just how to motivate her."

As Dede slipped out the door, Tony said, "You can only eat a cow once. But you can milk it over and over and over again."

Chapter 7

OCCASIONALLY, THE DOCKET in associate court was overrun with cases; and Tuesday was one of those days. Elsie had been so busy that she hadn't had a chance to leave the courthouse all day, not even during the lunch hour; and the last thing she'd consumed was the coffee she had shared with Breeon and Madeleine that morning. By five o'clock, she was tired and hungry, more than ready to head over to Ashlock's house for a relaxing supper.

After she locked up her office, Elsie slipped into the women's restroom on the second floor of the courthouse for a touchup. She pulled her hair out of the elastic band that held it in a ponytail and ran a brush through it with quick strokes. She had just unearthed a lipstick when she heard her phone buzz.

It was from Ashlock: a brief text that read *I need you over here. Now.*

She stared at the phone. It wasn't a booty call, that much was certain. This was business. Serious business.

With her lipstick case still in her fist, Elsie grabbed her purse and took off, running for the front door of the old courthouse.

She sped down the stone steps and across the street, to the Barton Police Department.

She raced up the stairs to the detective department, where the longtime receptionist, Patsy, greeted her.

"He's not here."

Elsie paused, catching her breath. Running was not her sport. "But he just texted."

"I know, honey. He told me to tell you: go to that old motel by the highway. The Rancho."

Elsie turned and headed back down the stairs she'd just ascended. She found her car in the courthouse parking lot and headed for the highway.

No need to seek directions. Everyone in the small town of Barton knew the location of the Rancho Motel. It was famous: a no-tell-hotel for illicit romance. If the truth be told, Elsie had occasionally checked into the Rancho in her youth, when she still lived under her parents' roof but had grown too old for the backseat of a car.

When Elsie pulled into the parking lot, she saw the familiar vehicles: Ashlock's police sedan, the county sheriff's patrol car, two other black-and-white patrol cars belonging to the Barton PD. Also, a shiny new van emblazoned with the letters: KY2: THE PLACE FOR YOU!

If the news buzzards were circling, something was going on. Something bad.

She surveyed the Rancho. It was set off I-44, the neon sign flashing at half strength; only fifty percent of the bulbs flashed out the motel's name. A painted placard boasted Kitchenettes, Cable TV, Daily/Weekly/Monthly Rates. Behind the vacancy sign, a dozen cabins perched in a semicircle. Ashlock's car sat beside the ninth cabin. A strip of DO NOT ENTER tape stretched across the entry.

Elsie shot off a text: *Ash. At Rancho. You in there?*

No answer.

Sitting in the car, she debated whether she should approach. Elsie didn't want to storm the crime scene; she knew important work was going on, work she couldn't do. Collecting physical evidence was the job of the police department. She wasn't a forensic investigator. Getting the evidence before a jury was her job.

She picked up her cell phone, willing it to buzz. Maybe she should just sit there for a bit. Surely he'd come out and bring her up to speed; he had practically ordered her to join him.

Ashlock didn't appear, though she waited patiently. Elsie opened the door of her Ford Escort, shivering in the November wind. She wished she'd thought to bring a coat, but it was back in her office at the courthouse.

When she exited the vehicle, the driver of the KY2 van hopped out and began to approach her. Elsie jumped back into her car and locked it.

The newsman looked like a kid, barely old enough to attend college. She could see the gel in his close-cropped hair. He rapped on her window.

"Hey," he said, smiling. Elsie ignored him. She pulled out her phone and checked her emails.

"Can I ask you a couple of questions?" The young man's head was so close to her car window, his breath fogged the glass. Elsie shot him a glance and shook her head, then returned her attention to her cell phone.

The young man persisted. "I'm an intern at KY2. Tad Brockman. Are you with the police department?"

Elsie dropped her phone into her bag and dug inside for a mint. It took a minute before she unearthed a box of Tic Tacs. She popped one and sucked on it.

"If you're a family member, I'd really like to interview you. The girl isn't here, anyway. I heard on the police band that they took her to the hospital."

Young Mr. Brockman was a fair source of information, Elsie thought. She turned on the ignition and rolled her window down an inch.

"What hospital?"

"Barton Memorial? How are you connected to the case?"

Elsie rolled the window up, put the car into Drive, and pulled to the hotel exit. Fortunately, she was moving at low speed; because a woman driving a car with out-of-state license plates tore into the lot, nearly clipping Elsie's headlight.

She hit the brake and rolled down the window. Shouting at the car as it sped into the Rancho lot, Elsie cried: "What the fuck?"

The woman slowed her car to an idle, right in front of the room marked with police tape; then the car reversed, swung around Elsie, and pulled back onto the highway.

Elsie watched the woman go. She'd noted that the driver had red hair, and the plates on the car were from Alabama. She wondered whether she should've recorded the license plate number; but she brushed it off. It was too late. Elsie wasn't a traffic cop. And she needed to get to Barton Memorial. She turned onto the highway, heading in the opposite direction of the Alabama car.

Ten minutes later, she arrived at Barton Memorial.

It was a modest local facility, almost phased out of operation by the major medical centers in larger communities in Southwest Missouri. Barton Memorial no longer housed a surgical facility;

they had been pushed out by competition. Even the maternity ward had closed a decade ago. At this point, the hospital had a small ER that served as a referral base to Joplin or Springfield. People with minor or moderate injuries were received and treated at Barton. As long as a patient didn't need sophisticated care, Barton would take them.

Barton Memorial also performed examinations of assault victims.

And victims of rape.

Chapter 8

ELSIE BYPASSED THE information desk at Barton Memorial. The silver-haired volunteer sitting behind the counter had proven to be uninformative in the past.

She headed for the emergency services doorway and pushed through. Ignoring the check-in personnel, she walked straight through to the head nurse's station.

"Hey, Alice," Elsie said.

A woman wearing white scrubs looked up. With a sad shake of her head, she said, "Right here in Barton. Who'd have thought?"

Elsie leaned over the counter and spoke in a whisper. "Can you bring me up to speed, Alice? Ashlock called to tell me about it, but I missed the call; and he's tied up."

Alice glanced over her shoulder, then beckoned to Elsie. "That little girl had the tar beat out of her. But she's not talking—not yet, anyway. Maybe when Ashlock gets here, she'll open up." She gave Elsie a steadfast look through tortoise shell glasses. "Or maybe you can try."

Elsie backed away a step, thinking. She had a fair amount of experience with young victims of crime. But the police department always took the initial statement.

Alice interrupted her reverie. “She is still back there, in the ER. We haven’t moved her to a room yet.”

Staring down the open hallway, Elsie was tempted to approach the girl.

“How old is she?” Elsie asked.

Alice rolled her eyes. “Eighteen. She claims. Doesn’t look a day over fifteen. Well, to the extent that I can make out.”

“What do you mean?”

“Her face is beat up pretty bad. You’ll see.”

Involuntarily, Elsie shut her eyes. Confronting the reality of violence against young girls was the toughest part of her job. She never became immune to the shock and horror of seeing it.

In a hushed voice, she said, “And sexual?”

Alice’s forehead wrinkled. “The physical exam is consistent with recent sexual activity. But there’s no ejaculate. Must have worn a condom.”

Elsie frowned. The use of a condom prevented the easy DNA match that could have been provided by a timely rape screen.

“Well?” Alice said.

Elsie glanced down at Alice, who was looking at her with an expectant face. “You want to go on back?” Alice inclined her head toward the hallway.

Elsie paused, pulling her phone from her bag. No texts, nothing from Ashlock. Sighing, she slipped the phone back into her purse.

“I’ll just take a peek.”

Alice nodded. “She’s in the second exam room. You know the way.”

Elsie walked through the white hallway, wrinkling her nose against the smell of disinfectant. The door to the exam room was open, and she stepped inside. A blue nylon curtain shielded the bed from view.

She moved to the bed on tiptoe, so her heels wouldn't clatter on the tile floor. Reaching out, she pushed the blue curtain with a careful hand, and saw a dark-haired girl lying beneath a white sheet.

The metal hooks connecting the curtain to the overhead rod rattled. One of the girl's eyes opened, the other was a bruised slit on her face.

"Who are you?" the girl asked in an unfriendly voice.

Elsie gave a sympathetic grimace as she studied the girl. The left eye was blackened, in addition to being swollen shut; her mouth was also swollen, her lip split. In a soft voice, she said, "I'm Elsie. Elsie Arnold."

"Are you a cop?" The girl's lips moved with an effort as she spoke; Elsie knew it must be painful.

"No. No, I'm not."

The girl whispered, "You ain't a nurse. You not dressed right."

"Not that either." She took a step closer to the bed. "I'm a lawyer. I work for the Prosecutor's Office."

The girl cut her eyes away. "I don't need no lawyer."

A metal stool sat in the corner; Elsie wheeled it over to the bedside and sat. "Mind if I keep you company?"

The girl shrugged her shoulders, then winced. Elsie wondered how extensive her bodily injuries were. The sheet was pulled up to her chin; not even her hospital gown was visible.

Alice appeared at Elsie's shoulder. Her white athletic shoes hadn't made a sound. She pushed the nylon curtain open wide and said, "Look who's awake. Mandy, have you met Elsie?"

Mandy nodded. Elsie looked up at Alice. "Do you need for me to step out?"

"No, I'm just taking her vitals." Alice walked to the other side of the bed and slipped a blood pressure cuff onto Mandy's arm. Elsie caught a glimpse of fingerprint bruises. Mandy stared at the cuff for a moment, then turned her face away, toward Elsie.

Elsie nodded in Alice's direction. "Mandy, Alice and I went to high school together, here in Barton. Of course it's been a while ago."

"Fourteen years," Alice said in her brisk voice.

"Thanks, Alice; now Mandy will think we're ancient."

"Hush." Alice had the stethoscope on the pulse inside Mandy's elbow.

Elsie lowered her voice to a whisper. "Where do you go to school, Mandy?"

"I don't." She didn't bother to whisper.

Even under the sheet, Elsie could detect the girl's slight form, her flat chest, and narrow hips. Mandy's feet didn't approach the end of the small bed. In an even tone, Elsie said, "What year did you graduate?"

"I quit."

Alice exchanged a look with Elsie as she pulled the Velcro and removed the cuff with a ripping sound. In a defiant voice, the girl said, "I'm eighteen. I don't have to go no more."

Elsie's eyes widened but she kept a friendly face. "Wow, eighteen. I wouldn't have thought."

Alice picked up the chart from the end of the bed. "Mandy, when you came in, they didn't get your next of kin. We'll want to tell your folks that you're here. How can I get in touch? With your mother?"

Mandy closed her eyes. "Dead."

Alice's breath caught, but she recovered quickly.

"I'm so sorry. Your dad, then?"

"Dead."

Alice looked up from the chart. "Goodness. Both parents?"

The girl's response was so soft that Elsie barely caught it.

"Dead to me."

Alice was marking on the chart. Elsie wanted to place a hand on the girl's arm, just to reach out; but she held back. "Mandy, hon. Who's your family?"

The girl opened her eyes and fixed them on Elsie. Deadpan, she said, "I take care of myself."

Elsie nodded. "Okay. How do you do that?"

The girl raised her head. With a challenge in her eyes, she said. "I'm a whore."

Alice dropped the chart. It clattered on the floor.

Chapter 9

Desiree Wickham sat cross-legged on the sofa in the little rock house where she lived in Barton with her mother. It was growing dark outside, but she didn't bother to turn on the lights. Her attention was absorbed by a series of texts on her cell phone.

The door that led into the house from the carport opened and then slammed shut. "Des?"

"In here, Mom."

Kim Wickham walked into the living room and flipped a switch. "What on earth are you sitting in the dark for?"

Desiree looked up in surprise. Pushing the tangled mane of curly blond hair off her face, she said, "I didn't notice it got dark. What's for supper?"

Kim held a plastic grocery bag bearing the name Tyler's Family Market. She turned toward the kitchen, carrying the bag with her.

"Chicken."

Desiree jumped off the sofa and followed her mother into the kitchen. "What kind?"

Kim slid two boxes onto the kitchen counter. One box held a Hungry-Man fried chicken dinner. The other box was smaller and displayed a picture of chicken and rice.

"I got you the Lean Cuisine," Kim said as she carried the boxes to the microwave. "I'll make yours first."

Desiree cast a longing look at the Hungry-Man box. "I'm kind of starving tonight. The school lunch was pizza, so I just ate the top off it. You said not to eat carbs."

Her mother pressed the buttons on the microwave before turning to her with a look of reproach. "I thought you said you had a modeling interview this week."

Desiree nodded. "Yeah. I think on Thursday. Dede's supposed to get back with me. I was just checking my phone."

"Well, we agreed that you need to slim down some. Models don't eat fried chicken. I'm pretty darn sure of that."

When the microwave dinged and Kim removed the plastic plate, Desiree examined the dinner with a resentful eye. "I don't see you eating a Lean Cuisine."

Her mother froze, with the plastic plate in her hand. "I'm not a model. I'm a grocery clerk at Tyler's Market." She ripped the cellophane film off the dish. "Lean Cuisine costs more than Swanson's and Hungry-Man. Did you know that?"

In silence, Desiree picked a clean fork from the dish drainer and carried her supper into the living room. She had nearly cleaned the plate by the time her mother joined her on the couch.

In a gentler tone, Kim said, "I don't mind making sacrifices. I never have."

Desiree scraped the last grains of rice onto her fork. "I know."

"Just look there." Kim gestured at the fireplace across the room. Fashioned of the same native rock that lined the outer walls of the house, the mantel was covered with dusty trophies, rhinestone tiaras, and pageant sashes.

The hanging fabric posed no fire danger. A gas log had been installed in the fireplace decades prior, but hadn't functioned since Kim and Desiree moved in. Over the cold fireplace, the pastel strips dangled, bearing glittered letters that read LITTLE MISS and BEAUTY TOT and MISS MISSOURI PETITE.

Desiree turned away from the display. The prizes had sat in the living room for so many years, she hardly noticed them anymore. And the life-size photo that they'd taken of Desiree at age five had started to curl at the edges.

She lost her baby teeth the year after the portrait was made, and they couldn't afford the false plates other beauty contestants used to cover their missing and incoming permanent teeth. Kim had looked into acquiring flippers for Desiree, but the cost was out of their reach, so she went without. It had a negative effect on Desiree's scores at pageants.

Kim was staring at the photo, which hung directly over the fireplace. In a voice of regret, she said, "If we just could've got on *Tots & Tiaras.*"

Desiree didn't like being reminded of that disappointment. They had tried to break onto the show, more than once. The last time they auditioned, she was ten; and Desiree's mom had come up with a talent routine that wowed the judges: Desiree's Houdini Act.

But they told her that she just didn't have "the look." Desiree had held back her tears at the rejection. She lifted her chin and took it like a pro.

But not Kim. Kim had cried out loud, all the way back to Barton. And then she gave up on their dream. No more pageants.

Four years had passed since then. It seemed like forever ago that she'd once been a winner, a girl who wore a sparkling crown on her head. Since she left the pageant circuit, she no longer experienced triumphs. She wasn't any good at sports. Though she'd tried her best, she didn't make the cut for the cheerleading squad. She didn't even play an instrument in the school band. As a prisoner of middle school, she was destined to walk a lonely path; until she connected with Taylor Johnson, and showed her the modeling pages. Desiree had a new dream, and a friend to share it with. She had moved on from the pageant days, and didn't want to go back; but she sometimes wondered whether her mom would ever get over it.

Desiree said, "I don't want to talk about that. About *Tots & Tiaras*, or any of that stuff."

Kim's head ducked. With a guilty expression, she said, "Sorry, baby."

She picked a miniature piece of chicken out of a compartment on the Hungry-Man plate, and held it out like a peace offering.

"You want my thigh?"

Desiree wanted it. But she shook her head. Because there was something she wanted more.

Chapter 10

ELSIE HEARD HIM coming down the hall. At the sound of his determined tread, the muscles of her shoulders relaxed.

Ashlock appeared in the doorway of Mandy's hospital room. The light dust of fingerprint powder clung to his dark pants.

He inclined his head toward the hospital bed where Mandy lay, her eyes closed. "Did you talk to her?"

"No. Well, yeah. Just a little." Elsie rose from the chair she'd occupied while waiting, a vinyl recliner in seafoam green. When she joined Ashlock at the side of the bed, she whispered, "She's in bad shape, poor thing. How did the PD get called in?"

"There was a noise complaint. Someone staying in the next cabin at the Rancho called the front desk, said he couldn't hear his TV show for all the shouting and screaming from the room next door. The desk clerk checked it out, got close enough to hear it, too. Shouted into the room, said to knock it off. By the time he decided to call in the PD, the officer found the girl alone in there." Looking down at the girl's still figure in the hospital bed, he shook his head, frowning.

"I didn't try to take her statement. Thought I'd leave that to you."

He nodded. Stepping over to the bedside, he cleared his throat. "Mandy?"

When she didn't respond, he said her name again, in a firm voice. "Mandy."

Elsie whispered, "She's been sleeping since they brought her up here from the ER. I've been keeping watch, kind of. It's been over an hour since they assigned her to this room."

He held a nylon portfolio in his hand. Unzipping it, he turned a pad of paper to a fresh page.

"Mandy, I'm Detective Ashlock."

Still no response. Elsie said, "Ash, I think she's out."

"Oh I think she's coming around. Aren't you, Mandy?"

Her eyes opened; only a slit of white showed in her blackened eye. But her uninjured eye looked Ashlock up and down.

"What do you want?"

Elsie winced before she could mask it. Clearly, Mandy wasn't happy to see Ashlock. The interview was off to a rocky start.

Ashlock picked up the other seat provided in the room, a small metal chair. He placed it near the bed and sat.

"I need to ask you some questions, Mandy. I'm with the Barton Police Department, and I need to know how you ended up here."

"Why?" Mandy's voice was flat.

Ashlock regarded her with a direct look. "So I can find the person who did this to you."

The girl laughed, a hollow sound that turned into a cough. She leaned over the side of the bed and retched. Elsie jumped forward to grab the plastic wastebasket in the corner, but Mandy waved her away.

"Leave me alone. I'm okay."

Elsie retreated, back to the green vinyl recliner. She posed awkwardly on the edge of the seat cushion as Ashlock attempted to continue the interview.

"Your first name is Mandy. Short for Amanda?"

The good eye blinked. "Sure."

The pen hovered over Ashlock's notepad. "The hospital staff doesn't have your last name. What is it, Mandy?"

"Candy."

Elsie did a double take but Ashlock remained unruffled.

"How do you spell that?"

"How do you think?"

"Tell me, please."

"C-A-N-D-Y."

"And that's your last name."

"Yeah." Her voice had a distinct edge. "It is."

"Do you have any identification? Driver's license, student ID? Credit card?"

"Uh-uh." After a beat she added, "I got nothing."

"Where do you live?"

"I move around."

"Age?"

"Eighteen. I told the nurse before. I'm eighteen."

Ashlock glanced over at Elsie; their eyes met. She gave him a bare shrug of her shoulders, and he raised a brow. He turned back to the battered girl. In a calm voice, he continued.

"What were you doing at the Rancho last night?"

There was a long pause. "I had a date."

"Date with who?"

"I don't know." Mandy sighed, a weary sound. "Some guy."

"When did you arrive? At the hotel?"

"After dark. Not sure of the time. It was late."

"What did you do once you got there?"

"Sat in the room. Watched TV. Waited for the guy to show. That's all."

"How did you check into the hotel? If you don't have a driver's license?"

She looked away from Ashlock, toward the window behind Elsie's head. It gave Elsie a chance to study her. The girl's face was wary.

Mandy said, "I guess he checked in first."

"Can you describe the man you had a date with?"

"Not really."

The pen in Ashlock's hand stopped moving. "Why not?"

"I just can't. Are we about done? I'm tired."

Mandy rolled onto her side in the hospital bed, her back to Ashlock. They sat in silence for a moment. Elsie could hear the ding of monitors in a nearby room, and the muted sound of the hospital staff talking at the nurse's station.

Elsie felt the tension mount. Mandy's expression was closed, her jaw locked. Elsie edged toward her, sliding to the end of the vinyl seat. "Mandy?"

Ashlock said, "Pardon me, Elsie. Mandy, did he have dark hair?"

An angry whisper from the bed: "I. Don't. Know."

"Any distinguishing characteristics?"

She didn't answer. Ashlock continued, unruffled. "Like a tattoo. A tattoo on his neck."

Mandy's good eye opened wide, and she sat up in bed, facing Ashlock. "What did you say?"

He reached into the portfolio and pulled out a document. He handed it to Mandy: a photocopy of a driver's license. Elsie craned forward to see what it depicted.

The photocopy was fuzzy, so dark it was nearly indecipherable. She surmised the Rancho's copier was probably on its last legs, like everything else on the property. The license photo showed an unsmiling man with dark hair, slicked back from his face. It appeared that his neck bore a tattoo; but Elsie couldn't make it out, any more than she could distinguish the features of his face. The quality of the photocopied picture was too poor.

But a tattoo on a man's neck: that wasn't something Elsie saw every day. While tats were growing more common, even in small-town Missouri, they generally appeared on arms and legs.

The last neck tattoo she'd seen was on the modeling page she had found on Breeon's office computer. But it had to be a coincidence. What were the odds of it being the same guy?

Ashlock said, "The witness at the Rancho Motel told me that this man checked into the room we found you in. His name is Tony. Tony Fontaine. Do you know Tony Fontaine?"

Mandy pushed the photocopy away from her, toward the edge of the bed. Shaking her head, she said, "No."

In a gentle voice, Ashlock persisted. "Is Tony the guy you had a date with?"

"No." She looked up and met Ashlock's eye. "He's not."

"Then how'd you end up in Tony's hotel room?"

Mandy lay back on the pillow and pulled the sheet up to her chin. Her breath was rapid; her chest heaved under the sheet.

"Did Tony hit you last night, Mandy? Did he beat you up?"

Leaning forward, Elsie silently urged the girl: *tell us. Give us the information so we can go after him.*

But Mandy pulled the sheet over her head.

"Go away."

Chapter 11

AFTER THE UNPRODUCTIVE attempt at unearthing information from Mandy, Elsie huddled with Ashlock in the hallway.

"I think we've gotten all we'll get from her today." He swiped a hand across his jaw, where a five o'clock shadow bristled.

As she nodded in agreement, Elsie's stomach rumbled. She was running on empty. She'd skipped lunch; and the Snickers bar and Diet Coke she had grabbed from the hallway vending machines an hour prior were not sustaining her.

She ran a finger down his bristly cheek. "Let's go to the Baldknobbers. We can get a cheeseburger, and try to figure out where to go with this."

He grimaced. "I need to get home, check on Burton."

Elsie pursed her lips shut. She knew better than to argue. Ashlock had gained primary custody of Burton the summer before, and he took his parental responsibilities seriously.

He reached out and tucked a stray lock of hair behind her ear. "You want to come by the house? We can talk there. Burton will be playing those doggone games on his phone, most likely."

Her stomach gurgled again. "Okay. I'll pick up carryout."

"Great." He bussed her cheek and they walked out to the hospital parking lot.

"Starving. I am fucking starving," she muttered as she buckled herself into her Ford Escort. She considered the takeout options. Barton, Missouri's culinary choices were limited. A McDonald's near the highway exit, flanked by a Denny's and a Taco Bell. None of those choices struck her fancy. The stretch of highway also boasted a KFC, not far from Ashlock's neighborhood. She turned her car in that direction.

When she drove up to the KFC drive-thru box, it was covered with black tape. A handwritten note said OUT OF ORDER.

"Shit," she said, pulling her car into a parking spot. "Shit shit shit."

Why she felt so violently inconvenienced at the prospect of walking inside, she didn't know; but it had been a frustrating evening. When she pushed through the door, a line of people stood at the counter ahead of her. A single cashier was taking orders, a girl who looked like she had yet to matriculate middle school.

Elsie waited, her impatience mounting. The grease in the air sent her hunger into overdrive. The frozen line barely seemed to move. Peering around the customers clustered in front of her, she checked out the counter and saw a second employee: a teenage boy with a lank ponytail. His nametag read FRANK, ASST. MANAGER.

He was wiping the orange plastic trays with a laconic languor. Watching him, Elsie's temper spiked.

"Hey, Frank! Are you the manager?"

He looked up, his brow furrowed. "Huh?"

"Frank, you've got a lot of people waiting here." Elsie gestured at the elderly couples and the family of five that stood in front of her, waiting their turn. "Think you could lend a hand? Step it up here?"

He set the orange tray on the top of the stack, dropped the rag in a bucket of cleaning solution and slowly scrubbed his hands in the metal sink. When he finally walked up to an unattended cash register, his face wore a pout.

"Who's next?"

The family of five pounced, and Elsie stepped up behind them. She shut her eyes, praying for patience while they fussed over the kids' meal choices. When at last they stepped aside, she walked up and met Frank's eye.

"I want a twelve-piece bucket of extra crispy; one large side of mashed potatoes and gravy; one large coleslaw." She paused, thinking. "And a large Diet Coke."

"Is Pepsi okay?"

She made a face. "I guess so."

He avoided eye contact as he pushed the buttons of the computer. In a miffed voice, he said, "That'll be thirty-seven fifty."

Elsie blinked. She had a twenty-dollar bill and some change in her purse; her cash on hand wouldn't cover the cost. Rummaging in her wallet, she found her debit card and handed it over.

At the next register, a silver-haired lady reached out and patted her arm. "Miss Arnold?"

Elsie looked over, smiling. "Yes, ma'am?"

"I was on one of your juries. Your speaking voice is so nice and clear. I didn't have a bit of trouble hearing you."

Elsie felt a bubble of vanity surge in her chest. "Why, thank you. So nice to hear."

"I told all my friends about you. Everyone in my church group."

Elsie's smile widened at the praise. She was about to speak when Frank interrupted.

"Declined."

Elsie's head jerked to face him. "What?"

"Your card. You don't have enough money."

A hot blush raced up her neck; she could feel the heat in her face. She fumbled in her purse again, hoping to uncover another stash of bills, but she came up empty.

"I can't give you the food if you don't have the money to pay for it." Frank's voice was loud enough to be heard outside the drive-thru window and inside the far stall in the women's restroom.

Elsie zipped her purse, muttering a garbled apology. When a uniformed employee stepped up with the bucket of chicken, Frank snapped at him. "Put it back. She can't afford it."

Elsie grabbed her car keys. Before she stepped away, she glanced over at her former juror. The silver head was looking pointedly in the other direction.

Elsie slunk out of the KFC and into her car, slamming the door so hard that it bounced back open. With a string of dark curses, she sped out of the parking lot and headed down the highway.

To McDonald's. Twenty dollars would work some magic there.

Waiting in the McDonald's drive-thru, twenty dollars poorer, Elsie's cell rang. She picked it up, checking the number: Barton Memorial Hospital.

She answered just as the bag of food was handed to her. "This is Elsie Arnold," she said into the phone.

"Elsie? It's Alice."

Her shoulders tensed. The nurse from Barton Memorial wouldn't have called to pass the time. "Hey, Alice; what's up?"

At the window, the young server asked, "You want a drink carrier?"

She nodded; and juggled the sodas through her opened car window, setting the ungainly cardboard tray onto the seat beside her.

In her ear, Alice's voice was high-pitched. "Elsie, she left. Just walked out. We didn't release her; we were holding her for another day. The security guard saw her slip out the door; he called out, but she got away."

Elsie gripped the phone. "When?"

"Not long; maybe ten minutes ago. I called the PD, but Ashlock's not there."

A horn blared behind her. Elsie was blocking the drive-thru.

"Which exit did she use? To get away?"

"The front door, if you can believe that. Wearing nothing but a hospital grown and a pair of slipper socks."

"Oh Lord." The driver of the car behind Elsie leaned on the horn. She honked back and thrust her hand out the driver's window, giving a one finger salute.

The McDonald's worker looked aghast. In a hesitant voice, he said, "Ma'am, you'll have to step aside."

Hitting the accelerator, she dashed out of the lot so fast that the tray of sodas flipped over, tumbling off the passenger seat and onto the floorboard.

Chapter 12

ELSIE HAD NO master plan in mind, beyond heading back to Barton Memorial. She could talk to the security guard, to the floor nurses. Get a feel for the motivation behind Mandy's sudden departure.

A cold rain began to fall; she turned on her windshield wipers, then reached for the phone. She just took her eyes off the road for a second, to push the contact for Ashlock's cell phone.

He picked up on the first ring. "Where you at, Elsie? I'm hungry."

"Mandy bailed. Walked out of the hospital."

"What? Did someone come for her?"

She didn't answer. In the beam of her headlights, she saw a ghostly figure, standing on the wet pavement in a flapping gown, her arm extended, thumb up.

"Well, I'll be damned. I think I've got her." She cut off the call.

Elsie veered to the side of the road and hit the brake. She reached over to open the passenger door. Mandy slid inside without pausing to check out the interior.

Once in the passenger seat, Mandy said, "Shit, the floorboard's all wet." Then she looked over at Elsie. "It's you again? No fucking way. I'm not believing this."

Mandy reached for the door handle, but Elsie moved faster, hitting the master lock button with her left hand.

In a cajoling voice, she said, "Mandy, it's a pretty nasty night to be out in your stocking feet."

Mandy slid down in the car seat. "My feet was drier out there."

"Sorry about that. Hey, you hungry?"

"No."

"I've got a Big Mac."

Elsie glanced over. Mandy didn't reply, but she didn't say no either. The smell emanating from the hot McDonald's bag on the console filled the car.

Mandy cut her eyes at the bag. At length, she said, "My mouth's too messed up. I don't think I can eat a Big Mac."

Elsie nodded, her eyes on the road. "Got a Quarter Pounder with cheese in there, too. That might work better. And there's fries."

A long moment of silence was broken when Mandy said, "I guess I could eat fries." She pulled the paper bag off the console and onto her lap.

"What did they feed you at the hospital?" Elsie kept her voice deliberately casual.

Mandy's head snapped to face her. "I'm not going back there."

"I didn't say you were." Elsie had reached the turn that would take them back to Barton Memorial. She drove in the opposite direction.

"They give me Jell-O. Some soup that was like water," Mandy said, speaking around a mouthful of fries.

"I can see why you wanted to break out. Sounds like they were trying to starve you."

Mandy chewed. After a moment, Elsie said, "Why'd you leave, Mandy?"

"I need to get back. And I didn't like that cop."

"Ashlock?" Elsie's kneejerk reaction was to launch into a defense of Detective Ashlock. She was, after all, an expert on his good qualities.

But she paused, and said, "What don't you like about him?"

"Too fucking nosy," Mandy said without hesitation. She pulled out the cardboard box that held the Quarter Pounder. "I can have this?"

"Sure."

Elsie braked at a four-way stop. She glanced over at Mandy, watching her open her mouth carefully, nibbling at the burger's edge with her front teeth.

Elsie drove through the intersection. They were entering the oldest part of town. Her car bumped over a set of railroad tracks.

"Are we getting close to the highway? I can thumb a ride on the highway."

Mandy leaned forward to peer through the windshield. The street they were traveling was poorly lit. Vacant buildings and empty storefronts faced the tracks. A single streetlight illuminated the corner where an ancient brick hotel sat. Elsie pulled the car to the curb in front of the hotel.

Mandy's voice was sharp. "Take me to the highway."

Elsie sighed. She turned off the ignition. "I've done some stupid things in my day. But I'm not crazy enough to dump a near-naked girl onto the highway in the rain."

Mandy was staring at the old hotel, shaking her head. "Is this the police station? I'm not going there. Ain't gonna do it."

"No, Mandy. This is a place for you to sleep. You don't want to go back to the hospital, don't want to talk to the police; I heard you. But you need a place to stay."

The brickwork of the building's exterior held a sign with a name chiseled in stone: BARTON HOTEL.

"Is this a hotel? I don't have any money."

Elsie shifted in her seat and faced the girl. "It won't cost anything. It's a shelter."

Mandy laughed, a mocking noise. "Oh that's fucking great. A homeless shelter. Just when I thought shit couldn't get any worse."

The door of the building opened. A woman whose gray hair hung over her shoulder in a long braid peered out. "Elsie?" she called.

Elsie pushed the button to roll the passenger window down. "Hey, June."

The gray-haired woman ran to the car, huddling her shoulders against the rain. She leaned her head into the passenger window and said, "I thought it was your car. Who do we have here?"

"This is Mandy. She needs a place to stay. Some clothes, too."

When the gray-haired woman extended a hand to touch Mandy's shoulder, the girl winced and pulled back.

June dropped her hand. Examining Mandy with an expert eye, she clucked her tongue and said, "You poor lamb. Let's get you inside, get you into some dry clothes."

Mandy turned to Elsie with a suspicious look. "What the fuck is this?"

But Elsie didn't answer. She was busy texting Ashlock: *Dropping Mandy off at BWC of the O. See U soon.*

June was trying without success to open the passenger door, but it remained locked. "Elsie. Open the door. We're getting soaked."

Elsie punched the button and held her breath. If Mandy ran away when she was out of the car, Elsie had no right or authority to stop her.

But June's calm spirit appeared to work its magic. Mandy followed her inside. Elsie sighed out with relief. Mandy was in good hands at the Battered Women's Center of the Ozarks.

Chapter 13

THE RAIN PELTED Elsie as she made a run for Ashlock's house. The front door was open, and she walked inside, bearing the soggy bag from McDonald's.

Ashlock's son, Burton, sat on the couch in the living room, his feet on the coffee table. "Finally," he said. When he looked up from the television screen and saw the bag Elsie held, he made an unhappy face.

"McDonald's? Seriously?"

Elsie tossed the bag onto the table, next to Burton's feet. She fought the urge to apologize; he was Ashlock's kid, not hers. His appetite wasn't her responsibility.

Burton opened the damp paper bag and pulled out a fry. "The fries are cold."

"Yeah, probably right." She dropped into the recliner that sat next to the couch, though it was officially Ashlock's preferred seat. But she needed to put her feet up.

"Someone ate half of the Quarter Pounder." Burton's voice held a plaintive note, the sound of a wounded little boy.

"Hey, Burton? I wouldn't mess with that Quarter Pounder if I were you. There's a Big Mac in there. It's still virgin. Untouched by human hands." She leaned back in the chair and closed her eyes.

Ashlock walked into the living room. He had changed out of his work clothes and into his civvies, and wore slippers on his feet. Elsie felt a prick of envy. She longed to shed her wet clothes and the unforgiving shoes that pinched her toes.

Ashlock said, "I thought I heard you come in. How'd it go at the BWC?"

Elsie opened her mouth to answer, but Burton spoke first.

"Dad, she brought McDonald's. And it's cold."

Elsie watched as Ashlock peered into the soggy bag. *Don't you bitch about it,* she thought. *Don't you dare.*

Ashlock didn't look at her. To Burton, he said, "I can fry you some eggs."

"I had eggs for breakfast."

"We've got a chicken pot pie in the freezer. I'll put it in the microwave."

With an aggrieved sigh, Burton dropped his feet on the floor and rose from the couch.

"I'll do it," he said, and headed to the kitchen.

Ashlock sat on the sofa cushion Burton had vacated. He lifted the top bun off the Big Mac, inspected it, and then pushed it aside.

"So," Elsie said. "She wanted to hitch a ride on the highway, but I persuaded her to go to the shelter. Thank God. If she'd disappeared, it would have been the end of the case."

He looked up. "I wouldn't say there's much of a case anyway, at this point."

Elsie sat up in the chair. "What the fuck? We have a girl who got the tar beaten out of her at the Rancho Motel, right here in McCown County. I'd charge it as a felony assault."

"Who're you going to charge? She won't cooperate."

"She will. Give it time."

He shook his head. His hand disappeared into the McDonald's bag. He pulled out a soggy French fry and dropped it back inside. "She's already denied that the assault was at the hands of the guy who paid for the hotel room: Tony Fontaine. I had to put that in my report. If she turns around and claims later that he actually did it, then there's a prior inconsistent statement."

She pulled a face. What Ashlock pointed out was correct; but Elsie wasn't ready to wave the white flag. "Mandy made it clear that she's a working girl. Maybe Tony is the pimp. What about the client? The john?"

"She says she doesn't know who he was and can't identify him. It's a blind alley."

"She wasn't ready to open up, that's all. When she's had time to think it over, she'll be more forthcoming. I've got a feeling about her."

"Then you've already given the defense its reasonable doubt argument. Because when she becomes more forthcoming, the earlier report will show that she initially lied to the police. You know how that will go down. 'If she's lied before, how can you believe her now?'"

Her brow furrowed. "Ash, you saw her injuries. We can't ignore this, just pretend no crime was committed."

He picked up the remote control and flipped through the channels. With his eyes on the screen, he said, "At this point the only firm case I've got is against her. For prostitution."

Elsie slammed the footrest of the recliner down with an audible bang. "Are you fucking kidding me?"

"Whoa!" Burton stood in the doorway with a steaming bowl in his hand. "Did she just say the f-word?"

Elsie exhaled, rolling her eyes. Ashlock had repeatedly asked her to keep a lid on her colorful vocabulary around his kids.

"Sorry, Burton. It slipped out," she said.

Burton took a bite of the chicken pie in the bowl and said, "Dad, you were going to look over my project tonight."

Ashlock stood up. "You want to do it now?"

"I've got it pulled up on the laptop, on the kitchen table."

When they left the room, Elsie leaned over to the coffee table and picked up the Big Mac. She took a tentative bite.

Ice cold.

She ate it anyway.

Chapter 14

My mom is gonna kill me.

The thought had become a recurring refrain as Taylor stood before the mirror in the women's bathroom at the Denny's restaurant near the highway in Barton. She held a mascara wand. Her hand trembled so violently that she poked herself in the eye with it.

"Ouch!" Taylor dropped the wand and rubbed her eye.

"Stop that. You're rubbing off your eye shadow."

Desiree stood at Taylor's shoulder, applying a coat of dark red lipstick to her mouth.

"Taylor, you need eyeliner," Desiree said.

Taylor gave her a reflection a worried look. "Desiree, I'm no good at it. I haven't worn eyeliner since Halloween."

The bathroom door opened and a woman in a Denny's uniform walked in. Before she entered the bathroom stall, she shot the girls a suspicious look. Taylor met the woman's eye in the mirror, then glanced quickly away. The waitress had a funny eye, which wandered sideways in the reflection.

Desiree dropped her voice to a whisper. "We have to look older, or it isn't gonna work out."

Taylor nodded in agreement; but privately she'd begun to hope that this plan would not pan out. She had a bad feeling about it. And if her mother knew what she was up to, there would be trouble.

Big trouble.

Desiree was slipping her feet into a pair of worn stilettos. "Did you bring shoes to change into?"

Taylor shook her head. "Couldn't find any."

"Doesn't your mom have any sexy shoes? To go clubbing in?"

Taylor rolled her eyes. "You know my mom. Clubbing isn't her scene. She just works all the time. All her shoes are the black ones she wears to court. They're ugly."

With a sigh of resignation, Desiree handed the red lipstick to Taylor. "Good thing you're tall."

The girls were surveying their appearance in the mirror when the Denny's waitress pushed between them to wash her hands. In a voice of disapproval, the woman said, "What are you kids up to in here? This bathroom is for customers only."

Taylor gave her friend an apprehensive glance in the mirror. Desiree lifted her chin.

"We're customers. We got a business meeting."

She flounced out the door, wobbling on her heels. Taylor followed behind. As they walked into the restaurant, Desiree paused.

"She's here. It's her."

Taylor had spotted her, too. A woman with elaborately styled auburn hair sat alone at a back booth, sipping from a coffee mug.

Stretching her mouth into a wide grin, Taylor followed Desiree to the booth. The woman looked up as they approached. She greeted them with a toothy smile.

"Are you my modeling applicants?"

"Yes, ma'am," said Desiree, as she slid into the booth. Taylor sat beside her. Her heart was hammering.

"I recognize you from the application pictures. But I'm happy to say, you're even prettier in person."

She focused on Taylor. "You have an excellent build. And the most beautiful skin." She reached across the table and stroked the skin of Taylor's forearm. Taylor's arm jerked reflexively. Embarrassed, she folded her hands in her lap.

Desiree spoke up. "Taylor was afraid she'd be too dark. She said all the models in the pictures you showed us are white and Asian. But I told her I bet it wouldn't matter."

The woman smiled, lifting her coffee mug. "Oh, we are an equal opportunity agency." After she took a sip, she said, "So Tony's met you on Skype. It's time for the next step. You excited?"

Taylor's heart was beating so violently, she was afraid the woman would see it hammering through her dress. "Why isn't he here?"

The woman's smile froze. "What?"

Desiree shot Taylor a look that said: Don't mess this up. Taylor cleared her throat.

"Tony. It's just—wasn't he supposed to be here? To interview us?"

As the woman pinned her with a stare, Taylor slumped back against the cushion of the booth. "I guess I misunderstood."

The waitress from the bathroom came up to their table. As she pulled out her pad, she addressed the girls with a cocked brow over her wandering eye. "What can I get you ladies?"

Taylor shook her head, preparing to say "Nothing for me, thanks." But Desiree spoke right up.

"I'll have a sweet tea."

The woman across the booth reached out and placed her hand over Desiree's on the vinyl tabletop. "Unsweet," she whispered.

Desiree nodded. "Yes, ma'am. Unsweet."

As the waitress walked off, the woman winked at Desiree and said, "You're a model now."

Desiree's face broke into a wide smile. Taylor saw that her friend had a streak of red lipstick on her front tooth.

"Really?"

"Really." She patted Desiree's hand; then giving Desiree a wink, the woman curled her upper lip and scrubbed her tooth with a finger. Desiree gasped, hastily imitating the gesture and swiping at her own offending tooth. The woman turned her attention to Taylor.

"Tony's career name for Desiree is Lola. And for you, sweetheart, he's come up with a beauty. You'll be Coco."

Taylor blinked. Why did she need a fake name? A question popped out before she could stop it.

"What's your name?"

The woman tucked a lock of hair behind her ear. "You can call me Dede."

"Okay," said Taylor. "Dede what?"

Dede's eyes narrowed. Before she could reply, Desiree spoke in a breathless voice.

"When do I get my first gig?"

The smile returned. "Well, Desiree—I mean, Lola—Tony is

ready to do a photo shoot for you this Friday night. Both of you." Her eyes cut to Taylor. "If you're interested."

"Yesss," Desiree said.

Taylor twisted her hands in her lap. "I've got a game Friday."

Her friend turned on her, with a disbelieving face. "Taylor. It's a photo shoot."

She was torn. Desiree was counting on her. They'd pledged to do this together. "But the team is counting on me."

"The team?" Dede's voice was cool. "Our application form is clear: this is for professionals. Young women who want a career. Not little girls who want to play ball."

Under the table, Desiree's hand snaked around Taylor's knee; the pressure of the squeeze made her jump. Desiree said, "Taylor's just kidding around. We're interested. What time?"

"Ten o'clock."

"In the morning?" Taylor said.

Dede dove into a turquoise blue handbag and pulled out a five-dollar bill. As she set it under the coffee mug, she said, "Ten P.M. Tony's busy all day. Ten o'clock is the only time this week that he can fit you in."

"That works," Desiree said.

"Good!" The waitress walked up with Desiree's glass of tea. Dede waited until she walked off, then added, "We'll even pick you up. That's how serious we are about your audition."

The girls exchanged a look. Desiree's eyes were bright, as if she might be on the verge of happy tears.

But Taylor felt a lump in her stomach. "Are you picking us up at our houses?" She didn't know how she'd explain this red-haired woman showing up at ten at night. Her mom would eat Dede alive.

"No, silly. We'll pick you up here. In the parking lot." Dede scooted out of the booth. "Don't be late, sugars. Tony hates it when his girls are late."

Taylor watched Dede walk off, her bright blue bag bouncing on her shoulder.

My mom's going to kill me, she thought.

Chapter 15

ELSIE HAD FULLY intended to arrive at the Friday morning docket meeting in Madeleine's office on time. But after court, she was pining for a Diet Coke; and there was a line in front of her at the coffee shop in the basement. A line of senior citizens.

Once she had her beverage in hand, she made a dash for the elevator, to save time that running up the stairs would require; but it was full. Full of the gray-haired proprietors from the coffee shop.

By the time she knocked on Madeleine's office door and stepped inside, she was the last to arrive. Madeleine sat behind her desk; Chuck and Breeon were already seated, studying copies of the printed docket sheets. Elsie plopped onto the sofa beside Bree, prepared to offer an apology. But Madeleine spoke before she had the opportunity.

"I'm assigning you to try the case on Monday."

Elsie looked around. "Who? Me?"

Madeleine gave her a slow blink. "Yes, you. Third degree assault case."

"A third degree assault? We're taking a misdemeanor assault to a jury?"

"Well. You are."

Elsie slumped against the back of the sofa, thinking: *that's why you should never be late to a meeting. Because you'll be volunteered for a job nobody wants.*

"What's the case name?" Elsie asked, pulling a pen from her bag. She didn't try to hide her glum expression.

Breeon scooted close to Elsie so that she could see the docket sheet. A case name halfway down the page was marked with a star in blue ink.

Bree said, "It's this one. *State of Missouri v. Sweeny Greene.*"

"Doesn't ring a bell," Elsie said, shaking her head. "I didn't file it."

Chuck shifted in his club chair at the corner of Madeleine's desk. "I filed it," he said.

"Then why aren't you trying it?"

He pinned her with a look. "Because, as chief trial assistant, I'm assigning it to you."

For the hundredth time, Elsie mentally cursed Madeleine for placing Chuck Harris in the number one spot on her staff, rather than giving the position to Bree or Elsie, who had more trial experience than he possessed.

What Chuck had that the women lacked—aside from expensive suits—was a father who was a big dog in the state Republican Party. Madeleine had ambitions to higher office.

"So, is it a domestic assault case? I can get into that," Elsie said with resignation.

"Fistfight," Chuck replied.

"A domestic fistfight?"

"No," he said, with exaggerated patience. "A fistfight between two locals. Outside of the Baldknobbers Bar."

Elsie screwed her face into an expression of disbelief. "A bar fight? We're trying a bar fight to a jury? Whose idiot decision is that?"

When Breeon gave her an elbow to the ribs, Elsie realized she'd spoken too freely. Madeleine's voice was icy as she said, "Mine."

Elsie backpedaled. "Oh, okay. Hey, you're the boss."

"I am. And as the chief law enforcement official in McCown County, I am sending a message that I will not tolerate lawless and violent behavior. Nor will I countenance brawling in public places."

Madeleine paused to draw breath; her stump speech was just warming up. But she was interrupted when the door to her office flew open and a man stepped inside.

"Where's the keys?"

The attorneys turned to see who dared to disturb Madeleine's chamber without an invitation. Elsie recognized him: Dennis Thompson, Madeleine's husband. Elsie had met him before, but rarely in this setting. He was an infrequent visitor to the Prosecutor's Office.

Madeleine's tone was abrupt. "Dennis, we're in a meeting."

"Well, this won't take much of your valuable time. You took the spare set of keys, and I need them for the safe." He paused; when Madeleine didn't reply, he said, "Would you look in your goddamn purse?"

Madeleine bent down and picked her handbag off the floor. As she hunted inside the purse, she said, "Dennis, this is my trial team. Have you met them?"

He gave the attorneys a cursory glance. "Yeah. Probably." His eyes focused on Elsie. "You're a regular over at the Baldknobbers, aren't you, honey?"

Elsie wanted to squirm; with an effort, she managed to remain still.

"Pretty much," Elsie admitted; because there was no point in attempting a denial. Then she had inspiration. "Madeleine, do you think that should disqualify me?"

"From what?" Madeleine clutched a set of keys in her fist and gave Elsie an impatient glare.

"From that third degree assault trial. Since I'm a regular at the scene of the crime, maybe Chuck should do it after all."

"Don't be ridiculous." Madeleine handed the keys to her husband and he thumbed through them. He pulled a small brass key off the ring and shoved it into his pocket, and then tossed the key ring back onto her desk. In a formal tone, she addressed her husband, saying, "I didn't mean to inconvenience you. I grabbed them off the key ring this morning on my way out the door. The spare set has my extra Mercedes fob. They're almost identical."

He didn't respond. Turning, he made his way to the door.

Madeleine spoke again, to his back. "Will I see you tonight? Or are you working late?"

When he answered, he didn't turn to face her. "Not working. Hunting."

Chuck looked up at Dennis with a face of polite interest. "That's cool. What are you hunting, Dennis?"

Just before he pulled the door shut behind him, Dennis replied, "Turkey."

Elsie shook her head. Chuck was such a transparent faker. Anyone could take one look at him and know he'd never shot wild game.

Ashlock, on the other hand, had grown up in the woods. If his schedule permitted, he'd be on the hunt all autumn long.

And that caused her to recall something Ashlock had said; something that made her brow wrinkle. Wasn't turkey season over? If Dennis got caught hunting out of season, he'd pick up a citation.

Elsie glanced at Madeleine, and considered whether she should mention it.

A look at Madeleine's face decided the issue. She should keep her mouth shut.

Chapter 16

On Friday night, Elsie sat at the kitchen table, wrapped in a terrycloth robe. Her laptop was open on the table in front of her, and she leaned close to it with absorption. The words on the screen were familiar to her: Missouri criminal statutes defining sex offenses. She clicked the computer, rereading the language of the criminal code, searching the language from a new perspective.

Her cell phone sat at her left hand. When her phone hummed, she picked it up without looking.

"Ash?"

A laugh sounded in her ear; it was Breeon, not Ashlock. Breeon said, "Well, I got lucky. Where are you?"

"Home. Sitting in the kitchen." Looking down, Elsie frowned as she plucked at a fraying patch on the worn terrycloth robe.

"Great. Excellent. Let's go see a movie."

Bree's voice had a lilt to it; like a kid out of school for a snow day. Elsie checked the time on the computer screen, and scowled.

"Naw, I can't leave. I'm waiting around for Ashlock."

"Elsie Arnold! Since when do you waste a Friday night waiting on a man?"

It was a reasonable question. A year ago, she would have been kicking off the dust of the week, lighting up the night spots; undeterred by the fact that the number of cocktail venues in Barton was pitifully small.

A can of Diet Coke sat on the table, and she lifted it for a swallow, but only the dregs remained. "He had to deliver Burton to his mom; it's her visitation weekend. They meet halfway. But he should've been here ages ago. I'm tempted to start drinking alone."

"Don't do that. Let me pick you up. If you don't want to see a movie, we can grab a beer somewhere."

The mention of beer motivated Elsie to rise from her chair and walk to the refrigerator. Staring at the contents, she beheld a six pack of Corona in bottles and a couple of cans of Coors Light.

Though her mother taught that a considerate hostess would save the best for her anticipated guest, he'd been keeping her waiting way too long. She popped the cap on a Corona and took a sip from the neck.

And a thought occurred. "What are you doing, drumming up a Friday night companion? I can never drag you out on Friday, no matter how hard I try. Is Taylor with her daddy in St. Louis?"

"No. After the ball game, she asked if she could spend the night with a friend. So, I find myself with a free evening. On a Friday, no less. And I've got no prospects. It's kind of pitiful, actually."

Elsie sat down on the kitchen chair and tipped back the bottle. "Who's Taylor hanging with? One of the basketball girls?"

"No, it's a new friend. Her name's Desiree. She's kind of an odd duck; not like Taylor at all. I think Taylor has taken her under her wing."

Elsie was only half listening; she heard footsteps approaching in the hallway outside her apartment; and they had a familiar tread.

"Bree, I think Ash may be showing up at last."

"Okay, hon. I'll let you go. See you in court on Monday."

When he knocked, she checked the time on the laptop: it was past nine. He was late. Two hours late.

She shuffled to the door in stocking feet and looked through the peephole before she unlocked it.

"Sorry," Ashlock said, walking in and shedding his jacket. "She got held up at work, and didn't get to West Plains till way past time."

Elsie nodded, with resignation. She wasn't actually surprised he'd been delayed. It was a commonplace occurrence.

"How was she? Jolly?" Elsie walked to the refrigerator and pulled out another bottle of Corona. She sawed a wedge of lime on the kitchen counter with a serrated knife.

"You should do that on a cutting board. You'll scar the countertop," Ashlock said.

She shoved the limes into the necks of the bottles. "Don't rat me out to the landlord." Looking over her shoulder, she made a face at him.

Taking the fresh bottle, he stood behind her and kissed her neck. "You sure smell good."

"I took a bath. Since I had the time."

He followed her to the living room; as they settled on the couch, she indicated the TV remote on the coffee table. "You want to watch TV? I'll let you work the remote."

He groaned and swilled from the bottle. "It's been a long week, and I just spent thirty minutes negotiating holidays. I'd just like a chance to relax." He put an arm around Elsie's shoulders and pulled her close to him. "Some peace and quiet, that's what I want."

He closed his eyes and rested his head on the back of the sofa. Since he had mentioned holidays, Elsie considered broaching her mother's Thanksgiving invitation, but decided to let him rest. So she drank her Corona; and when the bottle was empty, she went to the kitchen for a fresh one. After she opened it, she lingered by the kitchen table, clicking the computer mouse and looking at the screen of the laptop.

Ashlock opened his eyes and called to her. "What are you doing over there?"

She looked over at him with a perturbed expression. "Thinking."

"Thinking about something bad, from the look of it." He patted the cushion beside him.

She joined him again, scooting close beside him on the couch, but remained pensive. "I've read the reports. Been rereading the statutes. Lord knows, I am familiar with the case law."

"What are you going on about?"

"The assault at the Rancho. Mandy."

"Ah," he said, reaching for his beer. Deadpan, he said: "Mandy Candy."

She frowned. "Yeah."

"C-A-N-D-Y. That's how you spell it."

"Ash, it's really bugging me. I keep going back to the report."

He brushed her long hair off her back and over one shoulder, then massaged her neck with his fingers. "Well, I wrote the report. If there's a problem with it, I'm your man."

His hands were working familiar magic; as he tugged at her robe and rubbed her shoulders, she resisted the urge to drop the subject.

"Ash, every time I read the report, it sounds inconclusive. Like there's a question about whether a case can be made for assault. I don't feel like we're doing right by that girl."

He squeezed the tense muscles of her back with warm, strong hands. "The only thing standing in our way is her. Miss Mandy. Because she won't give it up. Not her name, not the facts, not the suspect. She's made it impossible to proceed."

Elsie's jaw tensed; but she slipped her arms out of the robe to give him better access.

"Not impossible. More difficult, yeah. But not impossible."

His hands kneaded her lower back; she stifled a moan.

After a quiet moment, she whispered, "Nothing's impossible."

He bit her shoulder; she squeaked in surprise. Shifting on the sofa to face him, she rubbed the tender spot with her hand.

"What was that for?"

He tugged at the belt of her bathrobe. "Are you buck naked under there?"

When he opened the bathrobe, he had his answer. He let out a happy sigh, pushing her down on the sofa with a firm hand.

"Don't you want to go to the bedroom?"

"Too far."

As he unzipped his pants, she raised up on one elbow. "Aren't we even gonna order a pizza?"

"Later," he said.

And later, they did. With pepperoni and sausage. Extra large.

Chapter 17

TAYLOR LEANED UP to the front passenger seat of the car and whispered in Desiree's ear.

"If my mom calls your house, what's your mom gonna tell her?"

Desiree turned her head toward the car window and spoke in an impatient undertone. "Your mom isn't gonna call. But if she does, my mom will tell her we went to Sonic for a slush."

"In the rain? After ten?" Taylor said.

In the driver's seat, Dede glanced over her shoulder. "Hey! What's going on over there?"

"Nothing," Desiree said, giving Taylor a look of warning over her shoulder. "Everything's good. 'Sall cool."

"How about you, Coco," Dede said, catching Taylor's eye with the rearview mirror. "Are you cool, baby?"

Taylor nodded and turned to stare at the raindrops spattering on the window of the back passenger door. Her knee jiggled, and she couldn't make it stop. She wished she could see a familiar sight out the window, but it was too dark. And they'd been driving for at least half an hour.

Now it seemed like a bad idea to her. A really bad idea.

When she and Desiree had plotted their adventure during lunch in the school cafeteria, it sounded glamorous and daring. And they agreed that it was really fortunate that they could confide in Desiree's mom; she was sympathetic to the plan.

Desiree's mom had always cherished big dreams for her little girl. When Des was a little kid, they invested every spare dollar and every weekend they had in the kiddie pageant circuit.

Desiree told her that the pageant career ended when she hit adolescence and couldn't bring home the trophies anymore; but her mom's big dreams were revived when Desiree found a Backlist.com ad for Marvel Modeling. Kim Wickham believed in Desiree; she told the girls so.

Taylor's mom, on the other hand, just didn't get it.

When Breeon came into the living room and saw Taylor watching *Project Runway*, or reruns of *America's Top Model* on cable, she laughed and changed the channel. When Taylor asked her mom to pick up a copy of *Vogue* at Barnes & Noble, Breeon returned empty-handed. Didn't even apologize, just said she forgot.

Sneaking out with Desiree had sounded like fun, and the prospect had given her a thrilling sensation of finally pulling one over on her mom. Taylor's mom was so bossy. Controlling.

But as she sat in the silent car on Friday night, listening to the flap of the windshield wipers, she wished with all her heart that she was home. With her bossy mom.

Taylor cleared her throat. "How long till we get to the audition?"

"Soon. Pretty soon." Dede reached onto the dash and pulled a cigarette from a pack. "I'll crack the window," she said as she lit up.

Desiree said, "Hey, can I have one?"

"Sure. Help yourself."

Taylor gasped. She'd never seen Desiree smoke before. The interior of the car soon filled with a cloud of cigarette smoke. She coughed, despite an effort to choke it back.

"That bothering you?" Dede said. "No problem, hon." She rolled her window down and tossed the butt onto the highway.

When Desiree tried to follow suit, the wind blew the lit cigarette into the backseat, where it fell on Taylor's bare arm. Shrieking, she knocked it to the floor.

Dede peered into the rearview mirror, causing the car to swerve into the left lane. "Fuck! Put it out. Are you burning a hole in the upholstery? This is Tony's personal vehicle."

The shrill voice in the front seat sent Taylor into an anxious hunt for the burning ember. She bent down to the floorboard, feeling for the cigarette with her hands. When she found it, she rolled the window down and flung it into the darkness.

Dede was cussing under her breath. The burn on Taylor's forearm smarted; she cupped her hand over it. In the distance a lit sign appeared: it said EconoMo Motel.

"We're here," Dede said. Her voice was grim.

As they pulled into the parking lot of the motel, tears slipped down Taylor's face.

Chapter 18

TAYLOR LAGGED BEHIND Dede and Desiree as they made a run from the car to the hotel room at the EconoMo. Desiree was squealing: "My hair is going to frizz."

Dede led the way, to the doorway of Room 217. She knocked first, even though she held a key in her hand.

Pressing her hands onto the door, she spoke in an urgent voice. "It's me."

Then she thrust the plastic key in the slot and opened the door partway, just far enough to stick her head through.

"Tony?"

Taylor had caught up to them. She wiped the tears from her cheeks. When she pulled her hands away, the light shining out of Room 217 revealed traces of mascara on her wet fingertips.

Following Dede's lead, they stepped inside the room. It was a double, with two beds. The mattresses were covered by dingy bedspreads in a pattern of tan and brown. A dark-haired man with a tattoo on his neck sat in a chair by the desk, his legs crossed: Tony.

When they walked inside and Dede shut the door behind them, he rose from his seat.

"Well, look what the cat dragged in," he said with a laugh.

He had an accent that Taylor couldn't place: not the Southwest Missouri twang, but a Southern drawl. He wasn't that tall, not nearly as tall as her dad in St. Louis; maybe about her mom's height. But he had the arms and shoulders of a body builder, and his ink-covered muscles were on display in a tight blue T-shirt.

"You girls are wet as sop. Dede, what have you done?"

Dede flashed a nervous smile. "It's pouring rain out there. They were wet when I picked them up."

Taylor could read the unspoken message in Dede's tone: *Not my fault.* She's scared of him, Taylor thought.

That made Taylor scared of him, too.

Tony walked over to the desk and adjusted the position of his laptop computer.

"Okay, girls. We're going to see what you've got."

Desiree gave a wide pageant smile. "Do you want to see me walk?"

Without waiting for an invitation, she pranced across the worn carpet, pivoted, and walked back, her hand poised on her hip. When she came to a stop, she flipped her curly hair over her shoulder.

"That's my sassy walk. I can do a fashion walk, too, if you want to see that. It's for the runway."

Dede and Tony exchanged a look. Dede coughed into her hand, while he put an arm around Desiree's shoulders.

"That was sweet, hon. Just darling. But we want something a little more grown-up. I've got a chance to get you in a lingerie catalogue."

Desiree's eyes glowed. "Love it!"

"So let's get y'all camera-ready. Dede, show them what we have for them to model."

Dede unzipped a black nylon suitcase. Taylor craned her neck to see what was inside: a jumble of wadded clothes. She made an involuntary face of disgust; they looked used, dirty.

Dede pulled out a pink teddy and a thong. "Pink would be good for her," she said, tossing it at Desiree. Digging deeper into the suitcase, she said, "Maybe red for the black girl."

Taylor's spine stiffened. "I'm not wearing that stuff."

The room fell silent. Desiree clutched the pink underwear to her chest, sending Taylor a pleading look. Dede shot a look at Tony.

Tony walked up behind Taylor and caressed the back of her neck. She jerked away from the touch.

"Oh baby," he said, his voice crooning. "You're all nervous. All worked up. Sit down, baby."

He took her by the elbow. She let him lead her to one of the beds, where she sat on the edge. He stood in front of her and squeezed her shoulders.

"Feel how tight you are. You need to relax. A girl's got to relax, if she's gonna be any good at this."

Taylor swallowed, staring down at the floor, focusing on her feet. She felt a scream building in her chest. If he didn't stop touching her, she was afraid the scream would escape.

But something about him kept the scream bottled inside. She wasn't sure what he'd do if she made a noise. His arms were on either side of her; she glanced over, saw that he had more ink on his forearm, a picture of a creature baring sharp fangs.

"Dede, make these girls a magic drink. So they can relax a little bit. Desiree, you hustle into that lingerie and hop up on that bed facing the laptop. You can go first, so your friend can see how it's done."

Desiree ran into the bathroom, closing the door with a click. Over on the dresser, Dede was pouring liquid into a cup. She dropped a couple of ice cubes into the cup and handed it to Tony.

Tony advanced on Taylor, holding out the red plastic cup. She shook her head.

"I don't drink."

He smiled, beaming down at her in approval.

"Well, that's just fine. That's real smart. Booze makes a girl's face all puffy. Did you know that?"

He loomed over her. He seemed to expect her to respond.

"No," she whispered.

"Well, it's the damn truth. Just look at Dede over there. Used to be tight as hell, but now that she's a boozehound, she's getting the old moon face." He raised his voice. "Ain't that right, Dede?"

Dede crossed her arms over her chest and stared at him with a pout. Taylor peeked around Tony and inspected Dede covertly. Actually, she could kind of see what Tony was talking about. Dede had puffy bags under her eyes.

Taylor shifted her gaze to Tony. His face was baggy, too. And he had broken veins around his nose.

He put an arm around her shoulder. "This little old drink doesn't have a drop of alcohol in it. Just try it, you'll see. Tastes like fruity punch. It'll hydrate you. Models need to stay hydrated."

Taylor accepted the cup and took a tentative sip. It didn't taste like liquor, not that she'd had much experience with alcohol. But he was right; it tasted like fruit punch, maybe with extra cherry flavoring.

And she was thirsty. Maybe because she was so nervous, and she'd sweated a lot during the basketball game. She tipped the cup up and drank.

Desiree emerged from the bathroom, dressed in the pink lingerie. When Taylor saw her friend in the overhead light, she gasped and looked away, mortified. The teddy was see-through. Desiree's nipples were visible; she could even see a triangle of dark blond pubic hair through the lacy thong.

Desiree cleared her throat. "Is this for Veronica's Secret or something?"

"Baby! You're gorgeous!" Tony rose from the bed, strode over to Desiree, and wrapped her in a bear hug. "You're so hot, you gonna set this room on fire."

When he released her, she stood uncertainly, her shoulders hunched, as if to keep the teddy from touching her chest.

"Is it a catalogue shoot? Who for? My mom will want to know."

A shadow crossed Tony's face. He picked a plastic cup off the top of the dresser and filled it from bottles that sat nearby; then lifted it and swigged.

After he swallowed, he said, "Tell your Mama? Y'all still at that stage where you've got to run everything by your mommy?"

His voice ended on an inquiring note, and he paused, looking at Desiree with a sardonic half smirk.

She hastened to say, "Not everything. I mean, I'm eighteen now. I do whatever I want."

"That's my girl." He took her by the hand and led her to the other double bed, the one that faced the computer. Setting his cup on the bedside table, he placed his hands on her shoulders and pushed her down onto the mattress.

"Now, when a place like, say, Veronica's Secret, wants to hire models, they have to see what a girl can do. How she can carry off the product. You got to make the lingerie look hot, baby."

Desiree scooted back onto the mattress, sitting with her legs thrust out in front of her. She still wore her Converse tennis shoes, the canvas soaked with rainwater.

He sat beside her. "Let's get these off, what do you say?" And he slipped the shoes from her feet.

"You ticklish?" He rubbed his fingers down the bottom of one foot.

From Taylor's vantage point on the next bed, she thought her friend looked nervous. Real nervous. Almost as keyed-up as Taylor had been. But Taylor was feeling better now. Almost a little sleepy. She sipped from her cup again. It tasted good.

Still, Taylor felt duty-bound to stick up for her friend. She said, "Des, if you're feeling weird about it, you don't have to do it."

"Oh baby girl—you turning nervy on me, Lola? You just need a little magic. Here." He picked up his cup and waved it in front of Desiree's face.

Her eyes grew frantic as she stared at the cup, then up at Tony.

His voice crooned like he was singing a lullaby. "Now this is a magic potion. Like in an old fairy tale. You drink up, and it will take all your nerves and worries away."

He put the cup to her lips. Obediently, Desiree drank; though she coughed violently between swallows.

Sliding her back against the headboard, Taylor lifted her own cup and followed suit.

Tony spoke to Desiree in a coaxing voice that sounded like warm honey. "Let me rub your shoulders a little. Get those kinks out. Dede, get over here with our makeup box. Let's get some color in her cheeks."

Desiree tried to hand the cup back to Tony. He held up a finger and spoke sternly. "Drink."

Taylor watched them in a daze as Dede brushed her friend's hair and painted her face. Tony stroked her arms and legs then placed her in position on the bed.

It looked like Desiree was starting to enjoy it. She got a fit of the giggles when he told her to be sexy, to open her legs to show them what she's got.

At Tony's urging, Desiree pulled off the pink teddy and tossed it aside. Taylor knew she should intervene. She should tell Desiree to stop, to cover herself up. She should get up and get Des's clothes out of the bathroom and hand them to her, so they could leave.

But she was sleepy. So sleepy, she couldn't keep her eyes open.

So sleepy, she couldn't move.

Chapter 19

At noon on a cold Saturday morning, Elsie turned the ancient brass doorknob and walked into the lobby of the Battered Women's Center of the Ozarks.

June, the director of the facility, looked up from her desk. Her gray hair had worked its way out of her customary braid; wisps fell over her forehead, were tucked behind her ears. From June's appearance, Elsie figured that it had been a rough night at the shelter.

"Hey," June said in greeting. Her face was drawn, but her eyes were sharp behind wire-rimmed glasses.

"Hey, you. Did you pull an all-nighter?"

June scrubbed at her head with a blue-veined hand, ruffling the gray tendrils of hair. "Mess of trouble in here last night, hon. I been running interference since the sun went down."

Elsie pulled a worn wooden chair across the tiled floor and sat down, facing June across the desk. "When you called me, you said Mandy's ready to talk."

"She better be. She's lucky I didn't boot her out of here last night."

A black landline phone sitting on the desk began to ring. June checked the caller ID before she picked up the receiver.

"Jeanette? You're late, hon."

Elsie watched as June's face twitched with weary resignation.

She sighed and spoke into the phone. "Well, if you're running a fever, go back to bed. I'll cover you."

She dropped the receiver into the base and stared at the phone. "No rest for the weary."

Elsie pressed her lips tightly closed. She volunteered two Sundays a month at the shelter; but this was a Saturday, and she had no intention of sacrificing her day to that wooden desk. *Don't do it,* she thought. *Don't tell her you'll take the day shift.*

Elsie had a full plate for Saturday. Prep for the Monday misdemeanor trial in Judge Calvin's court. Witnesses to talk to, examinations to write. And when she was done with her labors: cold beer to drink.

But June didn't beg for a favor. She opened the top drawer of the scarred wooden desk and pulled out a pint bottle of Old Charter and a pack of Parliament cigarettes. She tossed them onto the desktop.

"I don't know how on earth Mandy managed to get these. She don't look a day over sixteen, and doesn't have a scrap of ID, anyhow."

Elsie studied the bottle. It was half full.

"Shoplifted, maybe?"

"Not likely. The convenience store a block or so away from here keeps the booze and smokes under lock and key."

Elsie picked up the pack of cigarettes and opened the box. A few were missing.

"How'd you find them?"

June barked a laugh. "World War III broke out up there. After midnight, I heard someone hollering like they were being murdered. When I got up the stairs, I could smell the smoke. Lord, Elsie; this old fire trap could go up like a tinder box if we let the women smoke in here."

"What was the shouting about?"

"Mandy's rooming next door to Peggy Pitts. You know of Peggy?"

Elsie nodded. Peggy Pitts and her husband were regulars on the docket at the McCown Country Courthouse. Domestic disputes, drunk and disorderly, DWI.

"Peggy sniffed it out before I did. Wanted a share. But Mandy wasn't sharing. They were wrestling like a couple of cubs." She blew out an exhausted breath. "Peggy's got a new bald spot on her head to show for it."

Elsie's eyes widened. "Damn." Peggy Pitts was a big woman, probably outweighed Elsie by fifty pounds. And Elsie wasn't pint-size.

"Well, I told Mandy I was tired of her sass. Said if she wanted a roof over her head, it was time to get to the bottom of her troubles. She said she wouldn't talk to no cops. That's a quote. But she'd talk to you."

June pulled the drawer open, replaced the bourbon and cigarette pack. "So here we are."

Elsie picked up her bag. "Where is she?"

"In her room. Waiting for you. End of the hallway, number 18."

"I'll go on up, then."

"You do that." June rose from her seat with a groan. "I'm going to lie down on the cot in the back room. Wake me up if you need me."

Elsie walked up the stairs to the next floor. The carved walnut stairway was a remnant of the old hotel's glory days, when it had been built to accommodate a brief burst of railway traffic a century prior. The peeling wallpaper revealed dark wood paneling underneath, stained from ancient water leaks.

When she reached number 18, the door was shut. Elsie gave a brisk knock.

"Mandy? You in there?"

She heard footsteps; the door opened a crack. Mandy's black eye, now turning a purple shade, stared out. "Oh it's you."

She opened the door and walked to the bed. Elsie followed, taking care to leave the door ajar. She didn't fancy being shut up with a kid who was tough enough to tear Peggy Pitts's hair from her scalp.

Mandy lay down on the bed. It was a single, a twin with a blond 1950s headboard. Elsie glanced around, uneasy. There was no other place to sit.

"You want to go down to the lobby to talk?"

"No, I'm cool."

A rickety bedside table adjoined the headboard; but Elsie didn't dare sit on that; she was sure it would collapse under her. Instead, she moved over to the window. An old metal radiator sat beneath it. She leaned against it, ignoring the way the rungs pressed against her butt.

"I heard you had some trouble last night."

Mandy gave her a flat stare, didn't respond.

Elsie continued. "So I'm curious. How'd you score the Old Charter?"

Mandy blinked. "I didn't steal nothing."

"I didn't say you did."

"If anyone says I stole it, he's a fucking liar."

Elsie nodded; the vehemence with which Mandy spoke was convincing. "So where'd you get it?"

"At that store over there."

Elsie held her tongue. After a beat, Mandy said, "I gave him something for it."

"Ah," Elsie said.

Mandy's face twisted. "Ah," she repeated, in a mocking voice. She bent her head over the bedspread, picked up a piece of lint and dropped it on the floor. "He got a good deal. More than it was worth."

Elsie had a pretty fair idea of the barter Mandy had made with the store clerk. She asked Mandy yet again: "How old are you, Mandy?"

"Yeah, I keep telling you. I'm eighteen."

"Because it's a crime for men to have sex with you if you're underage. A crime for them. Not you."

"That so?" Her voice was flat.

"Yeah. That's the law."

Elsie fell silent again, willing the girl to open up. She shifted her weight on the metal radiator; it was cutting off the blood supply in her rear end.

When Mandy stayed mum, Elsie said, "Give me a break, Mandy. This thing I'm sitting on is busting my ass."

For the first time, Mandy smiled.

Chapter 20

MOVING CAREFULLY, AS if her injuries still caused pain, Mandy swung her feet from the bed to the floor. "If you wanna sit somewhere, we got to blow this dump."

When Mandy stood, she must have read the uncertainty on Elsie's face. The girl laughed again, with a scornful sound.

"Don't freak out. I'm not running off. Remember? Got no place to go."

She shuffled over to the corner and slid her stocking feet into flip-flops.

Elsie moved away from the metal radiator and rubbed her rear end in an attempt to get the blood flowing. "Where do you want to go?"

Mandy didn't meet Elsie's eye. As she headed out the door, she said: "For a drive."

Elsie followed her down the walnut stairway. Pausing in the lobby, Elsie considered whether she should duck into the back room and let June know what they were doing. But Mandy was swiftly making a beeline for the door, her flip-flops slapping across the porcelain tile of the lobby floor.

Elsie scurried to catch up. June was probably asleep, anyway. No need to disturb her.

Out in the weak November sun, Mandy hugged herself, rubbing her hands up and down her arms. She wore a pink cotton sweatshirt with matching sweatpants.

"Are you going to be warm enough?" Elsie asked in a doubtful voice.

"I will be as soon as you get me in your car."

Elsie clicked the locks on her Ford Escort and they slid inside. After she started the car, she turned up the heat. Mandy twisted around in the passenger seat, studying her.

Elsie said, "Buckle up, Mandy."

Mandy ignored the suggestion. "Didn't you tell me you're a lawyer?"

"Yeah. Sure am." She aimed the temperature control vents in Mandy's direction.

Mandy looked around the vehicle with contempt she didn't try to disguise. "So if you're a lawyer, how come you don't have a better ride?"

Elsie gave her a grudging smile. The Ford Escort—a law school graduation gift from her parents—was far from new and had no flash whatsoever. Her father, when he handed her the keys, had proudly claimed it would be "reliable transportation." It was dependable as Old Faithful, but she dreamed of a day when she could finally afford an upgrade.

"County prosecutors don't make big money. Take my word for that." She put the car in Drive and pulled away from the curb. "So where you want to go?"

"Let's get a smoke and a drink."

Elsie shook her head in wonder; the girl had some nerve. "I'll get you a soda at the convenience store."

"And a pint of something."

Well, Elsie thought, Mandy was certainly persistent. "And a pint of nothing," Elsie said.

"Then you'll get nothing out of me."

The one block drive was quick; Elsie pulled into the Jiffy Go market. Two gas pumps sat in the lot. They bore a large sign, printed in marker. PAY INSIDE B4 U PUMP!

Elsie pulled up beside the door. "You want to come inside? Introduce me to your buddy at the cash register?"

Mandy gave her a sulky look. "Just get me a Cherry Coke. And some Parliaments."

Elsie pocketed her keys and grabbed her purse. As she walked into the store, she did a mental checklist; was there anything in the car the girl might steal? Probably not. Elsie wasn't reckless enough to leave valuables in a car that sat in the courthouse parking lot all day and an open lot at her apartment at night. Maybe some change in the dash, but that would be slim pickins.

A buzzer sounded as she walked through the door, and the clerk did a swift turn at the counter, to check Elsie out. The clerk was a woman with a long ponytail. Elsie felt a twinge of disappointment. She had hoped to encounter the guy who'd bartered Old Charter for Mandy's sexual favors.

"Afternoon," the woman said. "Can I help you find anything?"

Elsie waved a hand. "I'm good, thanks." She opened the refrigerator case and pulled out two cold plastic bottles: a Cherry Coke and a Diet Coke.

At the counter, she fished three dollar bills.

"Anything else today?" The clerk smiled broadly. She was missing a canine tooth and a molar. Something about the woman was vaguely familiar. Elsie glanced at her nametag: Misty.

"Misty, are you from here? Did we go to school together?"

"Naw. I'm from Douglas County. Moved here five years ago with my boyfriend. My ex," she said, putting emphasis on the ex factor.

Elsie nodded. Maybe she knew her from a jury. Or the courthouse.

"I've seen you over to the Baldknobbers a time or two." The gap-toothed smile flashed again. "You sure know how to party, girl."

Elsie's face grew hot; though she knew that at the ripe old age of thirty-two, she should be past blushing over her misadventures.

"Yeah, probably back in the day. I'm not spending so much time there these days."

"I seen you there a couple of weeks ago. You was drinking beer like it was going out of style."

Her face was flaming; she could feel it. In an offhand voice, Elsie said, "Probably wasn't me."

"It was you. I seen you. You was hanging with some cops."

Well, that ended the debate. Elsie loved her hometown; but living in a goldfish bowl had its challenges.

Misty pointed at the three wrinkled dollar bills that lay on the glass countertop, above a display of Missouri lottery tickets.

"Those pops costs three twenty-nine."

"Sorry. Wasn't thinking." With a tight smile, Elsie shoved the bills in her purse and pulled out her debit card.

"You want anything else today?"

Elsie had the card poised to slide through the machine, but her hand stilled. She looked out the glass storefront, to where Mandy sat in her car. Through the windshield, she could see the purple bruise around her eye.

"I'll take a pack of Parliaments. And a Bic lighter." She plucked a pink lighter from a dispenser by the checkout. To the guilty voice whispering in her head, she said: *She claims to be eighteen. It's legal.*

Misty turned around to get the cigarettes. She placed them on the counter and rang up the purchase.

"Nine dollars and sixty-two cents."

Elsie swiped the card and punched in her PIN. Holding her breath, she waited, thinking: *Come on come on.*

When the word *Approved* appeared on the small screen, she exhaled in relief. Misty handed her a bag.

"I didn't know you smoked."

Elsie blinked, uncomfortable with the level of interest the woman exhibited. Then she shrugged, thinking: *Get over yourself, Elsie.* Before she walked out, she flashed a parting smile at the clerk and said, "Girl, you just never know what I might do."

Walking out, Elsie muttered, "And that's the damn truth."

Chapter 21

ELSIE GRASPED THE handle of the car door and pulled. It was locked.

Inside, Mandy grinned at her, her split lip stretching dangerously. Elsie pulled out her keys, clicked on the fob.

Mandy pushed the button on the armrest, locked the doors again.

Elsie rapped on the driver's window with her knuckles. Mandy shook her head, laughing.

Damn, I'm glad I don't have kids, she thought, as she rustled in the plastic bag from the Jiffy Go. Sometimes, the knowledge that her biological clock was ticking frightened her. She'd see pictures of babies and toddlers and grade school kids on her classmates' Facebook pages, and suffer pangs of longing. But babies grew up. And became teenagers.

She pulled the cigarettes from the bag and pressed them against the glass. Mandy's eyebrows shot up, her mouth made an O of surprise. Quickly, she pushed the button on the armrest to unlock the car.

Elsie was shivering as she settled into the driver's seat. If she'd known that her visit to the BWCO would involve a road trip, she'd have worn her winter coat. She handed the Cherry Coke to Mandy.

"Don't mess with me, okay, Mandy? It isn't funny."

Mandy unscrewed the bottle top. "I thought it was funny."

Elsie swilled a mouthful of her Diet Coke. "Not funny," she repeated.

"Give me my cigarettes."

Elsie held the pack of Parliaments and slowly pulled the cellophane wrapping from the top of the box.

"Technically, they're my cigarettes."

A layer of silver foil paper still covered the smokes. Elsie tucked the pack into the left pocket of her jeans.

"What the fuck?" Mandy whined.

Elsie shifted in her seat so she could face Mandy.

"I want to know exactly what happened to you at the Rancho."

Mandy's face shuttered. There was a long moment of silence. Elsie fumbled with the bag and pulled out the pink lighter. Then she grabbed the pack in her pocket and ripped off the silver foil, giving Mandy a calculating look. She slid a cigarette from the pack, tucked it between her teeth and lit it. Sucked the smoke into her mouth. Blew it out.

Mandy's face lost its guarded look. "You fucking faker. You didn't even inhale."

Elsie rolled the driver's window down halfway and took a grateful breath of cold air. She held the cigarette up.

"You want it?"

"Yeah."

"Why were you at the Rancho that night?"

Mandy sighed. "I had a date." She held out a hand. Elsie let her take the burning cigarette.

The girl inhaled deeply and blew the smoke through her nostrils. "Oh, that tastes good."

"Did you have a date with Tony? The guy who rented the room?"

"No. Some other dude." She took a puff, and said, "Some old asshole."

Elsie said, "So who's Tony?"

Mandy paused before she answered. "Tony's my boyfriend."

Elsie shook her head. "Sounds crazy to me. Your boyfriend, Tony, rents out a hotel room for you to have a date with another guy."

Mandy smirked. "Quit playing dumb. I already told you about me, back at the hospital."

Elsie put the car in gear as she thought about the right response. As she pulled onto the street, she said, "Well, you were on a lot of medication when you said it. I wasn't sure how you meant it."

Mandy pursed her lips and blew smoke at the windshield.

"How the hell would I mean it? I told you I was a prostitute."

"Not exactly. You said you were a whore, as I recall." Elsie coughed; the interior of the car was smoky. "I thought you might have been using the word in another sense."

"Huh?"

"Like, you know. 'Oh my god, she's such a whore.' Sometimes people say that. It doesn't mean they're talking about actual prostitution, as a profession."

The girl laughed. Rolling down her window, she threw the burning butt onto the pavement. "You're so lame. Give me another cigarette."

The car hadn't aired out from the first one yet. "You just had one."

"Come on. Do you want me to talk to you or not?"

Again, Elsie pulled the pack from her pocket. When she braked at a four-way stop, she handed Mandy another cigarette and the Bic lighter.

"Why did your date turn out so bad? If you're a pro in the business, what went wrong?"

Mandy lit up. "He wanted a backdoor/Fifty Shades special. Paid Tony extra for it. I wasn't down for that."

Clearing her throat, Elsie said, "Just to be clear—"

Mandy fumbled with the dash. "Ain't you got no ashtray in here?"

"Ash out the window."

Mandy rolled it down an inch, and nimbly tapped the cherry against the glass.

In a voice that carried a shade of hesitation, Elsie said, "So just to be clear—since this is actually my first time interviewing a sex worker—what was it he wanted?"

"He wanted to do it in my ass. And probably wanted to whup it. But that's no fun, I'm telling you. It hurts. I only do that if Tony gives me my candy."

"Excuse me?"

"My candy, bitch."

Elsie figured she understood the reference, but wanted to make certain. "What kind of candy?"

Mandy crowed with laughter. "My medicine. He forgot to bring my medicine to the Rancho. I don't do that without my medicine."

The girl sobered. "So I tried to offer up other services, you know? Something else, just not up the butt, no Fifty Shades. The dude got all kinds of pissed off. Called Tony, wanted his money back."

"Did the customer hit you?"

"No. Cussed me. Didn't hit me."

"What was his name?"

Mandy rolled her head back on her neck.

"They don't tell you a real name. Not unless they're doing the girlfriend experience—and I'm not classy enough for that business. That's what Tony says."

"So he never gave you a name?"

"Said to call him Johnny."

Elsie frowned. Not much to go on.

"He said to call him 'Johnny Dear.' Which I thought was weird as fuck. So I didn't call him nothing."

"Did he wait around for Tony? For his refund?"

She touched her eye gingerly. "Tony don't give no refunds. I heard them shouting outside. Then Tony came in." She sighed. "Shit, he was pissed off."

Elsie had been driving aimlessly through town, but they were nearing the highway.

She made a left turn and headed for the Rancho Motel.

"So. This Tony—your boyfriend—he's really your pimp, right? And he's the one who beat you up?"

"I guess so." Mandy extended her open palm. Elsie fished another cigarette from her pocket and handed it over.

"I intend to file an assault charge against Tony for what he did to you." She gave Mandy a sidelong glance. "I'll need your cooperation. On the witness stand."

Mandy clicked the lighter and stared at the flame. "Good luck finding him."

"Mandy, we've got his ID. He used a driver's license to check into the motel."

She snorted; a bubble of mucus blew from her nose, and she wiped it with the back of her hand. "You think that's his real ID? For a lawyer, you ain't that smart."

Elsie braked at a red light. The Rancho was a short distance up the road; she could see the sign through the windshield. Elsie pointed at it, for Mandy's benefit.

"So you can help us locate him. After the way he worked you over, I'd think you would hate his guts."

Mandy tucked the unlit cigarette behind her ear. "I guess I do."

The light turned green. Elsie drove into the entrance of the Rancho, then pulled into the parking spot in front of #9, the room where Barton police had found Mandy, beaten unconscious, bleeding onto the bed. They sat in silence until Mandy spoke, in a sad voice.

"But he ain't always so bad. He can be real sweet. Takes charge of everything. Sometimes I love him."

Elsie turned her head to Mandy; their eyes locked. The girl stared at Elsie, her mouth working.

The split lip began to ooze blood. Mandy licked it with her tongue and looked away.

"You don't get it. Sometimes I think he's the only person that ever cared about me."

"How'd you meet him?"

"I was outside a bus station. When I was hitting people up for spare change."

"Why?"

Mandy fixed Elsie with an incredulous look. "Why do you think? To get me some money. I'd say, 'I need to get home to see my mom on the bus, but I don't have the twenty dollars for a ticket. She's sick; I need to see her real bad.'"

"Was your mom sick?"

Mandy responded with a scoffing sound. "Pfftt. So I hit Tony up, and we started talking. He said he was staying at a hotel near the highway. Asked if I wanted him to buy me something to eat. Said we could party. I've been with him ever since. It's business, Tony says; but that's not all. We got a personal connection."

As Mandy stared out the window, a silence fell between them. Mandy pulled the cigarette from her ear and lit it, inhaling reflectively; while Elsie framed arguments in her head, hoping to persuade the girl that a man who assaulted and prostituted her was not a caring individual. She was about to launch into her pep talk when Mandy spoke.

"Even when it's bad, it's better than before."

"What was it like before?"

"Alone, on the street. That's scary. After I took off from foster care." She cut a look in Elsie's direction. "Because I turned eighteen," she added hastily.

"How'd you end up in foster care?"

Mandy blew out smoke as she answered. "Stepdad got my oldest sister pregnant."

Elsie bowed her head, then shook it with regret. As a prosecutor, she was familiar with such scenarios. "But wasn't he removed from the home? When he was prosecuted?"

Mandy stared at her for a minute, sucking on the cigarette. "He wasn't removed. Mom stuck by him. So the kids got removed."

Elsie was silent, searching for words to convey to Mandy: she had handled cases that were similar; she understood. But Mandy spoke again before she had the chance.

"Remember that stranger danger talk they gave us in kindergarten?"

At the steering wheel, Elsie tried to follow the sudden switch in topic. Remembering kindergarten was a stretch, but she tried to conjure it up.

"What was it, exactly?" Elsie said.

"Oh, you know, a cop came to school, in uniform. And they gave us a picture to color. The stranger danger picture."

Elsie hunted for a kindergarten memory that would be similar, but her kindergarten recollections were painted in hazy pastels. Swinging on the playground at recess. Sitting on scratchy carpet squares while the teacher read aloud from Junie B. Jones. Finding a pudding cup in her *Little Mermaid* lunch box at noon.

"I'm not digging up the same kind of memory," Elsie said.

Mandy took a hit on her cigarette and ashed out the window. "They gave us that picture to color. It was a little girl walking down the street. And a man was standing there with a big bag of candy behind his back."

"Oh. Okay."

"And after we colored the picture, the cop would give a speech. You know: Don't talk to strangers, don't get in the car, that old line."

"Right."

Mandy rolled the window down and threw the butt into the street. As she looked out the window, she said, "But you know what I remember about it? That bag of candy the man had in the picture. It was huge. All I could think was, I wonder what he's got in there. Must be something really cool."

Elsie glanced over at Mandy's profile. The girl was smiling.

Chapter 22

THE REMAINDER OF Elsie's weekend had not been ideal. On Saturday night, she brought Ashlock up to date on Mandy's revelations while they drank a Corona at the Baldknobbers Bar. Ashlock's reaction to the information goldmine she provided almost led to a fight. As she outlined the details of Mandy's relationship with her abuser, Ashlock played the role of devil's advocate, contesting her assertion that a charge should be filed at this juncture. He stressed that the sad story of Mandy's life didn't change the fact that she knew her attacker's true identity but had yet to reveal it to anyone.

By the time they left the bar, Elsie was so mad at Ashlock that she almost didn't want to have sex. Almost.

And on Sunday, she had no time to fret about Mandy. Although she thought it fruitless to conduct a jury trial over a bar fight, she nonetheless needed to prepare. Sunday was spent drafting jury instructions, voir dire questions, and arguments.

On Monday at nine o'clock sharp, Elsie and Breeon squeezed through the crowded hallways of the third floor of the courthouse. All the seats on the wooden benches that lined the marble hallways were occupied by county residents; those who weren't fortunate enough to snag a seat loitered in the halls and leaned against the railing of the rotunda.

The misdemeanor jury case set in Judge Calvin's court was gearing up on the third floor. Elsie kept her expression serene as she passed the potential jurors in the hallway; but behind the facade, she was grumbling. No county prosecutor wanted to invest the time and energy required to try a misdemeanor before a jury; but Elsie drew the short straw. She had sacrificed precious chunks of her weekend on the piddling case of *State of Missouri v. Sweeny Greene.*

"Jesus, how many prospective jurors did Calvin call in for this piece of shit case?" Elsie took care to lower her voice as she spoke close to Breeon's ear.

Breeon answered in a whisper. "The associate circuit judges don't get to try a lot of jury cases, not like the circuit judges on the second floor. Maybe he's excited about it—who knows?"

Elsie pulled a face. "Judge Calvin's gonna eat a glory sandwich, preside over a jury today. Meanwhile, I ate a shit sandwich all weekend, preparing for this dog."

She was speaking too loudly. At the phrase *shit sandwich*, a gray-haired woman seated at the end of a bench looked up in alarm.

Breeon pushed through the glass-paneled door into the courtroom, with Elsie at her heels. Eldon, the judge's bailiff, spun around in his chair to face them.

"Judge is waiting for you in chambers, Elsie. Public defender is already here."

Elsie nodded, and the women approached the door to Judge Calvin's office, adjoining his bench in the courtroom.

Elsie knocked, and called through the door. "Judge?"

"Come on in."

Elsie and Breeon entered. Josh Nixon, the assistant public defender, already occupied one of the two seats facing the judge's desk. Elsie nudged Breeon and said, "You sit. I'll stand."

Breeon nodded and took the empty seat. Judge Calvin fixed her with a quizzical look.

"Ms. Johnson, I was told Ms. Arnold would be handling the prosecution."

Nixon laughed, scornful. "Are you all double-teaming me? On a class A misdemeanor? You must be hard up for something to do in the Prosecutor's Office."

He flashed an irreverent grin and tucked his longish blond-streaked hair behind his ear. Though she struggled to suppress it, Elsie nursed a private appreciation for his casual, surfer look as well as his skill in court.

But he was a little bit of an asshole, most days.

She spoke up. "I'm trying it, Judge. Bree is just sitting in with me for jury selection. She had this same panel of prospective jurors in a trial in Judge Rountree's court last month."

Judge Calvin shifted his gaze to Nixon. "That okay with you, counselor?"

"Sure, no problem. If Elsie isn't confident in her ability to choose a jury to try this case, then by all means: let Breeon babysit."

Breeon turned to him with a mocking laugh. Elsie just kept a poker face. She and Nixon had faced off in court on countless occasions. He would try to make her lose her temper, if he could.

The judge continued. "Ms. Arnold, has there been any attempt to plea bargain this case?"

She stepped forward and grasped the back of Breeon's chair.

"Judge, we made a very reasonable offer: in exchange for a plea of guilty to the charge, the state will recommend three months in the county jail and stand silent on the issue of probation."

She would have said more, but Nixon broke in. "Judge, this charge should never have been filed in the first place. It's a classic scenario: a bar fight over a woman, outside the Baldknobbers Bar. Both parties were intoxicated. Both guys swear the other one started it."

Judge Calvin's brow rose. "And the man who was charged—"

"Was the guy who won the fight. My client. He got the better of the other guy. So when the police showed up, they sent the state's witness to Barton Memorial Hospital and threw my client in the paddy wagon."

The judge studied the computer screen on his desk. "And charged a class A misdemeanor. I'm curious; why is the public defender's office involved in a misdemeanor case? You all have bigger fish to fry."

"Because the prosecutor refuses to waive jail time," Nixon said, in a tone that conveyed his disbelief over their unreasonable stance.

Behind her stoic expression, Elsie privately agreed with everything Nixon said. The jail time stand had come from Madeleine; she was so unrelenting that Elsie wondered how the victim was connected to her boss. A political supporter, maybe; or more likely, an employee of Madeleine's husband.

If Elsie had her druthers, she'd plead him out to a reduced charge and recommend probation, just to wash her hands of it. But the offer was set by her boss; she couldn't alter it.

"Well, counselors, let's get going, then. I don't like to keep the panel waiting."

The three attorneys slipped through the doorway as Judge Calvin thrust his arms into the sleeves of his black robe.

They took their places at the counsel table. Eldon rose from his desk, holding on to a sheaf of paper that identified the jury panelists. A woman in her forties with her hair twisted into a bun on the back of her head settled down at the court reporting device. Elsie knew the court reporter; her name was Heidi Morris, and she was a member of Riverside Baptist. Elsie had seen Heidi in church on the rare occasions when Elsie attended services with Detective Ashlock and his son.

"All rise!" Eldon said. "The Associate Circuit Court of McCown County, Missouri, is in session, Judge Calvin presiding."

Elsie and Breeon stood until the judge invited them to be seated.

Adjusting his eyeglasses, he flipped open a file. "Before we bring the prospective jurors in, are there any remaining motions or evidentiary questions to be ruled upon?"

"No, your honor," Elsie said; and Nixon echoed her. This was not a case involving any complex legal issues.

"All right, then. Eldon, invite the panelists to enter."

As the door opened, Elsie swiveled in her chair to greet the McCown County citizens with a respectful smile when they entered the courtroom. She didn't flash her teeth, lest she leave the wrong impression, like she thought a criminal case was a party. Just a genial expression, to radiate warmth and confidence.

A glance at the defense showed Nixon ignoring the procession of jurors altogether. He had an arm around the meaty shoulders of his client, and was whispering in his ear.

Well, Elsie reflected; defense attorneys didn't have to uphold the same profile as prosecutors. Elsie was on the side of law and order; in court, she did her level best to keep a white hat on her head.

The benches inside the courtroom were filling up with the usual suspects: gray-haired women, a few farmers, some blue-collar men between thirty and sixty years of age (Elsie's favorite brand of juror), young mothers, a double handful of white-collar men and women. She picked up her legal pad, preparing to take fast and furious notes when the questioning of jurors began.

Then a screech assaulted her ear, followed by a string of high-pitched gibberish. Elsie looked from left to right, trying to identify the source of the noise.

When she saw it, she dropped her ink pen onto the floor. It was a monkey. An actual monkey, walking into court holding the hand of a gaunt middle-aged woman.

The woman and her monkey passed by Elsie's counsel table as they made their way to the jury box, where a few empty seats remained.

The creature wore a diaper—a dirty one, from the whiff Elsie caught. And a little striped shirt.

Elsie and Breeon exchanged a look. Elsie pinched her lips shut to keep from laughing.

After four years as a trial lawyer, she thought she'd seen it all. Apparently not.

She hadn't seen a monkey in court before.

Chapter 23

ELSIE LOOKED FROM the monkey to the woman who held it. Though she wasn't familiar, she had the look of a local: the prominent Appalachian chin, shoulder-length hair pulled behind her ears, starting to gray. Some of the folks on the jury panel had dressed up for court; but the monkey's owner wore faded jeans and a Hard Rock Tulsa T-shirt.

Eldon hurried over to the monkey's companion and placed a restraining hand on her upper arm. At his approach, the monkey jumped into his owner's arms and hid his head on her shoulder.

"Ma'am, what's that monkey doing in here?"

The woman stroked the monkey's back over its tiny shirt. "He has a name. It's Lester."

Elsie glanced at Breeon. Under her breath, Elsie said: "Lester." Clamping her lips shut, Breeon ducked her head and turned away.

"Well, you take Lester on home. This ain't a zoo," Eldon said.

Lester's owner wrapped a protective arm around his furry neck. "I take him with me everywhere."

A few of her fellow panelists snickered. When she scooted

inside the jury box to reach the empty spot, her seatmates shifted in the wooden chairs, leaning away from her. The judge tapped his gavel.

"Ma'am, what is your name?" Judge Calvin asked.

Though the judge's voice was not unkind, she looked up at the bench with a rebellious face. "Sally Mays."

"Ms. Mays, were you called for jury duty in my court today?"

"Yes. I got a postcard. It come in the mail." She scratched the monkey's head as she spoke.

The judge's face was grave. "Ms. Mays, we conduct important court business. Witnesses will testify, the attorneys will conduct argument. Jurors need to be paying close attention, so they can return a fair verdict. This is a criminal case."

"I'll pay attention."

Judge Calvin rubbed his eye under his black-framed spectacles. "The monkey. He's a distraction. Folks just don't get to bring pets into court."

She sat, pulling the monkey's head from her shoulder and tugging on his shirt, so that Lester sat on her lap, facing the judge.

"He's not a pet. Lester is my comfort animal."

Breeon was shaking her head, writing on the legal pad before her on the counsel table. Elsie leaned in to see the words on the page.

Breeon wrote "Service animal like seeing eye dog, for the blind—permitted in public places. But monkey?"

Judge Calvin took a deep breath. "Ms. Mays, please approach the bench. Counsel for the state and defense, come on up."

Elsie and Breeon joined Josh Nixon in front of the bench. It took a minute longer for Sally Mays to squeeze out of the jury box with the monkey in her arms.

When she joined the attorneys standing before the judge, Sally said, "This is Lester." She kissed him on the head and said, "Say hello, Lester."

The monkey smiled, baring square yellow teeth. Elsie took a step to the side. She'd been right about that diaper.

Judge Calvin might have smelled it, too; his nose wrinkled. Nevertheless, he leaned toward the woman and spoke in a calm voice.

"Ms. Mays, this panel was called into Judge Rountree's court back in October and I don't recall hearing that he had a monkey in here. And I believe I'd remember."

Lester was struggling in her arms. She got a tighter hold on him. "I couldn't come. Lester was sick."

"And you say he's your service animal?"

"That's right."

Lester wriggled out of her arms. She set him on the floor and held him by the hand. "For my anxiety. I have panic attacks."

The judge cleared his throat. "Did a doctor prescribe a monkey for treatment? Because I've never heard of such a thing, not in these parts."

The monkey stared up at Elsie and gibbered. It looked angry, she thought. So she backed away another step, bumping into Breeon.

"Don't step on my toes," Bree whispered.

The judge shot a glare at them, and turned back to Sally Mays.

"If you have written documentation from a licensed physician that you're required to be accompanied by this monkey, I'll need to see it."

"Are you calling me a liar?" The woman didn't bother to speak in a whisper. People froze on the benches, waiting to see what might happen next.

She pointed an accusatory finger. "My doctor says people are just taking a pill for everything. That's what's the matter with this country."

She turned a baleful eye to Elsie. "People who have struggled with addiction can't just pop a pill. It ain't so easy."

Sally's umbrage was rubbing off on Lester. He started to scratch.

Judge Calvin picked up a pen. "Who is your physician?"

"He's not from here. He's holistic." She looked over her shoulder and addressed the courtroom. "A holistic doctor."

She must have loosened her grip when she turned from the bench, because Lester got away. He bounded first to Elsie, grabbing at her leg. She shrieked and shoved him off.

Lester made a run for the jury box. A woman rose from her seat, trying to get away. She screamed. "It'll rip your face off!"

The courtroom erupted with noise. Five people made their way to the door and escaped into the hallway, despite the bailiff's protests.

Judge Calvin slammed his gavel while Elsie bent over to inspect the damage. Lester had torn through her hose and left scratch marks on her leg. One of the scratches was bloody.

"Son of a bitch," she muttered.

"Order!" the judge demanded. To Sally Mays, who was still standing dumbfounded at the bench, he said, "Get that critter under control."

She turned and barked at Lester; miraculously, he responded, scampering back and jumping into her arms.

Judge Calvin ran his fingers through his silver hair. "Ladies and gentlemen, I think we'll need to call a recess," he began.

But he didn't have the chance to conclude his sentence. At that very moment, a portly woman wearing a Tyler's Family Market uniform threw open the door; it slammed against the wall with a bang.

"Breeon! Breeon Johnson, I need to talk to you." Her face was puffy; tears rolled down her cheeks.

Eldon, the bailiff, scurried over to her, clutching at her arm while demanding that she hush; but she jerked free. Her voice rose to a dangerous pitch. "It's my daughter. It's my Desiree. I don't know where she is. You got to help me find Desiree."

Elsie looked from the hysterical woman to Breeon, who stared at the woman without comprehension. And Elsie thought, this courtroom can't get any crazier.

Then Lester stripped off his diaper and flung it across the room.

Chapter 24

After the monkey shed and shared his dirty diaper, Judge Calvin slammed the gavel, declared a mistrial on his own motion, and cleared the courtroom. The jury panelists fled.

But Desiree's mother remained, fighting through the tide of departing jurors and shouldering her way to the counsel table.

Breeon watched her approach with a wary expression. When the woman was within earshot, Breeon said, "Now what's all this about, Kim?"

The woman's face was haggard. "It's Desiree. She didn't come home."

Breeon's voice was measured. "I'm sure sorry to hear that. But I haven't seen her. And my daughter is at school. I dropped her off an hour ago."

Elsie watched as the woman's face crumpled. "No, don't you see—she didn't come home last night. She went for another photo shoot."

Desiree's mother drew a ragged breath. Elsie pulled out a chair from the counsel table. "Do you need to sit down, ma'am?"

The woman nodded, and dropped into the seat, her shoulders shuddering.

Elsie leaned beside her at the table. "I'm Elsie Arnold; I work with Breeon. You're Desiree Wickham's mom?"

"Yes." She swiped her wet cheek. "Yes, I am."

Over the head of Desiree's mom, Elsie shot a questioning look in Breeon's direction, but Bree lifted her shoulders and wrinkled her brow.

"What's your full name, ma'am?" Elsie said. Her shoulders itched, and she gave an involuntary shudder. Because she was getting a bad feeling, like bugs were crawling up the back of her neck.

"Kim. Kimberly Wickham." She grasped Elsie's hand. "We have to find her. She's all I got."

Breeon spoke up. "Why would you think she'd be with Taylor? I know they've become friends this year, and Taylor had a sleepover at your house on Friday. But I can promise you, Taylor was at home last night. She was working on her project for social studies."

"I know. That's the problem. Desiree went alone to the photo shoot this time, because Taylor was busy with her homework." Her voice cracked. "I shouldn't have let her go alone."

A chill ran through Elsie. In an urgent tone, she asked, "Where did Desiree go?"

"Another shoot. For a catalogue. He said she was gonna be in Veronica's Secret."

Elsie squeezed Kim Wickham's hand. "Who said?"

"Tony."

"Tony," Elsie repeated, dropping the woman's hand. The bugs under her skin multiplied, and began to hum in her ears.

Kim Wickham pulled a battered Veronica's Secret catalogue from her purse and smoothed it out on the counsel table. "She's been practicing. Her poses, her expressions. It's the happiest I've seen her since the pageant days."

Breeon's expression had grown forbidding. "How long has she been missing?"

"Since Sunday afternoon. I was working at Tyler's Market. I thought she'd be home before dark. She rode her bike to Denny's."

Elsie shook her head in confusion; why would she do a photo shoot at Denny's? Was the Tony at Denny's the same guy as the Tony who had assaulted Mandy at the Rancho? How had the child encountered him? Before she could ask, Breeon broke in.

Breeon's brows made an angry furrow between her eyes. "Your fourteen-year-old daughter has been gone all night? Have you called the Barton police?"

Kim rubbed the wrinkled catalogue cover reflexively. "No. I didn't know what I ought to do. I thought everything must be all right. It went real late the first time, when he photo'ed Des and Taylor together."

Breeon took a backward step. Her eyes narrowed. "What did you just say?"

"I said it went really late that night, and I worried about it then, but they got home just fine."

Breeon reached out and grasped the woman's arm. "What did you say about Taylor? Some man photographing Taylor?"

Elsie reached into her bag and pulled out her cell phone. She stepped away from the counsel table and dialed Ashlock. To her relief, he picked up immediately.

"What's up, Elsie?"

Voices at the counsel table were growing more agitated. Elsie walked to the jury box. "Ashlock, it's a missing person situation. A middle school girl. Her mom is here at the courthouse."

"How long?"

"Since yesterday afternoon. Not twenty-four hours, but Ash, she's a kid."

"Runaway?"

"No." She dropped her voice. "Supposed to be a photo shoot. For modeling." She paused for emphasis. "With a guy named Tony."

She heard him hiss into the phone; his substitute for swearing, when he was in the presence of others. Aside from Elsie, anyway.

"Do you want me to come to the courthouse? Or will you bring her over here?"

Elsie eyed the two women warily. Tensions were running high.

"I believe I'll bring them over to you."

"Them?" The phone was growing warn. She switched ears.

"Yeah."

"More than one?"

"Yeah. Breeon needs to come along, too."

She ended the call and approached the table, taking care to wear a businesslike face.

"Just talked to Detective Ashlock," Elsie said in a brisk voice. "He'd like to see you all." They looked up at her, and she added: "Now."

Breeon seemed to digest the summons for a moment. Then, with a nod, she picked up her briefcase. "Okay. Let's go."

Chapter 25

Elsie walked behind the two women as they exited the stone courthouse and headed over the lawn and across the street to the Barton Police Department. In contrast with the historic county courthouse, the police building was a squat, flat-topped, blond brick structure built in the 1960s.

They trod the steps to the Detective Division on the second floor. Desiree's mother clung to the bannister for support. Bob Ashlock met them at the top of the stairs.

Ashlock greeted the women with a nod. "Breeon, Elsie." He extended a hand to Desiree's mother. "Ma'am, I'm Detective Ashlock."

Kim trembled visibly as she grasped Ashlock's hand. "I'm Kim. Kim Wickham."

"Ms. Wickham, Ms. Arnold tells me your daughter has gone missing."

"Yes." She spoke with a gasp, and the tears began to roll again. "She's gone. Since yesterday afternoon. She shouldn't be out all night. She's just in ninth grade."

Ashlock led them into the second-floor conference room. The

space held a table and eight chairs; the cinderblock walls were bare. The sole window overlooked the town square. Glancing down, Elsie saw two women from the clerk's office shivering on a bench as they shared a cigarette.

Elsie turned her gaze from the window and took a seat at the conference table. Ashlock opened a file folder and pulled out a paper form. He set it before him on the table; it read MISSING PERSON REPORT.

He spoke in a calm voice. "Let's get this information down, ma'am. Your daughter's full name?"

"Desiree Wickham. Desiree Hope Wickham." She shut her eyes. "I've pinned my hopes on her since the day she was born."

"Date of birth?"

"May 18, 2003."

"Description?"

"She's a little thing. Curly blond hair, just like me."

Elsie cut her eyes to the woman's hair. It was curly; the frizzy locks brushed her shoulders. And the ends were yellow, but the roots were a much darker shade.

"Specifically. Height? Weight?"

"Five foot one, I think. Maybe a hundred pounds, something like that." She paused and rubbed her eyes. "Ninety-five? Could be ninety-five. Because she's been dieting."

Breeon exhaled; it sounded like an indignant snort. Elsie eyed her friend; it looked like Breeon was exercising rigid control to remain silent.

"Eye color?"

"Blue. Pretty blue eyes."

Ashlock marked on the form. "Can you tell me what she was wearing when you last saw her?"

"I can show you." The woman reached into her purse and pulled out the Veronica's Secret catalogue she'd displayed at the courthouse. With shaking hands, she fumbled through the pages until she reached one that had been dog-eared. She pointed at a picture of a model wearing a push-up bra and a thong.

"We went to Springfield and bought it special, for the shoot. Because it's pink, and they put her in pink at the audition. But she didn't like wearing the things they put on her and Taylor, because they was used and they wasn't clean."

Breeon stood so abruptly that her chair tipped over and crashed to the floor. The noise made Elsie recoil.

"This is the third time you've brought my daughter's name into this." Breeon's control had cracked; her eyes were blazing. "Do you understand that your false statements about Taylor constitute slander? Defamation?"

Kim looked up at her with a woebegone face. "It's not false. I'm telling the truth. Desiree told me. She said that Taylor said you wouldn't like it. That's why it had to be a secret."

Breeon's fist slammed down on the tabletop. "So you're informing me that someone is putting my daughter in dirty underwear and taking her picture?"

"I didn't know it was like that. Not at first."

"And who the hell are you, conspiring to hide this activity from me? I am her mother."

Ashlock stood. "Breeon," he said.

"Don't you 'Breeon' me. If someone is taking advantage of my child, then this woman was a party to it."

Desiree's mother opened her mouth wide, and wailed. "Your daughter is safe at school! My baby's missing!"

Ashlock set his pen down on the table, at a right angle with the paper form. "Elsie, would you like to take Breeon to my office while I conclude this interview? Maybe get her a cold pop so she can settle down."

Elsie shot an inquiring glance at Breeon. Bree's jaw was working. After a pause, Bree spoke.

"I'm not going anywhere."

"Then you'll need to refrain from speaking out, Breeon. So we can get to the bottom of this," Ashlock said.

With an air of dignity, Breeon bent down and righted her chair. As she sat down, Elsie reached under the table and took Breeon's hand.

Then she regretted the gesture as Breeon squeezed her fingers in a crushing grip.

As Elsie winced, she looked from Breeon's stony face to Kim's puffy red eyes and wondered again: was it all related? The name Tony kept popping up. Could it be a simple coincidence? And if not, could she have done something to prevent this from happening?

Her stomach twisted and she squeezed Bree's hand.

A box of store-brand tissues sat on the conference table. Ashlock reached out and pushed the box to Kim. She pulled three from the box and blew her nose into them.

He said, "What time did Desiree disappear on Sunday?"

She rubbed the tissues under her nose before she replied. "Well, I went into work over to Tyler's at ten. But she was supposed to be at Denny's at three."

"Three o'clock in the afternoon?"

"Yeah. I got home around six, and she wasn't there. Then I slept on the couch while I waited for her to get back. But I didn't worry until I woke up at two, maybe? In the morning? Because she should've been home by then."

Breeon interjected. "What's the deal with Denny's? Who's doing a photo shoot over there?"

"That's where Desiree goes to meet the agency. They pick her up there, then drop her off. It's open twenty-four hours, so it's real convenient."

Ashlock said, "Who picks her up?"

"The agency. Marvel Modeling. She had her interview with the agency at Denny's last Thursday afternoon. Then they met up in the parking lot on Friday night and Sunday afternoon."

As the woman spoke, Elsie scribbled on a notepad: "Denny's. Marvel Modeling. Th afternoon, Fri night, Sun afternoon." She turned and looked at Breeon, but Breeon was focused on Desiree's mother.

"So—who was it from the agency that picked Desiree up at Denny's?"

"Dede."

Ashlock's pen quit moving. "Can you spell that?"

"I don't know. Like it sounds, I guess."

"Last name?"'

"I don't know."

Ashlock's eyes narrowed. "Description?"

"I don't know. I never met her."

Breeon opened her mouth to speak, but Ashlock held up a restraining hand.

"Ma'am, you sent your fourteen-year-old daughter off with a stranger?"

Kim buried her face in her hands. For a long moment, they sat as she sobbed. Her shoulders shook.

When she recovered sufficiently to speak, Kim said, "Desiree wanted it that way. It seemed more grown-up."

Breeon's voice cracked like a whip. "But she's fourteen."

Kim shook her head. In a mournful voice, she said, "Des is fifteen. But they said they was eighteen."

Breeon dropped Elsie's hand. "Who said?"

When Kim met Breeon's eye, there was a spark of challenge in her expression. "Desiree and Taylor. When they applied at the agency."

Under her breath, Breeon said, "Sweet Jesus."

Ashlock interjected. "I need the names of anyone else who was involved, other than the woman named Dede."

"Tony. Tony was in charge."

Elsie tried to catch Ashlock's eye, but he remained focused on Kim. "Last name?"

"I don't know."

"Description?"

"I never saw him."

Elsie spoke up. "Did he have a tattoo?"

Kim shook her head. "I don't know, I told you. I never saw him. But it was Tony that took the pictures of Desiree." She paused before adding: "And the pictures of Taylor."

Breeon pushed away from the table and picked up her bag. As she made her way to the door, Elsie said, "Where you going, Bree?"

Without looking back, Breeon said, "I'm going to school. To see my daughter."

Chapter 26

AT ELSIE'S SUGGESTION, she drove Bree in her car, leaving Ashlock to ferry Kim across town. She thought it best to separate the two women, before a war broke out. And she wanted a private moment with Breeon, to broach a touchy topic.

As she studied on the best way to ask about Taylor's modeling escapade, Breeon looked around the interior of Elsie's car, wrinkling her nose with distaste.

"Why does it smell like smoke in here? Are you leaving your car unlocked? Smells like some hobo's been camping out in your backseat."

Elsie shook her head. "I took an assault victim for a ride, she had a cigarette."

"Why are you letting someone smoke in your car?"

"I wanted her to talk. It's that girl I took to the center, the one I told you about. Mandy. And she did finally open up. She told me a little bit about her pimp. His name is Tony."

She took her eyes off the road, glancing over at Breeon, to gauge her reaction. But Breeon didn't appear to be listening. The pulled up to a red traffic light, and Breeon sat forward in her seat, groaning at the delay. "God, will we ever get there?"

"Breeon. Breeon, did you hear me? The guy who beat Mandy up at the Rancho hotel: his name was Tony."

"Yeah." The light changed, and Breeon pointed at the windshield. "Drive."

As Elsie drove through the intersection, she persisted. "And Kim Wickham just said that the so-called modeling agent was Tony. Same name."

Breeon's head snapped to face Elsie. "Are you trying to make me lose my mind?"

Elsie spied the school building, and swerved toward the entrance. "No."

"Because I'm barely hanging on right now. Elsie, don't plant a false seed with me, telling me my daughter is tied up with a pimp. If you're suggesting that, you'd better have proof."

Elsie parked her car beside the middle school building, an antique brick structure on the west side of town. Nearby, the windows of the new high school sparkled in the late autumn sun. Repeated attempts to tear down and replace the middle school were defeated by taxpayers who believed the old school was built to last into the twenty-first century.

As soon as Elsie cut the engine, Breeon's hand fumbled for the latch on the passenger door. Under her breath, she said, "I'm getting to the bottom of this."

As Elsie dropped her keys into her purse, she protested. "You're the best mom, Bree. Whatever's going on, it's not your fault. Don't do this to yourself."

But Breeon slammed the door shut and took off for the school entrance at a run.

They met Ashlock inside, conferring with the principal. Desiree's mother was nowhere to be seen.

The principal, a middle-aged man whose necktie rested on a large belly, had his hand on the telephone receiver. "Ms. Johnson, Ms. Arnold," he said, nodding at Breeon and Elsie.

"Mr. Samson, I need to talk to my daughter," Breeon said.

"Yes, ma'am, the detective told me."

He picked up the receiver of a landline phone and pushed four digits with his other hand. "Marge Arnold? Please send Taylor Johnson down to the office." After a pause, he said, "Now, ma'am. Not after the test. Right now."

Elsie pressed her lips together, imagining her mother's response to the principal's command. Marge Arnold didn't like it when administrators interfered with class time.

To Ashlock, Elsie said: "Desiree's mom? Kim Wickham?"

He cut his eyes at Breeon, then leaned toward Elsie and said, "She's sitting with the girls' counselor right now. Seemed like the best idea."

Elsie nodded. They sat in strained silence, watching the principal check his email on his laptop, until Taylor appeared in the doorway.

When she saw her mother in the office, along with Elsie and Ashlock, Taylor's eyes widened.

"Mom?"

Breeon rose from her chair and seized her daughter in her arms, clutching her tightly to her chest.

Mr. Samson cleared his throat. "Will you need me to stick around for this meeting? I've got a conference call, but I can—"

"No, sir. Thank you. We just need a private space."

The principal didn't mask his relief. He ushered them into the vice principal's office. "Mr. Adams called in sick. I'll shut the door so you all won't be disturbed."

Once the door clicked behind him, Ashlock turned to Taylor.

"Take a seat, Taylor."

Two straight-backed chairs faced the desk. As Taylor and Breeon sat, Breeon scooted her chair close beside her daughter and took her hand. Ashlock sat in the principal's empty seat.

Elsie leaned against the office door with a queasy stomach, wishing she'd thought to stop by the bathroom.

Ashlock said, "Taylor, we're looking for your friend Desiree. She's missing."

Elsie couldn't see Taylor's face, but the girl's shoulders began to shake.

He said, "We need you to tell us about your modeling shoot. About a woman named Dede, a man named Tony."

The shaking had become palsied. Elsie heard Taylor say, "I don't know."

Breeon's head was almost touching Taylor's. "Don't know what?"

"Anything."

In a trembling voice she said again: "I don't know anything."

Ashlock leaned forward, his eyes fixed on Taylor. "Didn't you and Desiree go together to an appointment last Friday night?"

Taylor dropped her head. After a pause, she whispered, "Yes."

"In Barton?"

"No. Out of town."

"Where?"

"I don't know. It was dark."

"How did you get to the out-of-town appointment?"

"A woman picked us up. She drove us."

"Where did you meet her?"

"Denny's."

"What was the woman's name?"

Taylor didn't answer. After a moment, Ashlock prompted her. "Was it Dede?"

Taylor nodded.

"Last name?"

She shrugged. "I don't know."

"Can you describe the woman? Dede?"

"No."

"Why not?"

"I just can't." She paused before answering again, in a fierce whisper. "I can't."

"How far did she take you out of Barton?"

"Can't say."

"How many minutes did the drive take?"

She sniffled, rubbing her nose with a shaky hand. "Thirty. Maybe."

"Could it have been longer?"

"Yes."

The strain of the unproductive interview was starting to show; Ashlock's features tensed. "Or shorter? Than thirty minutes?"

"Sure. Could have been."

His jaw twitched. Elsie tried to catch his eye, but he didn't look up. "Did a man or woman take photos of you? Or of Desiree?"

"Nobody took pictures of me."

"What happened? Where did you go?"

"I don't know. It was late, I was tired. I fell asleep."

Her head remained bowed. Taylor repeated: "I don't remember anything." Her voice dropped to the barest whisper. "Leave me alone. Everybody, just leave me alone."

Chapter 27

DEDE'S HANDS WERE so full, she couldn't knock. She had to kick the door of Room 217 to get Tony's attention.

Slow minutes ticked by as she waited outside in the frigid air. She stepped to the left, checking the room next door: 218. She pondered whether she should give that door a kick, for good measure. Earlier that day, Tony had gone to the motel office and rented 218 as well as 217. The adjoining rooms were connected by an interior door. He said it would be good for business. He wanted to keep an eye on the new girl.

With a creak of door hinges, Tony finally opened 217. "Get on in here, Dede. I want my coffee." She hurried inside, shivering, and set the cardboard tray on the counter.

In a snappish tone, Dede said, "You know we could tell them at the front desk that our coffee maker doesn't work."

Tony pulled a chocolate frosted Long John doughnut from the white paper bag she had delivered with the coffee. He took a bite before he responded to her.

"I think I told you. I'm not too keen on having people snoop around in here."

He picked up a coffee in a tall foam cup and carried it to the desk, where he set it next to the laptop computer. Sipping from the cup, he studied the screen.

Dede walked over to the bed on the far side of the room and lifted the bedsheet, studying the limp form beneath it.

"I see you uncuffed her."

Without turning away from the computer, Tony said, "She's out. Don't need to keep her tied up if she's unconscious. Don't want to bruise that peach."

Dede reached out to the girl on the bed and pinched the fleshy part of her right arm. The girl didn't respond. She continued to breathe deeply, her mouth open. Her curly hair fanned out over the pillowcase.

Dede walked back to the desk and doctored the other coffee with cream and packets of Equal sweetener. "You absolutely sure they won't come looking for her?"

Tony snorted. "That girl is white trash. Guaranteed. They'll figure her for a runaway."

"How can you be so sure?"

"Shit, Dede. What kind of girl you think trolls through the ads on Backlist.com?"

"They still might look. She's a missing kid."

"Let them. They won't find her."

"What if her friend talks? Coco, the black girl?"

"She won't. I took care of that. Coco gonna keep her lip zipped. I'll keep tabs on her."

His fingers scampered across the keyboard, typing fast. "We've got a live one," he said, smiling. "I've hooked him."

Dede bent over his shoulder to read the words on the screen. He jabbed her in the gut with his elbow and said, "Back off. I don't want to smell your stinking breath while I'm working. You need to gargle some Listerine."

She walked to the empty bed with an injured expression. Kicking off her shoes, she sat and reclined against the headboard. After a moment's silence, she said, "We gotta move on."

Tony didn't answer.

Dede spoke again, more forcefully. "I got a feeling. There's too many things going to shit around here. It's risky. Let's pack up. We can leave her here. You've got the pictures; they're being downloaded already, on the P2P network. You'll make your profit off her."

Tony let out a deep sigh. "We're not leaving money on the table, Dede."

"I've got a bad feeling."

He swiveled slowly in the chair. Pointing at the sleeping girl, he said, "Do you know the payday I've got lined up for that over there?"

When Dede opened her mouth to speak again, Tony cut her off. "Since when have your instincts been worth a shit? If it wasn't for me, you'd still be working the massage parlors in Mobile. If they'd have you; they can get those Asian girls now. They're younger than you, better looking. And they don't even have to pay them anything. Those bitches don't speak English."

Dede drank her coffee. She didn't argue.

He said, "You've come up in the world since you started listening to me. Just try to deny it."

She shook her head. The red waves obscured her face.

"Remember at the Happy Ending Massage? You'd turn tricks for ten to twelve hours straight; then sleep on the floor of the back room. I felt sorry for you, I've told you that. It's one thing to work those Chinese like that; but goddamn, you're an American."

Tony left his chair and sat beside Dede on the bed. He massaged her thigh with a tattooed hand. "What did I tell you back then?"

She shook her hair back from her face. "That we could get out, do it on our own instead of working for someone else."

"Damn straight."

"And if we grew it, I could be management."

"See? Was I right? That's what we're doing right now." He pointed again at the unconscious girl. "Everything's cool. I'll know when it's time to move on. I always do. Remember when they busted the parlor in Mobile? Jerked his license? I could feel it coming. We got out in time."

A knock on the door caused him to jerk his hand away. In a sharp voice he said, "Who is it?"

"Housekeeping," said the voice on the other side of the door.

Tony rose from the bed. He unlocked the door and cracked it open. He smiled as he spoke.

"My girlfriend's still running a fever. Just hand over the towels and stuff."

A woman's face appeared in the opening, as if she was trying to see inside.

"She still sick? How long has it been?"

Tony whistled. "It's bad. You don't want to catch it, ma'am. Just drop all that by the door. I'll pick it up."

Dede could see the woman's eye at the crack of the door. "What about the sheets?"

"Later," Tony said, as he pushed the door shut and locked it again.

In a fierce whisper, Dede said, "See? Even the hotel maid is sniffing after us."

She would have said more; but Tony's phone rang, and he shot her a warning look. He picked up the cell phone, checking the number on the screen. His face was guarded as he answered.

"Who's this?"

As he listened, his expression transformed to one of satisfaction. He flashed Dede a triumphant grin.

"Is that right? I ought to let you sit down there and rot, you little bitch."

Dede sat up straight on the bed. She whispered, "What?"

He shook his head in warning before speaking into the phone again.

"Have you been behaving yourself?"

The voice on the other end of the line filtered into the hotel room: a girl's voice. Dede couldn't make out what she was saying.

Tony dumped the remaining doughnut from the paper bag and snatched up a pen. "Slow down," he said. He smoothed the bag on the desktop and began to write on it. "Okay, tell me where."

A moment later, he ended the call. To Dede he said, "Remind me never to listen to you."

She edged away from him, scooting back toward the headboard.

"What was it?"

"Baby's coming back." He balled up the paper bag and threw it at Dede. It bounced off her chest and rolled across the bedspread. "There's the directions. Go get her. We are back in business. I knew it. Good thing we got an extra room."

Dede picked up the paper ball. "You sure it isn't some kind of setup?"

Tony fished the keys from his pocket. He crossed to the bed and handed them to Dede. Before returning to the chair, he gazed at his reflection in the mirror over the dresser, running his fingers through his hair.

"The problem with you, baby, is that you're so fucking negative. That's why you can never make it on your own."

Their eyes met in the mirror. Tony smiled suddenly, showing his teeth like a wolf.

"Mandy misses her daddy. And she needs some candy."

He picked up one of the bottles on the desk and shook it. The pills inside rattled.

"Now get off your lazy ass, she's waiting."

Chapter 28

I told you so.

Elsie was dying to say it. The words jiggled on the very edge of her tongue like a spoonful of Jello. The air between Elsie and Ashlock sparked with the unspoken reproach. He avoided her eye as he rummaged in a drawer of his desk.

In her head, she recounted the warning signs she'd provided to him. The last Friday, she had told him she was unhappy with the report on Mandy at the Rancho; that they weren't doing right by her. And on Saturday, when she'd filled him in on Mandy's background, Elsie had let him know that Mandy's pimp, Tony, was responsible for the brutal assault. He'd brushed it aside.

And now they faced another serious mishap: at the hands of a man named Tony.

She couldn't resist the impulse to speak. But she attempted to phrase it in a more political fashion. No one liked to hear the words *I told you so.* Perching on the edge of his desk, she spoke in a reasonably pleasant voice.

"I worried that something bad was going to happen."

He didn't respond; just kept digging through file folders.

She took a breath and tried again. "When that incident went down at the Rancho Motel, I had a feeling. Something wasn't right. I could sense it."

When he slammed the metal drawer shut, she jerked backward and nearly fell off the desk.

Ashlock said, "I've got important work to do. I need to get an Amber Alert out. And I have to contact the Feds."

Elsie's brow wrinkled. "The Feds always treat us like hillbillies. Why don't you start with the state highway patrol instead? They worked together on a trafficking case with local law enforcement over in Greene County. I saw it on the news last summer."

He shook his head. "This is shaping up as a kidnapping. I need the FBI."

"Okay, but before you call them in, let's piece this together."

He reached for his phone; but paused before he dialed. "Aren't you supposed to be in trial today?"

"The jury trial got canceled. Kind of a wild story, actually. But I'm freed up today, don't have anything set. So I'm thinking—do you want me to bring Mandy by the PD? To see if there's any connection between her Tony and Desiree's Tony? I know it may seem like a long shot, but it's totally worth following up. Let's get her on the record, ask whether she's ever heard of Marvel Modeling. And see if her pimp, Tony, ever did photo shoots of her, or of anyone else. I can run by the BWCO and get her."

"I need to get on the Amber Alert."

Elsie nodded. The procedures for an Amber Alert weren't uncomplicated; and dealing with the FBI always involved a challenge for local law enforcement.

"How can I help?" she asked, briskly.

He made eye contact. "You can head on back to the courthouse and let me get to work here."

Affronted, she jumped off his desktop. In a brittle voice, she said, "Fine. Sorry to bother you."

His countenance was tense. With his hand on the computer mouse, he focused on his computer screen. "I appreciate you bringing Breeon and Kim Wickham over here. I'll check in with you later. Maybe we can eat."

She grabbed her purse and opened the door to his office. "Maybe."

Fuming, she walked across the street of the town square and up the stone steps to the courthouse. Ashlock was playing the cop card. She got the message: stick to the courtroom. Let the law enforcement professionals handle the investigation end.

With a flip of her hand, she bypassed the security station at the courthouse entry. The deputy greeted her, and she nodded in response. She'd almost reached the worn marble stairway when she had a thought.

Denny's.

The people who lured Desiree and Taylor had met up with them at Denny's. Someone on the staff at Denny's might have information about the meeting, maybe a description of a suspect. For a bare second, she considered passing her thought on to Ashlock, before discarding the notion. He'd made it abundantly clear that he wanted to work with the FBI, and that the first order of business was the Amber Alert.

But there was nothing to prevent Elsie from cruising over to Denny's. It was a public place. Maybe she'd show Ashlock that her investigatory instincts were legit.

She paused at the bottom of the stairs just long enough to unearth her car keys. Then she headed for the back door of the courthouse at a fast clip.

In her car, she turned the radio on, tuning in to the primary country music station for the region. If an Amber Alert was issued, there was no way she would miss it. It would be preceded by an earsplitting metallic squeal.

But by the time she pulled into the Denny's parking lot on the highway, Miranda Lambert's voice belted through the speaker without interruption.

She marched into the restaurant with a determined step. A young woman in a loose-fitting black uniform met her with a smile. Grasping a plastic menu, she said, "Just one today?"

Elsie shook her head. "I need to talk to the manager."

The waitress's smile faded. "He's in the back. He's busy."

Elsie lowered her voice and pinned the girl with a fierce stare. "I'm with the county Prosecutor's Office. And I need to see him now."

The girl scurried away and reappeared shortly, accompanied by a man in his thirties, wearing a black shirt that bore the Denny's trademark on its sleeve.

"Hey, Elsie," he said, "I'm Dwayne Meyer. We went to Barton High together."

She beamed at him, though she barely recalled him from school. "Dwayne, thanks for seeing me. I need you to help me with an important matter. You have to check your work records. Tell me who was working here last Thursday in the afternoon."

He looked reluctant. "How come?"

Elsie squared her shoulders, giving him her no-nonsense face. "It's police business."

"I didn't think you was a policeman. Thought you was a lawyer."

Give me a fucking break, she thought; but she held her temper in check. "A teenage girl was in your restaurant last Thursday, for an interview. She has gone missing. It's important that I talk to the server who waited on her."

He didn't say anything. Elsie stepped closer to him, clearly violating his personal space. "It's imperative."

They were drawing an audience. Two other members of the Denny's wait staff had wandered within earshot. Even the short-order cook left his station and was peering through the kitchen door.

"Well, what time on Thursday? Before three or after three? We have a shift change."

Elsie paused, trying to remember; what had Desiree's mother said?

A woman volunteered, "After three. About four o'clock."

Elsie looked at her. She was leaning against the cash register behind the manager's shoulder. Graying hair was pulled back from her face, revealing a forbidding expression. Elsie locked eyes with the waitress, then glanced away.

The woman had a wandering eye: literally. One eye was fixed on Elsie. The other deviated, turning in the opposite direction.

The manager turned to the waitress. "How do you know?"

"I saw them. One of the girls was curly headed, the other black. They was looking for trouble."

Elsie could hardly believe her stroke of luck. "Can we sit down somewhere? We have to talk."

The deviating eye spun again. "I've got an order up." She turned on her heel and walked off, leaving Elsie with the manager. In an apologetic tone, Dwayne said, "We're kind of busy. She'll go on break later; about one-thirty."

The waitress reappeared, bearing a large tray loaded with plates of food. Elsie blocked her. With a decided move, she took the tray from the waitress and handed it off to the manager.

Elsie said, "She's going on break right now."

The manager turned to the waitress with a befuddled look. "What am I supposed to do with this?"

"Table eighteen, in the back corner," she said.

As he walked off with the tray, she added, "I'm keeping the tip."

Chapter 29

ELSIE FOLLOWED THE Denny's waitress down an aisle and scooted into a booth across from her.

"This is my section," the waitress said, looking around with a frown. "They'll be wondering why I'm not taking care of them."

Elsie rummaged in her purse and pulled out the notepad she'd used to jot notes at the PD. Under the handwritten scrawl that read "Marvel Marketing," she circled "Denny's" and "Th afternoon."

"I'm sorry to inconvenience you. This is really important." Glancing at the nametag on the woman's chest, she added: "Brigitte."

Brigitte grabbed a stray napkin and began to scrub the table with it. "The busboy is just plain lazy," she muttered. She wadded the napkin into a ball and stuffed it into the pocket of her black nylon apron. "You need me to get you something? Coffee?"

Elsie would have killed for a cup of coffee; but asking the woman to wait on her felt wrong. She needed to treat her as a witness rather than a server.

"No, ma'am. Thank you. Can you give me your full name, Brigitte?"

"It's Clifton. Brigitte Diane Clifton."

Elsie looked up from her pad. The left eye was moving again; so Elsie fixed her focus on Brigitte's right eye.

"And you're from Barton?"

"All my life. Do you not know me? Because I sure recognize you."

Elsie faltered, struggling to recall the woman. Brigitte was too old to claim a high school kinship; and she didn't recognize her as a courthouse regular. From her grim vibe, it was unlikely that they'd shared a beer and a laugh at the Baldknobbers Bar.

Elsie hazarded a guess. "I bet it was here. At Denny's?"

Bingo. Brigitte nodded, and her eye steadied momentarily. "I don't see you so much these days. A while back, I used to work the graveyard shift. You'd come in after you were drinking. Order breakfast."

The blush started to crawl up Elsie's neck. She huffed a regretful laugh. "Back in my old college days, I bet. My wayward youth."

"Not so long ago as that. You'd come in with that policeman."

Elsie drew up in her seat, with an air of injury. "Brigitte, Detective Ashlock can't be accused of stumbling into Denny's under the influence."

"Not him. The other one. The good-looking cop." Her face was stern. "And he wasn't the one doing the stumbling."

Oh Lord. Elsie's history was biting her in the ass again: Noah Strong, her cop boyfriend from the bad old days. The woman's memory was probably accurate.

Which was embarrassing for Elsie, but good for the interview. She was glad to know the woman had strong powers of recollection.

"Let's talk about last Thursday. You waited on the two girls you described?"

"I didn't just wait on them. I saw them in the restroom first."

At the mention of the restroom, Brigitte smoothed her hair with her hands and tightened the elastic band that held it away from her face.

"The restroom? Here at Denny's?"

"Yeah. They were painting their faces like a couple of Jezebels. Couldn't have been old enough to be in high school yet."

Elsie shook her head, trying to envision Taylor Johnson wearing makeup. She had a perfect complexion. Elsie had never seen the girl with any look other than a scrubbed face.

She asked, "Did you observe anything else in the bathroom?"

"The short girl with the curly hair was putting on a pair of high-heeled slippers. Looked three sizes too big for her."

It occurred to Elsie that the waitress had missed her true calling. With her sharp recall of detail, she could've worked for the CIA.

"Did you overhear their conversation? Did they say what they were doing there?"

"I told them. I said the restroom was for customers only. Because it is." Her lips thinned into a hyphen on her face.

"Anything else?"

"Not then. Next thing, they turned up in my section."

Elsie edged closer to the tabletop. "So, you waited on them?"

"If you want to call it that. Didn't hardly order anything."

Elsie's heart began to pound in her chest. She felt adrenaline surge in her veins as she asked: "Was anyone with them?"

Brigitte nodded.

Elsie kept her voice under control as she asked: "Can you describe the individuals who met the girls?"

Her hand clenched the pen, ready to write. Waiting for the words.

Brigitte tilted her head to the right. "It was a woman."

"A woman?"

"Yeah. About your age. Had a cup of coffee."

"Was she alone? Are you certain?"

"Yeah. Until the two girls joined up with her at the table."

Elsie looked down, trying to hide her disappointment. She'd hoped to score a description of Tony, the man with Marvel Modeling. But at least she would get a description of the woman.

"What did the woman look like?"

The waitress fixed her good eye on Elsie, looking her up and down. "Skinnier than you. Not as tall. Shoulder length red hair, all curled up in a fancy hairdo."

"Any distinguishing features?"

"She wore a lot of makeup. And she had an accent. Not anything from around here. More Southern than us."

She dropped the pen on the pad. "Did you pick up any of their conversation?"

"I don't eavesdrop on the customers. Or waste time on chatter. Not like some people around here. I do my work. It's a job, not a social time."

Elsie nodded politely. She sneaked a glance at her watch. When she saw the time, she reached for her purse; Madeleine and Chuck would have her head on a platter for being out of pocket so long.

"But I remember one thing. The black girl didn't ask for anything, not even water. The curly head wanted sweet tea."

She paused, as if giving Elsie the opportunity to respond. So Elsie nodded and repeated the words: "Sweet tea."

"But the woman grabbed her arm, said no sugar. Not if she wanted to be a model."

Elsie dropped her purse and snatched up the pen again. As she scrawled detailed notes, recording every scrap the waitress recalled regarding the red-haired woman and her meeting with the girls, Elsie completely forgot about the time.

But Brigitte had her eye on the clock.

"It's almost noon. If I don't do the lunch business, this day will be a loss for me."

Elsie had exhausted her questions; she put the pad into her purse. Smiling at Brigitte, she said, "I really appreciate your help today. I know it was a sacrifice, breaking into your workday like this."

"You're right. It was. So, thanks. But I didn't do it for you."

Taken aback, Elsie waited to see if the woman would speak again.

"I did it for your mama." The waitress scooted out of the booth, preparing to walk away.

But Elsie held out a restraining hand. "What do you mean?"

The waitress looked down. Elsie had to steel herself, not to glance away from the roaming eye.

In a whisper, Brigitte said, "She was my sixth-grade English teacher. At Barton Middle School, right before you were born. Back then, they called me names at school. Wall-eye, Cock-eye, Cross-eye. They had a lot of them."

Elsie stared into the stationary eye, trying not to blink.

"Your mama put a stop to it. To this day, I don't know how she did it. She was a saint."

Before she walked away, Brigitte had a parting word. "With a mother like that, you ought to know how to behave better."

Chapter 30

ELSIE DROVE AWAY from Denny's on autopilot, rehashing the conversation she'd had with Brigitte in her head. Clearly, Taylor was holding out on them. She hadn't mentioned anything about the meeting that she and Desiree had attended in the prior week. A bright girl like Taylor should have been a wealth of information. Why had she neglected to mention the interview at Denny's? To confirm that the woman at Denny's on Thursday was the same Dede who drove them out of town on Friday night? Why not mention her distinctive hair color? Her Southern drawl?

Something was whispering in the back of Elsie's brain. A connection was just out of her grasp. What was it? What was she missing?

The sign appeared on the opposite side of the road: RANCHO MOTEL. DAILY/WEEKLY/MONTHLY RATES. KITCHENETTES. She couldn't miss it; since they widened the highway, the sign nearly leaped off the curb.

Elsie had almost reached the courthouse before she remembered. A car tearing out of the Rancho parking lot, with Alabama plates. Driven by a red-haired woman, on the day Mandy was found in the motel room, beaten like a dog. That car had nearly sideswiped Elsie in the lot.

As Elsie circled the town square and headed north, she dug in the console of the car, hunting blindly for loose change. She knew she'd need to offer up a bribe if she wanted Mandy to talk. And she was determined to make her talk, to back up Elsie's suspicions. That Mandy knew the connection between the Rancho incident, and Desiree's disappearance, and Taylor's involvement, and the red-haired woman at Denny's—who had to be Dede. And Tony. Tony, with Marvel Modeling.

When her hand unearthed a fistful of quarters and dimes, she smiled. She could afford a trip to Jiffy Go.

After she parked across the street from the Battered Women's Center, she dropped the coins in her purse before she trotted across the street. Inside the lobby, she was disappointed to see that June wasn't in her usual spot. Instead, the desk was occupied by a woman in her twenties, bent over a paperback book.

Elsie strode to the desk. "Hi. I'm Elsie Arnold, with the county Prosecutor's Office. I volunteer at the center on the weekends."

The young woman folded the corner of the page and closed the book. "I'm Jeanette."

"Hey. I'm looking for Mandy. She's been staying here this week. Room 18, I think.

Jeanette wore a loose-fitting blue sweater; the sleeves were so long that she had to push them up before she turned to operate the computer on the desk. "Last name?"

A wave of impatience started to build inside Elsie's chest. "Not exactly sure. But I know her, I swear; I'm the one who brought her here."

Jeanette stared at the computer screen, frowning. "I don't see a Mandy."

Elsie stepped away, scanning the empty lobby. "Where's June? June knows who I'm talking about."

"She comes in at five. You can come back then."

Elsie headed for the stairway. "I'll go check in on her. I know where she is."

She hustled up the stairway, her shoes making the wooden treads creak. Jeanette's voice echoed from the bottom of the stairs, but she ignored it, and marched up to Room 18.

The door was ajar; but she knocked anyway. When she didn't get a response, she pounded on the door with the side of her fist.

"Mandy? You awake? It's Elsie. Want to go for a ride?"

She pushed the door slightly; the hinges complained, screeching like an ancient soprano in the church choir. Sticking her head through the door, Elsie repeated: "Mandy?"

The room was deserted. The narrow bed was unmade, the sheets shoved to the side, as if someone had left it abruptly. Elsie stepped inside, heading for the closet and jerking open the door. It was empty.

Jeanette appeared in the doorway, her face pink with indignation. "You can't just barge in here like this. We have a policy."

Ignoring her, Elsie walked into the minuscule bathroom, barely large enough to hold an ancient sink and toilet, and a rust-stained bathtub. A sliver of miniature soap sat in the soap dish. Other than that, there was no sign that Mandy had ever occupied the room. Not even a toothbrush was left.

Thinking aloud, Elsie said, "She didn't have any money. No belongings, not even a coat, as far as I know. The last time I saw her, she was wearing flip-flops on her feet. In November."

Jeanette stood in the bathroom doorway. "If you don't leave immediately, I'm going to have to call someone."

Elsie shut the bathroom door in her face; she didn't want to argue. As it clicked shut, she was inches away from the only evidence of her stay that Mandy left behind.

The hospital gown hung on a hook on the back of the bathroom door.

The door swung open with a strong push. Elsie didn't back away in time; the heavy wood clipped her on the forehead.

"Damn," she howled as she bent over, clutching her head. "Shit."

Jeanette backed away a step. "Are you all right?" she asked, apologetic.

"No, I'm not all right." She rubbed the sore spot, inspecting it in the age-speckled mirror over the sink. "You almost cracked my head open."

When she emerged from the bathroom, Elsie saw that an audience had assembled inside Room 18. Three of the residents were standing in the doorway, watching the show.

Peggy Pitts stood in the front. Elsie noted the raw spot at the front of her scalp; an injury inflicted by Mandy, she surmised.

Touching her forehead with careful fingers, Elsie eyed the three women before asking, "Do any of you all know where Mandy is?"

Three sets of eyes darted from her gaze. No one answered.

Elsie said, "She was here on Saturday; I talked to her. Did she take off? Did anyone see anything?"

A wan woman in her thirties with birdlike features spoke first. "I didn't really know her. She kept to herself."

Elsie pinned Peggy with a gaze. "Peggy, you had a run-in with her."

Peggy's face was blank. "Yeah."

After no more information was forthcoming, Elsie said, "When's the last time you saw her, Peggy?"

"Today. This morning."

Elsie struggled to keep the impatience from her voice. "What was she doing when you saw her last?"

"Leaving."

There was a heavy silence. Elsie turned to Jeanette, who answered the unspoken question with a shrug. "I didn't know. June didn't say anything."

Elsie focused again on Peggy, forcing her to meet her gaze. "Did you tell anyone? That Mandy was taking off?"

"Nope."

Elsie shook her head in dismay. "Why not?"

"She asked me to keep quiet. So, I did."

"But why?"

"Just being a friend."

Then Elsie noticed Peggy Pitts wore a white men's T-shirt with a front pocket. Inside the pocket, she could make out the outline of a crumpled pack of Parliaments. And a pink Bic lighter.

Chapter 31

THE GRAY CLOUDS looming over the Battered Women's Center held a swollen threat. Elsie made a run for her car, grateful for its protection. Once she was safely inside, she pulled out her cell phone and began a long text to Ashlock, her thumbs typing so fast that autocorrect made the message almost incoherent.

But she sent it, knowing he'd get the gist. Then she checked the texts she received in the past hour. One was from Madeleine, all in capital letters.

WHERE ARE YOU?

Groaning inwardly, she headed toward the town square. In her head, she enjoyed a lengthy debate with Madeleine, in which she defended her absence in a series of pithy zingers which rendered Madeleine speechless, remorseful, and unable to disagree.

By the time she parked in the courthouse lot, the gray skies had opened up, pelting her with cold rain as she dashed to the side entrance of the building. Once inside, she shook her hair like a horse's mane, scattering drops of water onto the tiled floor.

She took the stairs slowly, thinking about the information

she had gained over the past hour and a half. About Mandy's abrupt departure. And Taylor and Desiree's meeting with the red-haired woman at Denny's: Dede, from Marvel Modeling. A meeting that Taylor neglected to mention when they talked to her at school.

When she approached the entrance to the Prosecutor's Office, she saw a huddled figure seated on the wooden bench outside the front door.

Oh Lord, she thought. It was Kim Wickham, Desiree's mom.

Only a heartless person would bypass her; and Elsie wasn't guilty of that. She walked up to the bench with a concerned expression.

"Ms. Wickham," she said.

The woman raised her head. Dark roots made a Rorschach pattern along her bleached hairline. Her eyes were swollen from crying.

"They sent me away."

Elsie cocked her head. "Who sent you away?"

"The police. They said to go home, they'll tell me when they hear something. I can't go home. I want to talk to the FBI."

Elsie sat beside her on the hard bench. "Ma'am, this is the McCown County Courthouse. There aren't any federal offices in this building. The nearest FBI office is in Springfield."

Kim Wickham didn't appear to be listening. Her voice rising, she said, "The detective took our computer, for evidence. Now I can't even look for her on the computer. Or look for somebody from the modeling agency. I want to see somebody. I tried to talk to Taylor's mother again, she won't see me. I want to see the prosecutor, that Madeleine Thompson."

She turned wet eyes to Elsie and said again: "I want to talk to somebody."

Elsie took her hand and gave it a gentle squeeze. "Do you have family nearby, Ms. Wickham? Anyone I can call?"

"I've got nobody. Nobody but my baby girl. And somebody took her away from me."

Kim Wickham dropped her head and began to weep, with the involuntary wails that accompany profound suffering. The tears ran in tracks down her face and snot ran from her nose.

"I'm going to get you some Kleenex," Elsie said. Stacie kept a box on the reception desk, to use for her cosmetic applications.

Inside the office, Elsie saw Madeleine, Chuck, and Breeon clustered inside the interior hallway that led to the attorneys' private offices. They were speaking in angry whispers. Elsie edged over and stuck her head through the doorway.

"No way. I refuse to have anything to do with that woman," Breeon was saying.

In a harsh undertone, Madeleine said, "She asked for you first."

Breeon advanced on Madeleine with an expression so fierce that her boss backed away a step. "I already heard what that woman has to say. She endangered my daughter, for God's sake. You better not put her in the same room with me unless you want to see real trouble."

Madeleine glanced away, with a guilty face. "Chuck, you talk to her. Don't bring her inside the office. Just get rid of her. Convince her to go home."

Chuck raised both hands in protest. "I know nothing whatsoever about this situation. And I'm due in court in ten minutes."

Madeleine pursed her lips and squeezed her eyes shut, like a harried mother counting to ten. After tense moments, she exhaled, opening her eyes and glaring at the group huddled in the hall.

Elsie pulled a face. "Jesus fucking Christ. I'll do it. I'll give her a ride home." Tossing her wet hair over her shoulder, she turned her back on them; but before she walked off, she added, "Damn, you all are cold."

"Where have you been all day?" Madeleine said.

Elsie snatched the Kleenex box off the reception counter and left the office without offering a reply.

Chapter 32

ELSIE PULLED HER car into the narrow driveway of a small rock house in an old neighborhood of Barton, braking before she entered a battered carport fashioned from corrugated metal.

Putting the car in Park, she examined the woman in the passenger seat. Kim Wickham's head was bowed, her chest heaving; but the open-mouthed sobbing had subsided.

"Can I walk you in? Make you some coffee?" When Kim didn't answer, Elsie fidgeted, uncomfortable. She broke the silence with the first thing that popped into her head.

"Or Diet Coke? Want me to get you a Diet Coke?"

The woman shook her head, but remained in her seat. Elsie hoped she'd make a move to open the car door, but Kim sat, her hands limp in her lap.

Elsie peered at the nearby houses, praying that a neighbor might come to her rescue, but the sidewalks were deserted. She tried again.

"Is there someone I can call? A friend at work? Or a neighbor?"

Kim shut her eyes and shook her head. Finally, she spoke. "How will I get my car back? It's at the courthouse. I need my car."

Elsie took a moment to reflect. She had thought it imprudent to let Kim Wickham drive, in her emotional state of extreme distress. That had motivated Elsie to insist on ferrying her home. But the gesture left Kim without transportation.

"I'll talk to Detective Ashlock. When you feel up to it, he can send a patrol car over. They'll give you a lift to the courthouse."

She hoped she wasn't making a promise she couldn't keep. Ashlock hadn't been in touch since she left his office that morning.

Elsie cleared her throat. "Ashlock gave you a card, right? With his number. I can give you one of mine, too. You can call me if you remember any additional details. Or if you want to talk."

Her purse was in the backseat. She had to twist around and fumble inside for long moments before she found a business card. It was wrinkled and slightly grimy, but her office phone was legible.

When she offered the card to Kim, the woman didn't reach out to take it. She fixed her eyes upon Elsie with a fierce red-rimmed glare.

"I want to talk to the FBI."

Gently, Elsie dropped the card onto Kim's denim-covered left leg. "I'm sure you do. Ashlock is going to be in touch with them. I bet they'll call. Real soon."

"I want to talk to them now."

"Kim, I don't have a personal contact in the FBI. I don't know anyone who works there."

"I got to talk to them."

Her voice grated with need. Elsie couldn't brush it off; even though she was chagrined to admit she didn't have any confidence that a federal agent would take her call. She twisted back to reach into her purse again; fortunately, locating her cell phone was an easier task than unearthing the business card.

She tapped in her code, then did a Google search: FBI Missouri. Scanning the results, she found a contact number. "Let's call them right now," she said with a brave smile.

The search gave two options: St. Louis or Kansas City. She chose KC; McCown County was in the Western District of Missouri, so she assumed the KC branch had jurisdiction.

Elsie punched the number into her phone. As it rang, she reached for Kim's hand, and gasped when Kim clenched it in a bruising grip. She pulled free, ashamed to withdraw support; but Breeon had crushed the bones of the same hand earlier that day.

When the call picked up on the other end, Elsie shot her an encouraging look. The recorded voice on the line in Kansas City shouldn't have come as a surprise; it wasn't a pokey little office like the McCown County Sheriff's Department of the Barton PD, where human beings still answered the phone.

Elsie drummed her fingers on the console as the polite female voice talked in her ear.

"You have reached the office of the FBI. If this is a life-threatening emergency, please hang up and dial 911."

Elsie hung on. As the options rolled by, Kim Wickham tapped her shoulder. Ignoring the silent inquiry, Elsie squeezed her eyes shut, waiting.

"For employment information, press four."

"Jesus," she whispered.

"What is it? What are they saying?"

Elsie shook her head, and Kim fell silent. Finally, she was told to press a number for "all other matters" and an operator would answer.

Elsie pressed the digit. When a woman answered, Elsie breathed out in relief.

"Hi. This is Elsie Arnold, assistant prosecutor in McCown County. I'm with a mother of a fifteen-year-old girl. We believe the girl has been abducted."

The voice on the line was calm. "Have you dialed 911?"

Elsie's heart rate amped up. "Yes, she contacted local law enforcement. And they are investigating. But she'd like to talk to someone in the FBI. She's right here. I can hand off the phone."

Kim Wickham tore the phone from Elsie's hand. "I want the FBI. This is Kim Wickham, Desiree's mama."

Elsie could hear the voice say, "Okay. One moment. I'll connect you."

Kim shot Elsie a look of triumph, and Elsie responded with an encouraging nod. But another recording buzzed through the phone, saying: "I'm away from my desk, please leave a message."

Kim's face crumpled. She handed the phone back to Elsie, saying, "There's no one there."

Elsie slipped the phone into her pocket. "Let me get you inside. It's cold out here."

Without speaking, they walked up the drive, under the carport. As she unlocked the side entrance to the rock house, Kim gave Elsie a pleading look.

"Will you come in, just for a minute? I got some Diet Shasta in the fridge."

Elsie longed to fly back to her car, rev it up, and race back to the courthouse. But she followed the woman inside and accepted the cold can of soda.

In a distracted voice, Kim said, "I can get you a glass, but I don't have ice. Ice maker isn't working too good."

Elsie popped the top of the Shasta and took a swig. "I like it from a can."

She followed, watching as Kim wound through the kitchen and into the living room. The woman moved in slow motion, as though it took all her strength to put one foot in front of the other. When they reached the sofa facing the rock fireplace, Kim froze so suddenly that Elsie stepped on her heel.

"Beg pardon," Elsie said; but Kim wasn't listening. Her face focused at the display on and around the fireplace mantel.

Elsie's eyes squinted in disbelief as she studied the childhood trophies. Some of them were huge, two and three feet tall. They sat on the floor framing a gas log in the fireplace. Colored sashes hung from the mantel like stockings on Christmas Eve. The sashes varied in color and length; but they were clearly child-size. The display gave off a distinct JonBenet Ramsey vibe that chilled her.

She stared at a large photo over the mantel: Desiree, obviously as a tot; with one hand resting on her hip and the other holding on to a tiara, poised on a riot of curly blond hair. Struck with a sick fascination, Elsie took a step toward the fireplace; but halted when Kim stumbled ahead of her, with her arms uplifted.

With reverent hands, the woman took down a glittering rhinestone crown, fashioned to sit high upon a small head. Sinking onto the floor, Kim cradled the crown in her arms and began to weep again.

"My baby," she said, repeating it like a refrain. "My baby, my baby."

Elsie's stomach clenched, and she looked away from the raw display.

Chapter 33

When Elsie left Kim Wickham at the rock house and returned to her office, she spent the remainder of the day in fruitless efforts. She tried to nail down Marvel Modeling on the internet; but all of her searches revealed nothing. Even Google turned up no website by that name.

Haunted by the image of Kim Wickham huddled over a miniature beauty pageant crown, Elsie had called the FBI office twice again in the afternoon; but she managed to communicate only with recorded voices. She even reached out to the U.S. Attorney's Office; but couldn't punch a hole through that iron curtain either.

"Fucking Feds," she muttered as she slammed her landline office phone into its cradle.

Elsie also made repeated attempts to follow up with Ashlock. But though she tried to contact him by phone and text, she hadn't communicated with him since leaving his office that morning.

After five o'clock, she started her car and headed for Ashlock's house. After all, he had mentioned eating dinner together when they parted that morning. She didn't need a formal invitation, she thought, as she pulled into Ashlock's driveway. Elsie hurried to the front door, anxious to compare notes on Marvel Modeling. She hoped to hear that Ashlock had experienced more success than she. Surely he had.

She pressed on his doorbell, not easing up till the door flew open. Burton stood there, a "WTF" look on his face.

"Is your dad here?"

"Yeah," he said, as Elsie walked past. "He's in the kitchen."

When she appeared in the kitchen doorway, Ashlock looked up in surprise. "Hey, Elsie. I wasn't expecting you."

He stood over the stove top. Two hamburger patties were sizzling in a cast iron skillet. A can of Van Camp's pork and beans sat on the counter nearby, beside a bag of salad.

"Seems like you mentioned it earlier, at the PD. I guess it was a maybe," she said.

She looked pointedly inside the skillet before aiming an inquisitive glance at the chef. Ashlock shrugged, unapologetic. "I'm afraid I'm cooking for two tonight, Elsie. I've got another can of beans in the cabinet; and we'll share our salad, if you're interested."

But not your burger. That's true love, she thought, slightly miffed.

She leaned over the vinyl kitchen countertop and lifted the bag of salad to inspect it. Tossing it down, she said, "My mom won't buy those bagged salads. She thinks they're dangerous."

Ashlock flipped the burger patties without answering. Elsie went on.

"She said that somebody found a dead bat in one of those bagged salads. Marge wouldn't feed a bagged salad to her worst enemy."

When he spoke, his voice was sharp. "Maybe I should feed my son a cold McDonald's."

She swung around, regarding him with a challenge in her eye as he tended the stove.

"Ouch," she said.

Elsie waited for him to speak. To take it back. When the silence stretched to the point where it became almost hostile, she broke it.

"I didn't hear an Amber Alert. Didn't get it on my phone either."

She could see him exhale. He pushed the frying pan off the hot burner. "Well, we're still working on that."

"I don't know what you mean."

He turned to face her, his expression grim. "There are strict requirements for an Amber Alert. Our situation with Desiree doesn't fit all of them."

"Why not?"

"For an Amber Alert, there has to be an abduction."

Their eyes locked.

"She was abducted."

"Not precisely. She went with them voluntarily."

"So what? They are holding a minor, without her parent's knowledge or consent. She has been kidnapped."

"For an Amber Alert, we need a description of the vehicle and the abductor. No one can provide that."

"That's bullshit."

Ashlock didn't respond. Elsie said, "I can provide a description of the abductor."

"You've never seen the abductor."

"I believe I have. I saw a woman who matches the description of the person who met the girls at Denny's. I saw her at the Rancho, in the parking lot. She's the same woman the Denny's waitress saw interviewing the girls."

"You don't know that. Not for certain."

"Jesus, Ashlock. Did you get my texts? Did you read them?"

He reached for a bag of hamburger buns. "We're taking care to follow the procedures correctly. We haven't had this situation before. We're talking to some law enforcement people in the bigger counties, for guidance."

"Who's this 'we'?"

"Me and the sheriff." He paused, and added. "It's been just twenty-four hours."

"So you're waiting for tomorrow? What the hell for?"

"The sheriff wanted to wait for the twenty-four-hour mark."

"The sheriff is a dumbass."

Ashlock ignored that observation. He slid the patties onto buns, opened the can of beans, and dumped the bagged salad into a bowl.

Elsie stepped closer. "The sheriff is a moron."

He peered over her head, into the living room. "Burton," he called. "Supper."

Elsie persisted. "What about the FBI?"

"I've been in touch. They said to keep them advised." He pulled a spoon from a kitchen drawer and dished cold beans onto two plates.

Elsie watched, horrified. "Aren't you going to heat those beans up in a pan?"

He dropped the spoon into the sink with a clatter. "If you just want to criticize my parenting, I wish to God you wouldn't show up at suppertime."

Elsie held up both hands in a gesture of surrender. "I would never criticize your parenting. You're a great parent. Your cooking, on the other hand, is kind of terrible."

Burton entered the kitchen. As if on cue, he said, "Burgers. Excellent."

As the boy dished salad onto his plate, Elsie whispered to Ashlock. "Ash. I've got the solution: the Amber Alert. Taylor can describe the driver, the woman. So can Brigitte Clifton, a waitress at Denny's. And I can describe the vehicle. I saw it at the Rancho, that first day."

"What vehicle? What are you talking about?"

"I knew you hadn't paid enough attention to the texts I sent you today."

"There were about fifty, seemed like. And in case you weren't aware, I was busy."

Growing animated, Elsie explained that she'd seen a red-haired woman in the car with the Alabama plates at the Rancho Motel. Ashlock listened; but when she was done, he shook his head.

"You're still trying to tie 'Mandy Candy' to this out-of-county deal with Desiree Wickham? You've got no factual basis for that, aside from red hair. A lot of people have red hair. Don't even have to be born with it."

"I've got a feeling."

He laughed at that; but with resignation rather than amusement. "Elsie, honey. As a lawyer, you know better than anybody. A feeling, an instinct, a hunch? That's not probable cause. Not for a search or an arrest or nothing."

Ashlock picked up a bottle of ketchup, squirted it on his burger, and forked some salad onto the plate. Eying the dinner, Elsie said, "That looks like a meal at the Fyre Festival."

He looked up, his brow wrinkled. "What are you talking about?"

She waved it off. Ashlock didn't keep up with trending news on Twitter. As he joined Burton at the kitchen table, she followed behind.

"Give me the FBI agent's contact info."

He looked up from his burger, wary. "What for?"

"I want to talk to him. About the sex trafficking angle."

Ashlock's jaw tensed. "We don't have sex trafficking in Barton."

"How can you be sure of that?"

"Because if we did, I'd know."

"Then how do you explain this whole deal? The meetings with Taylor and Desiree, and Desiree's disappearance?"

"It didn't happen in Barton, in McCown County. It happened someplace else."

"What do you mean? The girl was picked up at Denny's, in McCown County."

"I know that. But it could be argued that she went willingly from McCown County to another location, where she has been held against her will—and we're still trying to figure out where. That's why the FBI needs to be in charge."

"'It could be argued'? What are you, the public defender?"

"Back off, Elsie. I've never issued an Amber Alert before. I'm going to get it right."

Burton was following the exchange with rapt attention. Ashlock pointed at the boy's plate.

"Eat," he said. Then he bit into his own burger.

Elsie listened to the chewing for a few moments, trying to devise an argument that would persuade Ashlock to accept her point of view. When the eating continued, she jerked her purse onto her shoulder.

In a steely voice, she said, "I'm leaving."

Ashlock nodded, swallowing. "See you later."

"Just so you know. I'm going to do some investigating on my own."

She turned on her heel, ready to depart; but Ashlock launched out of the kitchen chair and caught her by the arm before she reached the door.

"Elsie, that's not your place. Stay out of this. Don't muddy the waters."

She jerked her arm out of his grip. "I told you, I've got a feeling about this."

He leaned in so close that their noses almost brushed. "Stop playing goddamned Nancy Drew."

"I'm not playing. I'm going to follow up on it."

As he watched her leave, Ashlock said, "Elsie. I'm warning you. Goddamn it, you can do more damage than six tornadoes."

Once she was outside, starting up her car, she turned over his statement in her head. And decided that it was a compliment.

Whether Ashlock intended it that way or not.

Chapter 34

THAT NIGHT, WHEN Dede walked into the motel room, Desiree was tugging on the handcuffs that chained her to the bed, her arm muscles taut.

Dede shook her head at the girl, her mouth puckered. "No point in fooling with those cuffs, honey. They're not a toy. They're the real thing. Tony got them on the internet."

Desiree's head jerked as she focused on Dede with frightened eyes. She made a sound, but it was garbled behind the strip of duct tape covering her mouth.

Dede held a plastic cup in her hand. Lifting the cup, she said, "I got some water for you. You thirsty?"

When Desiree's head bobbed in a nod, Dede clucked her tongue. She set the cup on the bedside table and sat on the mattress beside the girl's prone figure.

"I'm unlocking one of your hands, okay? So you can hold the cup. And I'll get the tape off your mouth." She raised a finger in warning. "But if you fuss when this comes off it'll go right back on and I'll cuff you back up and you'll stay thirsty."

Desiree nodded. Dede's hands moved delicately, pulling the duct tape from Desiree's mouth with gentle pressure.

"There. Didn't hurt a bit, did it?"

Then she unlocked the cuff restraining Desiree's left hand. She handed the cup over to Desiree and watched her grasp it from her hand, lifting it and drinking greedily. The girl didn't stop until the cup was empty.

As she drank, Dede said, "That tape's tricky stuff. If you're not careful, it can pull your skin off. And we want to keep your mouth pretty, don't we? Because you're a professional model now."

Desiree's voice came out with a raspy sound. "I want to go home."

Taking the empty cup from Desiree's free hand, Dede walked into the bathroom and turned on the faucet in the sink. As she refilled the cup, she said, "Don't be silly, Lola. You're a working girl. You work for Marvel Modeling."

"I don't want to be a model. I want to go back home. Please."

Dede leaned against the door frame of the motel bathroom, gazing down on Desiree with mock surprise. "Don't want to be a model? Are you messing with me? Honey, you signed a contract."

A look of confusion clouded Desiree's face. "A contract? I don't remember."

"Well, you were tired. You'd been partying. Maybe that's why it's a little fuzzy. But you signed on the line for Tony. Marvel has a five year exclusive on you."

The blue eyes widened with dismay. "Five years," Desiree croaked.

Striding back to the bed, Dede put an arm around the girl's shoulders and held the cup to her mouth. Closing her eyes, Desiree drank deeply, using her free hand to grasp the cup over Dede's fingers and tip it back.

When Dede set the empty cup down again, Desiree fixed her with a pugnacious look, though her mouth trembled. "I can't sign a contract. I'm not twenty-one."

"Oh, you don't have to be twenty-one to sign a contract. Just eighteen. And you're eighteen, Lola. You said so."

The trembling in her lips had overtaken her; her head shook with a palsy. "It wasn't true. I'm not. I'm in ninth grade. Fifteen."

Dede gasped. "No!"

"It's true." She used her free hand to grasp Dede's arm. "I turned fifteen on my birthday, two months ago."

"Are you telling me that you lied? On your job application? That you filled out online?"

When Desiree nodded in reply, Dede's head dropped. She said, "Oh no. No no no."

"What?" Desiree asked, her voice tightening into a squeak.

"Lying on the internet, giving false information. It's fraud. It's a crime." Dede's voice dropped to a whisper. "Do you know how much trouble you're in?"

Desiree's body began to tremble. "I didn't know. I just wanted to be a model. To try it out. But now I'm ready to go home."

Dede stroked Desiree's hair away from her face with a tender hand. "It's too late for that. But don't you worry, Lola. Tony will take care of you. He won't let the cops arrest you and take you to jail. Tony will take care of everything. He'll pay for your food and clothes and room. You don't have to worry about a thing, not anymore."

Desiree's voice came out in the barest of whispers. "But I want to go home."

Dede ignored her, combing through Desiree's curly hair with her fingers. "The only thing you have to concentrate on is doing a good job for Tony. In the photo shoots. And you'll have to entertain important clients. It's part of the job."

"I don't understand."

"Tony has some high-end connections. Really rich dudes, the kind that can make you famous. Help you hit the big time. But you've got to be sweet to them. There's one man right now who's dying to meet you. You'll need to be real sweet to him. Do what he wants. And the plus side of handling the clients—it will make you a better model. Sexier, more grown-up."

Desiree blinked. With her free hand, she rubbed her eyes. Dede lifted the girl's chin with a finger, staring at her intently.

"Are you starting to feel better? Relaxed?"

"A little sleepy, I guess."

Dede picked up the water cup and studied the interior, where a few powdery grains remained at the bottom.

"You'll feel good again, real soon." She turned to face Desiree with a bright smile.

Desiree's gaze grew unfocused, but she spoke again. "But my mom. She'll be worried. She'll be looking for me."

"Lola! You said you were ready to move out. You told Tony so when you talked on Skype, I remember it. I was in the room when you said it."

"I didn't mean it. I need my phone. I got to call my mom."

Dede stood and looked down at Desiree. "Tony took your phone. You don't need it anymore. But when you get all settled in, Tony will get you a new one. He'll pay for it."

Desiree's head dropped onto the pillow. Her eyes closed. When she spoke, her words were slurred. "My mom will worry."

"No, she won't. Tony got in touch with her. He said you're

moving on, joining the agency. Your mom was really happy for you. She said to tell you good luck."

Dede watched over the girl until her face went slack, her breathing regular. Dede reached out and gave the handcuffed wrist a jerk, to ensure that it was secure. Then she slipped back through the door to the adjoining room.

Chapter 35

The following morning, Elsie dodged into the courthouse coffee shop. Unbuttoning her coat, she called to the proprietor, who stood beside the grill with a metal spatula in hand.

"Tom, I need an egg sandwich. Need one real bad."

The man nodded, wiping his hands on his apron before cracking an egg onto the grill. The sizzle sent a thrill of anticipation up her spine.

"Hey, Elsie."

She glanced over to the round table where Public Defender Josh Nixon sat, his feet propped up on an empty chair. He nodded in her direction. "Join me?"

Casting a longing glance at her frying egg, Elsie walked over to the table occupied by Nixon. Staring down at him, she said, "What do you want?"

"Damn, you're grouchy in the morning. I was going to talk about pleading out some cases."

She sighed, dropping her briefcase onto the tiled floor. Nixon slid his feet off the neighboring chair, and she sat in it with a weary huff of breath.

He studied her with a curious eye. "Are you hungover? Big night last night?

"What's that supposed to mean?" Injured, she scooted the chair backward, intending to march away; but Tom arrived with the egg sandwich. And a hot cup of coffee.

"You want me to put it on your tab, Elsie?"

She sighed out in genuine gratitude. "Tom, you're the best. A lifesaver, honest to God."

"No need to take the Lord's name in vain," he said as he walked back to the grill.

She grabbed the saltshaker. "What cases are you trying to get rid of, Nixon?"

Nixon pulled his phone from his pocket and tapped the screen with his thumb. "How about Samuel Mason?"

She took a bite of the sandwich. As she chewed, she tried to recall the case name. The only name currently burned into her brain was Desiree Wickham. She swallowed before she spoke.

"Which one is that?"

"Assault."

"Which assault?"

A shade of impatience crossed his face. "We just had the preliminary hearing. Your witness, the homeless guy. You couldn't get him to ID the defendant in your direct."

"Oh yeah. That one."

"You want to make me an offer?"

She wanted very much to plead it out; but she couldn't offer without Madeleine's stamp of approval. So she hedged.

"What would you be able to get him to agree to?"

He stared at her, like a card shark at a poker table. "How about time served? He's been in lockup for two weeks."

Elsie was poised to snatch another bite of the breakfast sandwich; but at Nixon's statement, she dropped it back onto the plate in disgust.

"You're messing with me. Totally. Time served? For a felony assault?"

He tucked his long hair behind his ear. "I think that's reasonable."

"I think you're crazy. Batshit crazy." She took a gulp of coffee. It was growing tepid. "What else have you got?"

"Our recent mistrial in Judge Calvin's court. *State v. Sweeny Greene.* Misdemeanor assault."

"Oh god."

"Yeah, that was exciting. Have the police found the missing girl?"

Elsie's stomach twisted. The egg sandwich was losing its appeal. She'd awakened in the wee hours of the morning, obsessing over the plight of Desiree Wickham. "Not yet."

As if on cue, a deafening screech sounded from Josh Nixon's cell phone. He glanced at it. "Amber Alert," he said.

"Desiree?"

He studied the screen. "Yeah.

"Oh thank God; he got it done. It just took him a while. Jesus. Well, that's a step in the right direction." She plucked a piece of the muffin and lifted it to her mouth before she changed her mind. Dropping the bread back onto the plate, she said, "Have you ever defended a trafficking case?"

His brow rose. "Not me. The federal P.D.'s do that."

"I know there's federal jurisdiction. But we have state statutes now, outlawing trafficking at the state level in Missouri. It's part of the criminal code, Chapter 566.200."

"Just because it's on the books doesn't change things. At the state level, we're still dealing with the twentieth century perspective. State prosecutors haven't altered their mindset. Not yet, anyway."

She cocked her head. "Meaning what?"

He leaned forward and rested his elbow on the table. "Trafficking prosecutions view the prostitute as a victim. State law enforcement still regards sex workers as criminals."

She studied on the statement as she toyed with the sandwich, tearing it into pieces on the plate.

"That's not true," she said.

Behind her, she heard Madeleine Thompson speak.

"Tom, I need a cup of hot water with lemon."

Elsie turned in her seat, in time to see Tom bang the steaming cup onto the countertop.

"No charge," he said, frowning.

As Madeleine picked up the cup, she looked over at the table where Elsie sat with the public defender.

"Aren't you supposed to be in your office? It's past eight thirty."

Elsie scrambled out of the chair. "We were talking business. Assault cases."

As she followed Madeleine out the door, Josh called: "*State v. Sweeny Greene.* Time served!"

"Jesus," she muttered, shaking her head.

"Lord's name!" said Tom.

Madeleine walked down the hall at a fast clip; Elsie had to break into a trot to keep up.

"Did you hear the Amber Alert?"

Madeleine shuddered.

"Why do they insist on accompanying the announcement with that ear-shattering, blaring noise? It makes me shudder."

"I think that's the point."

Madeleine didn't respond. She made an abrupt turn onto the marble stairway.

"Madeleine, have you seen the reports on the girl who was assaulted at the Rancho Motel?"

"They're on my desk. Why?"

"I'm just thinking it's not a coincidence."

"What do you mean? I don't see it." As she reached the second floor, Madeleine shot Elsie a guarded glance. "Did the girl from the Rancho provide new information?"

"Yeah, she did. I got some background on the victim, some information on her relationship with the suspect. Her pimp beat her up. I made handwritten notes afterward. I can work up a memo and email it to you."

"Did she identify him? Provide his full name, a location where he can be found?"

"Well, no." Elsie paused, trying to form an explanation on Mandy's behalf, but Madeleine spoke before she had the chance.

"It's just as well. I'd hate to put the young woman on the stand as a state's witness."

The revelation riled Elsie. "Why do you say that?" she asked, though she anticipated that she knew what the answer might be.

"No jury will sympathize with a hooker. Or give credence to her testimony. Because she's a lawbreaker."

When Madeleine headed into the office, Elsie lagged behind, eager to place physical distance between them.

She couldn't bear to stand close behind Madeleine at that moment. Because she was tempted to plant her foot in Madeleine's skinny ass.

Chapter 36

LATER THAT MORNING, Elsie sat on the hard wooden chair at the counsel table in Judge Calvin's courtroom. It was an ordinary Tuesday. She was required to chime in on standard traffic charges and small-potato matters only.

The judge listened to a gray-haired defense attorney as he made his bid for leniency in a DWI sentencing. The lawyer, Billy Yocum, stood over his client with a supportive hand on the man's shoulder as he waxed eloquent on his many virtues.

Elsie slid her hand into her briefcase and pulled out her iPhone. Hiding it in her lap, she entered her passcode and returned to the Google page on Safari. She changed to a different search engine, looking again for the umpteenth time: Marvel Modeling.

She found comic books; software and engineering pages. What she didn't find was Tony.

"Ms. Arnold?"

She looked up, taking care to cover the phone with her hand. Judge Calvin was staring down at her with an expectant expression.

"Your honor?" she said.

"And what is the state's position?"

She glanced over at the gray-haired attorney. He smirked at her, looking pointedly at the hand that hid the phone in her lap. She cleared her throat, as she rose from her seat to a half stand. "We recommend shock time in the county jail. Two weekends."

"I know that," Judge Calvin said, his tone testy. "I'm asking your position on the submission of these letters from individuals writing on the defendant's behalf."

Bill Yocum held a sheaf of pages in his hand. His mouth quirked as he said to Elsie, "Would counsel for the state like to examine them?"

She shook her head. "No need to examine them. Objection, your honor. Hearsay."

"Overruled. It's sentencing." He extended his hand and accepted the sheets of paper that Yocum offered. Elsie settled back into her chair; and as Judge Calvin adjusted his glasses and began to read the letters, she uncovered her phone.

This time, she returned to Google, her old standby, and tried "Tony's Models." Nothing. She was getting nowhere.

Judge Calvin spoke up. "Mr. Yocum, there's a substantial amount of material here."

"Yes, your honor," the attorney said with a solemn face.

"I'll review them in my chambers." He tapped the gavel. "Court is adjourned for twenty minutes."

Elsie stood as the judge walked off, his black robe flying. Yocum sidled over to her.

"You young people can't leave those doggone phones alone. That ought to be contempt of court. That is what's wrong with the world today."

Elsie ignored him. She and Billy Yocum locked horns on a regular basis; but she had no time for a pissing match that day. She hurried into the hallway and called Ashlock, wild to know whether progress had been made in the hunt for Desiree Wickham.

When Ashlock didn't pick up his cell, she dialed his office number. Patsy answered.

Elsie kept her voice casual. "Where is he, Patsy?"

"Elsie? Detective Ashlock is on the run today. He told me not to expect him back before five."

"Where's he headed?"

"Out of town. Got a meeting with the highway patrol. Maybe someone from the FBI will be there, too." Her voice rang with excitement. "Can you imagine?"

"When did he leave?"

"Not long ago. He said he was stopping by the sheriff's office. See whether Sheriff Earl wanted to join him."

Elsie heard the ancient ding of the elevator bell. As the door opened, a familiar figure in uniform walked out: Sheriff Earl in the flesh, with a brass star pinned to his tan shirt.

"Thanks, Patsy," Elsie said, ending the call. "Sheriff!"

He was walking away from her; she hurried after him, calling out. "Sheriff Earl! Hold up."

He turned with a swagger, regarding her with a curious look. "Miss Elsie?"

She hated that title. It always rubbed her the wrong way when the sheriff played the part of Matt Dillon on *Gunsmoke*. Elsie had seen enough of Sheriff Earl's case work to hold a low opinion of his investigative skills. He embodied the old expression: all hat, no cattle.

"Where's Ashlock?" she asked him, still clutching her phone in her left hand.

"Ma'am?" he said, his eyes shuttering.

"Patsy told me he was going by the sheriff's office to pick you up; that you're going to accompany him to an out-of-town meeting with the highway patrol."

He sucked his teeth before he answered. "I'd best have a word with Ashlock about old Patsy. I don't believe she's supposed to share confidential information with a civilian."

Elsie's eyes snapped. "Civilian? What is this, the military?"

He studied her for a moment before saying, "If I see him, I'll tell him you were asking after him."

"Damn it, Earl; I want to know what's happening with the Desiree Wickham investigation."

"Lower your voice." He bent his head close to her ear. "This is a delicate law enforcement matter. You need to keep your nose out of police business and do your own job."

"It is my job," Elsie hissed.

The sheriff laughed.

"That's what I heard, this very morning. It's all the talk. You think you're a dad-blame Nancy Drew."

She gasped. That was the term Ashlock had used to describe her only the night before. Would Ashlock mock her to the sheriff? Was it even possible?

Eldon, Judge Calvin's bailiff, opened the courtroom door and bellowed down the hallway.

"Elsie! Elsie Arnold!"

The sheriff nodded in the direction of the courtroom. "You'd best run on down there. Do your prosecutor tricks. Let the lawmen take care of the police work." He reached out and squeezed her arm, just a little too hard.

"We'll find her," he whispered.

Elsie jerked her arm from his grasp. "You couldn't find your ass with both hands," she said, not bothering to lower her voice.

Then she turned on her heel and marched back to the court, ignoring the shocked expressions on the faces of people within earshot.

Chapter 37

ON TUESDAY AFTERNOON, Taylor sat cross-legged on her twin bed, poring over a worn paperback copy of *Lord of the Flies*.

A spiral notebook rested at her right hand, atop the kelly green comforter her mom bought after she won MVP in basketball in seventh grade, when they redecorated her bedroom in school colors. She set the book down, holding her place with an index finger while she jotted notes in the spiral notebook.

A burst of music sounded. Taylor looked up, startled. Her cell phone's ring played on the desktop, from its spot inside her green backpack. She dropped her pen and eased off the bed as the phone continued to play. She pulled it out of her backpack and read "Unknown caller." Pinching her lips together over her teeth, a sick look of dread settled on her face.

She didn't answer the call. Taylor tossed the phone onto the desk as if it burned her fingers, where it landed with sufficient force to knock over a cardboard-framed photo labeled: BARTON MIDDLE SCHOOL TRACK & FIELD, 8TH GRADE.

After another moment, the phone fell silent. Taylor opened her mouth and expelled the breath she'd been holding as she backed away from the desk.

Then the phone started up again. She lifted the gray cardboard frame that had fallen over it, and stared at the screen again: "Unknown caller." After the ring continued five times, she reached out and snatched the phone off her desk.

She pushed Answer but didn't wait for a greeting from the other end. She whispered into the phone.

"What?" she said.

Tony's voice crooned into her ear. "You alone, Coco?"

She glanced around the room fearfully, though she was the only person in the house. "My name's not Coco."

Abandoning the friendly tone, he said, "Answer me. Are you alone?"

Taylor's eyes closed, her chin dropped. "Yeah. Mom's at work."

With a note of warning, he said, "Baby, have you been behaving yourself? Like we talked about?"

Taylor paused before replying. "Yes," she said, then added in a rush: "What about Desiree? Where is she? Her mom is going crazy. The policeman came to my school."

He laughed. "Lola? Little Lola is just fine. She said to tell you you're a total loser for missing out. Lola's doing photo shoots every day, all day. We've got her lined up for a spread in a magazine."

Taylor breathed into the phone, clutching it to her ear with fingers that had grown damp. She didn't dispute him; but disbelief made her narrow her eyes to a squint

After a pause, Tony spoke in a voice that was deliberately casual. "Speaking of pictures. What did you do with those pictures of you? The ones I sent to you, the last time we talked?"

Taylor gasped at the mention of the pictures, and her mouth twisted. She said, "I deleted them."

"All of them?" His tone was incredulous. "Didn't even keep one, for a souvenir? They sure are pretty."

Taylor's hand on the phone shook. She placed her other hand on her stomach, to still the queasiness.

"I don't feel good."

"Just chill, baby. As long as you keep your part of the deal, do what I say, I'll sit on those pictures. They'll be our little secret."

She was silent. Her eyes squeezed shut, as if trying to block out an image she didn't want to recall.

Tony's tone on the other end of the line grew sharp.

"Coco? You hearing me, baby?"

When there was still no answer from Taylor, his voice dropped to a growl. "Coco. Did you hear me?"

Taylor drew a shaky breath. "Yes."

"Good." He chuckled, then said, "Sweet. Because hot pictures like those? If I let them slip, they gonna flat explode. Go fucking viral. You know how fast something like that can spread?"

Taylor's shoulders shook; she sat on the side of her bed, so she wouldn't fall down.

"Coco? Don't you know?"

"Yes."

A sound of rattling paper came through the phone. "I copied something off here. Cause I was looking over your application for Marvel Modeling, that you filled out when you said you wanted to work for me. You filled it out, put down all that contact information. I've got your daddy's cell phone number right here. 314-723-8961. That a St. Louis area code?"

When Tony recited the phone number, Taylor's vision tunneled.

All she could see was a green circle of her bedspread, surrounded by a cloud of gray.

"Stop it," she whispered, almost inaudible.

"You know how easy it would be for me to send those sexy pics to your daddy?"

"Please. No! Please don't do that."

He sighed into the phone. She could almost feel the hot breath in her ear.

"It's up to you, Coco. Totally up to you. You behave yourself, do what I tell you, and these pictures will be just between us."

Taylor registered a guilty sense of relief at the promise; but she tried one last time to make a stand. "But what about Desiree? When will she come back?"

"Don't you worry about Desiree."

"She's not eighteen. I told you already. She's in middle school. She's not supposed to be on her own."

"Girl, don't you watch TV? Lots of young girls work as models and actresses. They got a manager to take care of them; Lola's got me. Baby, my little Lola is happy as can be. She's partying, having fun, getting her shot at being famous. She feels real sorry for you, stuck in the Podunk town. Lola told me that last night. I'd put her on to tell you herself, but she's getting ready for a meeting with a director. If you want to tell her hi or anything, just give me the message. I'll pass it along."

Taylor opened her mouth to say more, but her throat closed and she couldn't speak.

"Okay then. Remember, Coco: if you talk about me, say a single word to your mama or some teacher or a cop or whatever—I'll know it. And everybody will be feeling real sorry for you, if it happens. You won't like the consequences. Am I making myself clear?"

Taylor dropped the phone onto the floor without ending the call. She leaped off her bed and ran out of the room, barely making it to the bathroom on time. As she retched into the toilet, tears rained into the porcelain bowl.

Chapter 38

By Wednesday, Elsie was still getting nowhere in her online hunt for Marvel Modeling. She was determined to speak to Desiree Wickham's mother, Kim. It would be nice if she could give Kim a ring on her cell phone; but Elsie didn't have the contact information. Ordinarily, Elsie would have asked Ashlock to give her the phone number. But she hadn't talked to him in nearly forty-eight hours, since they'd exchanged tense words at his house on Monday night.

So, after work on Wednesday, she pushed open the door of Tyler's Family Market and walked inside the grocery store.

Though the market had three checkout lanes, only one of them was occupied. Tyler's, a small family-owned store, had lost a lot of business when they built a Walmart Supercenter on the highway. Glancing around the deserted aisles, Elsie felt a twinge of guilt. As a Barton native, she should be supporting local business, shopping at Tyler's. But she had been lured away by the low prices and the one-stop shopping convenience that Walmart provided.

A harried-looking man was checking groceries for a customer;

and after ringing them up, he bagged them with angry thrusts, as if he hoped the canned goods would crush the egg carton and the bag of Doritos. Elsie stood to the side, waiting for the customer to push her cart away before she spoke.

"Hi there. I'm Elsie Arnold, with the county Prosecutor's Office. I'm looking for Kim Wickham."

A flash of irritation passed over his face. "Well, she's not here."

"Okay. When's her next shift?"

He barked a humorless laugh. "We haven't seen her nor heard of her since Monday."

With a sympathetic face, Elsie nodded to show she understood.

He went on. "I totally get it; her daughter is missing. But she doesn't call in or nothing. She's a no-show. It's making it tough on me."

The nametag on his chest read MIKE JONES, MANAGER.

Elsie clutched her car keys. "Thanks, Mike."

"Checking groceries isn't part of my job," he said.

Mike had more to say on the subject, but Elsie didn't stay around to hear it. She hurried to her car in the parking lot.

It was already growing dark. She flipped the headlights on as she drove away from the neighborhood grocery store and headed for the stretch of highway.

When she came to the four-way stoplight, she glanced over as a vehicle pulled up beside her: a shiny black GMC truck, with a luxury cab.

Elsie recognized the driver: it was Madeleine's husband, Dennis Thompson, who occupied the left turn lane.

When his head angled her way, she smiled, lifting her hand in a friendly wave. He didn't acknowledge it.

The snub irritated her. Who did he think he was? In a snit, she tapped her horn, waving again. Thompson turned his face away from her, angling his head in the opposite direction.

A flush crept up her neck. Fuming, she rolled down her window, determined to make him recognize her. "Hey! Mr. Thompson! It's me, Elsie Arnold."

The left turn arrow lit in the traffic light that hung overhead, and Dennis Thompson gunned his engine. Elsie's eyes narrowed as his taillights disappeared down the highway, moving toward the outskirts of town.

"Snob," she said, as she turned in the opposite direction, toward the old section of Barton.

When she arrived at the rock house on Cherry Street, there was no mistaking it. The windows of the house glowed in the November gloom. Every light in the house was on. A lit bulb even shone in the window of the attic.

When Elsie rapped on the front door, the hinges creaked and it inched open. She stared at the open doorway in surprise; and when no one answered her knock, she nudged it further ajar.

"Ms. Wickham? Kim? It's Elsie Arnold."

After a moment, a voice called out. "Come on in."

Elsie walked inside, taking care to push the door securely shut behind her. She saw Kim Wickham lying on the couch in front of the TV, covered in an afghan crocheted in a faded rainbow of colors.

Kim was staring at the television screen. When the woman failed to glance in Elsie's direction, Elsie ventured over to the couch and spoke softly.

"Kim? How are you?"

Turning her head from the TV, Kim blinked her bloodshot eyes and gave a blank stare. Elsie kicked herself for asking such an asinine question. Kim's child was missing; how would anyone be getting along, under those circumstances?

A coffee table sat beside the sofa. A box of Franzia wine sat on the tabletop beside a jelly jar that served as a wineglass. Kim picked up the jar and took a swallow.

"You want some wine?"

Elsie regarded Kim with a worried look. "No, thanks. I wanted to check in with you. Make sure you're okay." She paused, then added, "I know you're not okay. I just wanted to let you know I've been thinking about you. And Desiree."

Kim's eyes wandered back to the television screen. She pointed at the TV set with the jar she held, half-full of pink liquid. "There she is. The time she won the Grand Supreme."

Elsie studied the image. The volume on the set was muted; but a DVD had captured Desiree as a preschooler, strutting across the stage in a pink dress made of such shiny fabric it reflected the footlights.

"I made that dress," Kim said, as if she'd read Elsie's thoughts. "I sewed it on my mother's old Singer. Stitched the lace petticoats by hand underneath the skirt."

Elsie reached out and pressed the woman's limp fingers where they rested on the top of the sofa. Her hand felt icy. "That's incredible. I never learned how to sew."

Kim's eyes remained glued to the screen. "Desiree, she just had it. She had that stage presence. She was a winner."

A chill ran down Elsie's spine. Desiree's own mother was speaking about her in the past tense. She gave Kim's fingers a gentle squeeze, to get her attention.

"Did the FBI get in touch with you?"

Kim looked up with vacant eyes. “Somebody called yesterday. I was asleep.”

“Did you call back?”

“I tried to. I got that recording.” Her gaze drifted back to the TV screen again.

Elsie dropped Kim’s hand and looked around, trying to see a way to help Kim snap out of her inertia. “Kim, how about if I get you something to eat? I could make you a sandwich, or a soda pop. Or I can run and get you something. Anything you’d like.”

Kim shook her head. “I’m not hungry. People from work brought food yesterday.” She took another swig of wine. “You can have it, if you want.”

Desperate to pull Kim from her comatose state, Elsie dodged into the kitchen, hoping to locate a coffeepot. As Kim had indicated, there was plenty of food to be found. CorningWare, Pyrex, and foil casserole dishes covered the kitchen counter and the stovetop. Apparently, she had deserted them in a frozen state; and now moisture pooled around the containers.

She left the perspiring casseroles where they sat, though she could hear her mother’s disapproval in the back of her head. Beside the sink, she found the coffeepot; but the Maxwell House can was empty.

With a muttered curse, Elsie found another jelly jar in the cabinet, still bearing the remains of an orange marmalade label. She filled it partway with water and added a couple of ice cubes encrusted in the bottom of an ancient ice-maker.

“Here you go,” she said, as she returned to the sofa. Kim accepted the glass and took a swallow without looking at the contents. Elsie walked around the couch, knelt beside the coffee table, and spoke to Kim in an urgent voice.

"I have an idea. I think I should track down the modeling agency."

Kim raised to a sitting position and pointed at the TV. Glancing over, Elsie saw that the screen was dark.

"You want to see another one? I've got the last pageant she ever was at. Where she won the talent competition for her Houdini Act."

Kim reached for the nozzle of the wine box, but Elsie pushed it away. "Kim, I tried to find the agency online, but I didn't have any luck. How did Desiree find them? Do you have that information? Or did they find her?"

Kim gave her head a sodden shake, as if she was attempting to get her brain to work.

"Des had found it. She followed modeling stuff from things she read on the internet."

"But where on the internet?"

"Oh Lord. I'm trying to remember. Was it Backlist?"

Elsie pulled out her phone and typed in a note. "Backlist."

"Yeah. Backlist.com. Or one of those type pages, anyway. They post a lot of ads for models. You don't even need experience. She responded to one of them, and they got back with her. Said they were Marvel Modeling. They sent her an application, with information about the agency. It looked like this. She sent me a screenshot." With a fumbling hand, Kim dug her cell phone out of the sofa cushions and checked her photos. Elsie held her breath, waiting.

Finally, Kim handed it over. "That's it. Marvel Modeling."

It was on that trashy Backlist, Elsie thought, as a flush of triumph washed over her in a wave. "I'm going to send this to myself. Okay?"

"Okay." Kim's voice was flat. She lay back down.

Elsie punched in the text and placed the phone onto the coffee table. "Does Ashlock have that, Kim? Did you show it to him?"

She shook her head, listless. "I was too upset. Wasn't thinking straight."

"Don't worry. I'll send it on to him," Elsie said. She texted the image to Ashlock, without a comment. Rising, Elsie stared at the woman, trying to form words that would be a source of comfort.

"I'm going to try to find her, Kim. I'm going to do my best."

The tears welled in Kim Wickham's eyes. "I did my best. And look what happened."

Chapter 39

DEDE SAT BY the computer studying the screen. Behind her, Tony dozed in bed, his bare feet resting on a jumble of soiled bedding.

She bent toward the screen and squinted, rereading a recent message. Reaching around, she stroked Tony's bare foot.

He jerked awake, kicking her hand away. "Stop that."

"You've got a new applicant, Tony. From the Backlist ad. You want to check her out?"

He stretched his arms overhead with a weary moan as he shifted to a sitting position on the mattress. "How does she look?"

Dede shrugged, noncommittal. "Not bad. She's blond."

"How young?"

She barked a harsh laugh in response, scooting away from the screen. "Take a look. Here's the selfie she sent. This girl ain't no kid."

Tony crawled on all fours to the edge of the bed. He looked at the screen with an ambivalent expression.

"Tessie from Miami, Oklahoma," he said. "That could work. She's not that far away from here."

Dede scooted her chair back, to enable Tony an unrestricted view. "Her application says she's twenty-five. Lying whore. That girl ain't a day younger than me."

Tony held up a finger to silence her as he scanned the information on the computer screen. When he was done, he crawled back to the headboard and rolled onto his back.

Then he smiled, baring his teeth. "She can't hook the Daddy clientele, it's true. And that's the major score."

Dede nodded, triumphant. "That's just exactly what I was thinking."

"But that old Okie gal don't need to go out to pasture, not yet. She can hook some hillbilly Bills to get a nut off with her. We'll go for high volume with Tessie, since we can't go with high dollar."

Dede pulled the chair up to the computer and poised her hands over the keyboard. "You want to meet her on Skype first?"

"Yeah. Probably should. Make sure she don't have three eyes or three tits or something."

As Dede pounded on the keyboard a tentative knock sounded. It came from the interior door, connecting Room 217 to the adjoining room next door.

Dede rose from the desk and stalked over to the connecting door, unlocking it and pulling it open. In the doorway stood Mandy, her bruises hidden by a thick coating of makeup.

"Am I going out tonight?" she asked.

Dede looked to Tony for direction, but he didn't answer immediately. Instead, he rolled out of the bed and approached the open doorway where Mandy stood.

"Why are you asking? You got some big old plans?"

Mandy wrinkled her nose at him with an impish face, put a

hand on her hip and popped her knee forward. The hand resting on her right hip betrayed a tremor.

She said, "Even if I had a key to this room, I can't bring anybody back here tonight." With a voice that betrayed resentment, she added, "Can't do business in here next to the little blond princess."

Tony stood within inches of her, but his eyes strayed to the figure in the next room.

Desiree's blue eyes were wide open, staring at Tony. Through the duct tape covering her mouth, she was trying to speak. Tony bypassed Mandy and walked to the bed. He sat beside the girl, rubbing a hand down her bare leg.

"Hey, Lola. How you feeling, baby?"

The eyes grew wide as blue saucers, and she made muffled noises behind the duct tape. Tony continued to stroke her leg, talking in a soothing voice.

"Those pictures I took of you are selling like hot cakes. As soon as you're feeling up to it, we'll do another shoot. You gonna be famous, Lola."

Her eyes grew wild, and she shook her head back and forth until Tony stopped the movement by grasping a handful of her frizzy hair.

His voice lost its crooning quality as he said, "This is what you wanted, baby. You signed on for this."

Her legs, bound together at the ankle with yellow nylon rope, began to flail on the bed. Tony raised a hand and gave her a smart slap across the cheek. "Settle your ass down."

Dede appeared at Tony's elbow. "Tony, honey. She's got a big date coming up, don't forget. You want her to be pretty, don't you?"

Mandy walked up behind Dede and shoved her shoulder. "That's real funny, coming from you. You never worried about me."

The tattooed hand buried in Desiree's curly hair gave it a vicious twist. The girl responded with an involuntary groan behind the tape, squeezing her eyes shut.

Turning his face to Dede, Tony spoke in an angry undertone. "I am sick and tired of women back-sassing me every step of the way."

Dede nodded, her chin working like a marionette. "Oh you're right, Tony. Nobody best forget that you're the boss here."

Tony released the fistful of hair he'd been holding. The girl fell back on the bed, breathing heavily through her nostrils. Standing over her, Tony smiled.

"You've got a cute way about you. And men gonna think your country accent is sexy when we head up north. You'll be my little hillbilly Lolita. But we'll sell that cherry first, for high dollar. After that, we'll move on down the road."

Tears seeped down the side of the girl's face, wetting her hair before they fell on the pillow.

Chapter 40

Elsie checked her appearance in the bathroom mirror. She'd gone back and forth on the makeup question: at the age of thirty-two, did makeup make a woman look younger? Or older?

She lifted her chin, checking for foundation lines, but her makeup inspection looked satisfactory. She'd purposely purchased grocery store cosmetics: CoverGirl products in pink and brown, the shades that younger women purchased. She even used a pink lipstick. When she smiled, it made her teeth look yellow.

Elsie started to frown at her reflection before she stopped herself: she didn't want frown creases to appear in the makeup. Not today, of all days.

She sat down in the kitchen chair in her breakfast nook: the padded red chairs and gray-topped table that had once occupied her grandmother's kitchen.

She adjusted the angle of her computer screen. Behind her, only a blank wall was visible. Elsie checked the clock: it was showtime.

Now that she was so close to meeting the villain, her armpits grew damp. She jumped from the chair, wiping them with the dishtowel that hung on the oven door handle.

Back in the kitchen chair, she adjusted the spaghetti straps of the aqua nightie she'd purchased at Walmart for the occasion. Her breasts, freed from the confines of her bra, were clearly on display.

She sat straight up in the chair, thinking *they are falling out of this flimsy scrap of nylon*. She worried that they looked too big. Were they starting to sag? One thing she'd always been confident about was her rack.

Her inner debate was silenced: a ding on the computer informed her that Marvel Modeling wanted to chat.

She accepted, her hand a shade shaky. When the screen on the other end appeared, Elsie adopted an ear-wide grimace of delight.

"Hey, there," she said, with a twang that was pure Ozarks. "I'm Tessie!"

A sour-faced woman with auburn hair faced her on the screen. "Well, hey, Tessie. I'm Dede, with Marvel Modeling Agency."

Elsie pursed her pink-tinted lips into a pout. "Mighty pleased to meet you, Miss Dede. But where's Mr. Tony? Ain't he in charge?"

Dede's eyes darted to the right. "Tony's here. I'm his assistant. I'll do your preliminary interview."

"Well, okay then. I'm happy to talk with you. But you know—" and she heaved a dramatic sigh "—I was real excited about meeting Tony today."

At that juncture, a dark-headed man popped onscreen, over Dede's shoulder. He studied Elsie through slitted eyes before he spoke.

"Hi, baby. It's Tessie? That right?"

"Right as rain! And you're Tony, ain't you? I can just tell."

Tony's smile thinned. "Say, honey, how old are you?"

Elsie could feel blood rush to her face. She hoped it might give her a youthful, rosy glow.

"Tony, I'm twenty-five. And I read your ad on Backlist. You are looking for models between twelve and twenty-five. When I saw that, I went: Phew!" Elsie pretended to wipe sweat from her forehead. "Just barely made it!"

Dede glanced up at Tony. Elsie could see the skeptical look she gave him. Tony glanced down at Dede, then resumed talking to Elsie.

"Tessie, baby, how big a girl are you?"

"I'm five-eight, I hope that's tall enough. I know you'uns all like models to be real tall."

His mouth twitched. He said, "What do you weigh?"

Elsie sat back in the chair, slumping against it before she remembered to sit up straight. Good posture put her at her best advantage.

When he raised his chin, the tattoo inked across his neck came into view: a snake. It danced when he took a swallow from a red plastic cup. The sight gave Elsie an involuntary shiver, recalling the fuzzy driver's license photo bearing a neck tattoo she'd seen when Mandy was hospitalized after the beating at the Rancho.

He set his cup down and said, "Don't be shy, honey. We're a modeling agency, it goes with the territory. Now come clean. How big a girl are you?"

Elsie gave the computer a *Mona Lisa* smile. She turned in her seat so he could see her in profile, and took a deep breath.

"I wanna be a plus-size model," Elsie said.

There was silence on Tony's end. She broke her profile pose, turning her head to peek at the screen. Tony was staring at her, nodding his head.

"Looks like you got great tits," he said.

Elsie flashed a triumphant smile and swiveled back around in her seat. "Oh my goodness gracious sakes. You sweet talker!"

"Let's see them."

Elsie's face went blank. She hadn't expected a test, a game of striptease, not at this juncture.

Her face must have amused Tony; he burst into laughter.

"Just look at you: like the Catholic schoolgirl being told to drop her drawers. Didn't you just say you were twenty-five? Twenty-five years old?"

Elsie nodded, with a little toss of her head.

"Then you've surely bared your tits before. This is business, baby. I'm a modeling agent. And you are not young, or tall, or thin, or beautiful. You do have nice hair."

Elsie's hand jumped to the high ponytail she'd pulled her blond hair into, and pulled it over her shoulder.

"Yeah, good hair. But mostly, what you've got is good tits. Now let me see them."

Elsie froze again. Then Tony lifted his brow and said, "Are we all done here? Is this it? Because it'll be the end of the road."

Desiree, she thought. *Mandy. Taylor.* She forced her hand up to the spaghetti strap on her right shoulder. She pushed it down.

Tony nodded with approval. "Okay. Keep going."

She pulled the other strap and shimmied the nightgown down to her waist. Her breasts were bared to his view on the screen. She had never felt so exposed.

"That's my girl. Pull your hair out of that band. Let it fall down."

She did, following his orders like an automaton.

"Now arch your back and make a pouty face."

She complied, her heart pounding.

He smiled. "Great. Just great, baby."

He leaned in and kissed the screen.

"You're a natural."

Elsie twisted her mouth into a smile, though it took tremendous effort.

Tony said, "I think we ought to meet in person. What you doing Friday afternoon? Got some free time in your calendar?"

Elsie was amazed at how natural her voice sounded as she said: "I got time for you, Tony."

Chapter 41

DESPITE THE CHILLY weather, Elsie's sweaty hands left damp prints on the steering wheel as she pulled into the motel parking lot on Friday.

She'd left McCown County behind forty minutes prior. She had dodged out of the office before the end of the workday, feigning illness. All day, she'd taken care to tell anyone who would listen that she felt sick, thought she might be coming down with something. Because it was not her habit to take unwarranted sick days, no one argued when she made a dash for the door in the early hours of a Friday afternoon.

She glanced around the area, getting her bearings. This city was a metropolis, by Ozarks' standards. It sat on a major highway. On the outskirts of town, motels and gas stations and fast food businesses dotted the landscape.

As she checked out the parking lot, she saw it: the sedan with Alabama plates she'd seen at the Rancho. Craning her neck, she could read the license plate. She grabbed a pen from the console, and found a Sonic Drive-in receipt on the floorboard. After looking to ensure that no one was watching, she scribbled the license plate number on the back of the receipt and tucked it into her cup holder.

This was really happening, she thought. She checked her face in the mirror, reapplying the pink CoverGirl lipstick with a hand that trembled.

The motel rooms loomed before her. Before she walked into the unknown, Elsie pulled out her phone. As she held it, she debated which number to push.

And decided on her mother. She sent Marge a quick text: *Doing some investigating on a case. Meeting at EconoMo Motel off I-44 in Bodine County. Room 217. If you don't hear from me by midnight, call Ashlock.*

After the message was sent, she approached the motel and climbed the stairs to the second floor on shaky knees. As she approached Room 217, her stomach clenched with a fierce spasm.

Maybe, she thought, she should call Ashlock. Give him a heads-up. Time to break the silence between them.

But the door cracked open, and an auburn-haired woman peeked through. "Are you Tessie?"

Elsie smiled, though she felt her mouth tremble. "That's me."

"I thought so. Come on in."

The woman opened the door wide, a silent invitation. As Elsie stepped inside, her eyes darted around the motel room, searching for evidence of Desiree or Mandy.

But the room was empty. The two beds were unoccupied, made up with shabby bedspreads. No one sat in the sole chair at the plywood desk. The bathroom door was open, but she couldn't detect activity inside. No running water, no voices.

When she met the woman's eyes, Elsie saw her penciled brows raise, wrinkling her forehead.

"You looking for something?" she said.

Elsie ducked her head, letting a bashful laugh escape.

"No, ma'am. I'm sorry. I just thought it would look like a studio or something, like you see on TV."

The answer appeared to appease Dede; she smiled and said, "Oh, that's not how it works. I'm Dede, by the way. I saw you on Skype, remember? I'll do your interview."

Elsie nodded, with a look of anticipation. "That's cool."

Dede stepped over to the dresser, where a bottle of vodka sat. "Let's have a cocktail."

The suggestion shouldn't have taken Elsie by surprise. She had tried numerous sex cases in her career. She knew that predators used alcohol and drugs to keep women compliant. But she needed to keep her wits about her.

Dede was pouring the vodka into a red plastic cup, topping it off with a measure of Diet Coke. Elsie watched her make the concoction. It looked deadly.

In a bright voice, Elsie said, "What you got there?"

Dede didn't look up. As she made a second drink, the woman said, "Where I come from, we call this a skinny black bitch."

Elsie's eyes narrowed with distaste at the name Dede gave to the beverage; but when Dede glanced into the mirror and checked Elsie's reflection, her face cleared.

"I'm partial to beer," Elsie said, grinning.

Dede snorted. "I can tell that. By looking at the size of your ass."

For fifty cents, I'd kick your ass across this room, Elsie thought; but she took care to act like she enjoyed eating humble pie.

Elsie kept her tone friendly as she said, "I'm thick, that's all. Some dudes like it. I hear being thick is coming back in style."

"Not fast enough for you."

Dede handed Elsie the cup, then sat in the desk chair. Elsie stood awkwardly, as if she didn't know what to do.

Dede nodded at the bed. "Sit down. Let's get started. How old are you, really?"

"Twenty-five."

Dede rolled her eyes and took a swallow from the red cup. "Okay. Where you from, Tessie?"

"Miami, Oklahoma."

"Born there?"

"Naw." Elsie crossed her legs, pulling her skirt up to reveal some thigh. "I'm from all over. But I landed in Oklahoma a while back."

Dede nodded, as if she approved of Elsie's answer. "Marital status?"

"Single." Elsie cleared her throat. "Is that something that's required? For modeling?"

Dede flashed a phony smile. "We need to know. For tax reasons."

"Oh."

"Do you live alone?"

Elsie's radar buzzed like a live wire. Tell her you're all alone in the world, she thought; just like a girl in a Grimms' fairy tale.

"Yeah. I don't know that many people in Miami. Just some folks from work."

Dede's eyes sharpened. "Employment?"

"I'm between jobs, kind of."

"What did you do? When you were working?"

"Hospitality industry."

Dede shook her head. "What's that mean?"

"I was a cocktail waitress. At one of the Indian casinos in Miami, Oklahoma."

"Which one?"

"Do I have to say? Because I don't think the manager will give me a very good reference." Elsie twisted her face in a pout.

"Why's that?"

Elsie hung her head, sighing. She had thought out this part of her fake background in advance. "I got in a little trouble. They said I was flirting with the customers at the casino."

She peeked up at Dede to evaluate her response. The woman was smiling. *Good,* she thought.

"And they said they thought I was drinking on the job."

After that, Elsie lifted her own cup and took a gulp. She nearly choked, but swallowed it down with a valiant effort. Dede had poured a Coke-flavored martini.

Dede rose from the chair, and tipped Elsie's plastic cup with her own.

"You sound like you'll fit right in, honey. Here's to your career at Marvel Modeling."

When Dede drank, Elsie followed suit. This time, she was ready. She managed not to gag.

Chapter 42

"ARE YOU READY?"

Dede watched Elsie with a bright-eyed look that bordered on flirtation.

Elsie hid her trepidation. "Ready for what?"

Dede winkled her nose and laughed out loud. "To meet the boss man in person. Tony."

"Sure." Elsie took another swallow of the Diet Coke–laced vodka, to fortify herself. Then it occurred to her: if she got too lit, she might be ill-equipped to pull off her charade.

She reached in her purse and pulled out the pink CoverGirl lipstick, but when she opened the tube, Dede shook her head.

"Don't worry about that. I'll make you up. I'm an expert."

When Dede rose from the chair and approached an interior door beside the dresser that connected to the adjoining room, Elsie's heart began to race. She jumped off the bed and joined Dede as the woman rapped on the closed door.

Dede looked over her shoulder at Elsie, irate. "Don't dog my heels, Tessie."

Elsie took a half step back, baring her teeth with a big smile. "I want to make a good impression. On Tony."

"Then get your ass back over to the bed. He don't like a snoop."

Elsie poised on the bed nearest the door, hoping for a peek into the adjoining room; but she was disappointed. Tony slithered through the door, pausing only to whisper a harsh order to someone in the other room.

She thought she heard him say, "Keep her quiet."

He closed the door with a firm click of hardware and fixed his eyes on Elsie.

She sat up straight on the bed, meeting his gaze. The snake tattoo she'd seen on Skype was covered by his shirt collar; but even without the tats, he gave off a dangerous vibe. He eyed Elsie like she was a lamb ripe for slaughter.

Her knee-jerk reaction was to rise to the challenge; but when his eyes narrowed, she remembered to assume her role. Tessie from Miami, Oklahoma, wouldn't try to win a staring contest with a wolf. Her eyes shifted, and she toyed with the hem of her skirt.

"What do we have here?" he said.

Dede spoke up. "This is Tessie. Y'all are really going to hit it off."

"You think?" Tony walked to the foot of the bed where Elsie sat and stared down at her, appraisal in his eyes. Elsie peeked up and gave a nervous giggle.

"Hope so," she said.

Dede picked up the cup Elsie left on the plywood desk, and stepped up, handing it to her. "You want me to make you a drink, Tony?"

"Sure, baby. Let's all chill."

He reached into the pocket of his jeans and pulled out a pill bottle. "You want some candy, Tessie?"

Elsie pulled a face. "What kind?"

"Whatever makes you feel good."

She cocked her head, checking out the bottle. "That looks like medicine."

"It is, honey. It sure is."

Elsie lifted her shoulders in a friendly shrug. "I ain't sick."

Dede and Tony laughed, exchanging a look. Dede disappeared into the bathroom and returned a moment later holding a bag of makeup in one hand and wad of underwear in the other.

Elsie began to sweat again. Because the stakes were getting high, and she didn't know if she could pull it off.

When Dede dropped a multicolored jumble of bras and thong underwear on the bedspread, Elsie spoke up.

"I don't think we'll need that. I'm wearing my best lingerie. Real sexy stuff."

Dede turned to Tony; he made a noncommittal face at her. She settled onto the bed beside Elsie and closely examined her face.

"You got good skin. Let's just glam you up a little, hon."

Elsie sat still as a statue, submitting to the application of Dede's cosmetics. As Dede rubbed foundation onto Elsie's face and brushed blush onto her cheekbones, Elsie suppressed a shudder, wondering what germs the cosmetic brush harbored.

Don't be a germophobe, she thought, keeping her face still. *This is the least of your problems.*

When Dede pronounced that the makeover was complete, Tony came over to inspect her. He nodded with approval.

"Looks better. Okay, Tess, I've got the computer all set up for you. You're going to scoot on over to that other bed."

He paused; when Elsie didn't move, he snapped his fingers at her. She jumped up and crossed over to the other bed.

He laid a hand on her shoulder. "Now we're going to get started. I want you relaxed, chill, sexy. So, you're going to take a magic pill." He winked. "Doctor's orders."

Elsie held out her hand. He placed a tablet in it; she was pretty sure it was Vicodin. She'd prosecuted an armed robbery case where opioids were taken from a pharmacy. But she didn't want to examine the pill too closely.

She placed it on her tongue. "I'm going to swallow it with some water," she said, and started to rise; but he pushed her back onto the bed.

"Dede, hand Miss Tessie her drink."

Dede obeyed.

Elsie lodged the pill between her cheek and her jaw. She took a swallow from the cup, and coughed into her fist, spitting the pill into her closed hand.

When she looked up at Tony, she pulled a face. "Sorry. I choked."

He gazed down, his jaw twitching. He then grabbed her fist and forced her fingers open, revealing the wet tablet in Elsie's hand.

He plucked it from her fingers and grasped her by the neck. Bringing his face close to hers, he spoke in a gravelly growl.

"Some girls have to learn the hard way."

With his free hand, he pried Elsie's jaw open and placed the pill on her tongue. As his fingers gripped her chin, he covered her open mouth with his, using his tongue to force the pill down her throat. She tried to twist her head away, but his hand held her neck like a vise.

The pill went down; she tried to cough it up, without any success. Tony backed away and watched, wiping his mouth with the back of his hand. Dede stood at his shoulder, her face grim.

Elsie stopped coughing and gasped to catch her breath. She looked at Tony with trepidation.

He said, "Are you going to follow orders now? Or am I going to have to teach you a lesson?"

Elsie just breathed, trying to pull together shreds of composure.

He said, "Who's in charge here, Tessie?"

Elsie whispered, "You are."

He relaxed. "Okay, then."

Dede spoke in a small voice: "Her lipstick got smeared onto her face."

He nodded. "Fix it. Then we'll get to work."

Chapter 43

THESE DAYS, BY the time Friday afternoon rolled around, Marge Arnold wondered whether it was time to retire.

She walked the aisles of her empty classroom with a metal wastebasket in hand, clearing stray papers from desks and trash from the floor. Each time she stooped to pick up an item from the scuffed tiles, her lower back clenched with pain.

Marge carried on until the job was done; and dropping the basket by the desk, she lifted a nylon bag and draped the strap over her shoulder. Today, the bag was stuffed with assignment papers on *Lord of the Flies*. She would spend Sunday afternoon grading them.

Pulling her purse from the bottom drawer of her desk, she spent a moment hunting for her phone, before she remembered that she had left it hooked up to the charger in the living room of her house that morning. It had been dead as a dog by the end of school on Thursday; and she hadn't remembered to plug it into the charger until bedtime.

I'm getting more forgetful every blessed day, she thought, giving her head a rueful shake.

Before she left her classroom, Marge checked the doorknob to be sure she'd locked the door behind her, and then limped down the empty hallway. She had to maneuver a steep stairway to access the parking lot; and her hip joined the ache in her back as she carefully made her way step-by-step in her black Sketchers shoes.

She didn't feel up to cooking dinner tonight, she decided. She'd send George out for carryout at Little Hong Kong. They could eat cashew chicken and egg rolls while they sat in their recliners and watched the evening news.

Marge had a hand on the crash bar of the back exit when she heard voices. Kids' voices.

Her ears pricked up. The halls should be empty. The janitorial staff left early on Fridays. And no student activities were planned for the afternoon.

Forgetting the hitch in her hip, Marge turned from the doorway and retraced her steps. Her rubber-soled shoes made no sound on the poured concrete floor of the old school building.

The sound registered again: a girl's voice, pleading, followed by boys' laughter. It came from the direction of the locker room.

With a stern face, Marge marched toward the voices. Thirty-five years of middle school experience taught her the value of a surprise attack: she burst into the boys' locker room, swinging the door wide with a bang.

"What's going on in here?"

Four heads looked up, their faces regarding her with uniform expressions of horror. Marge advanced on them.

"What are you doing in here? School's shut down for the weekend."

She knew them, had all of them in class at one time or another. Burton Ashlock, Paul Wallace. A husky boy whose name she couldn't quite place.

And Taylor Johnson. What on earth, she wondered, was Taylor Johnson doing in the boys' locker room?

The husky boy held an iPad in his hand. It must be the source of the mischief, she surmised. There was no evidence of drugs or alcohol, not even a whiff of tobacco. And neither Taylor nor the Ashlock boy would be likely to be a party to that brand of shenanigans.

"'Fess up. What's all this about?"

While Marge frowned down at them, the boy holding the iPad dropped it onto the floor as if it had burned his fingers. The clatter of the iPad broke the spell. Paul Wallace snatched the device from the floor and tore through the door, with the husky kid at his heels. The big boy's shoulder caught Marge in the chest and nearly knocked her down. Her collection of *Lord of the Flies* papers spilled onto the locker-room floor.

She turned on her heel, shouting at the departing figures.

"I'm going to report you to Mr. Samson."

The threat had no effect. She heard a door slam. They were gone.

Marge swung around to face the remaining two teenagers. Taylor was shaking, her face tear-stained. Burton's eyes were trained on the floor.

In a gentler tone, she said, "Two of our very best students, hiding out in here after hours, breaking school rules. I'm surprised at you. Both of you should know better."

Taylor blinked rapidly, lifting a hand to wipe the tears from her face. "We weren't doing anything."

"Then why did those two take off running? Paul and—" Marge paused, trying to recall the other boy's name. She couldn't bring it to mind. More evidence that she was getting too old for this job.

In her younger days, no student would dare to storm away while she was talking to them. She rubbed the spot where the husky boy's shoulder had struck her chest.

Burton bent down and commenced to pick up the papers that were scattered across the locker-room floor.

"I'll get that," Marge said. But he continued, stacking them together in a pile.

"We were talking," Taylor said. "That's all."

Marge studied the girl. Taylor was a bad liar. And she was petrified.

"Did those boys tease you?" Marge cleared her throat, embarrassed to ask the follow-up question, but Missouri had a mandated reporter law, and the teachers were subject to it. "Did someone make an improper advance?"

Taylor shook her head, but Marge wasn't convinced.

"What were they showing you on that iPad? Were they showing you a dirty picture?"

At that, Burton's head jerked up, as if Marge had touched a nerve.

She said, "Burton, what were they up to? What was on that iPad?"

Burton looked up at Taylor, whose head was shaking with palsy.

"Nothing. No. Nothing," the girl said.

Marge knelt down to meet Burton's eyes as he squatted on the floor with her papers. Her lower back knifed with pain, but she ignored it.

"Were the boys showing images on the iPad that aren't permitted in school?"

Burton nodded. Taylor said, "Don't."

Marge ignored her. "If they do that, it's not just breaking a rule. It's a harassment issue. Teachers have to know about that. To protect the students from it. It's not right. You understand that, Burton. Don't you?"

Taylor's voice pleaded. "I have to go. My mom is expecting me. She'll be worried."

Marge held Burton's gaze. "Burton, you know your daddy would want you to tell the truth."

He nodded, his chin wobbling.

"Were there pictures on the iPad?"

"Yes," he said in a whisper.

"Stop it," Taylor said.

"Burton," Marge said, her voice low, "what were those pictures?"

He was breathing fast, almost hyperventilating. "Taylor."

Marge Arnold's head cocked. "What?"

"They were pictures of Taylor. He saw them on his dad's iPad."

Taylor wailed like an infant who'd been stuck with a pin. Startled, Marge glanced over at her. The girl looked like she was about to faint.

"Why would he have pictures of Taylor?"

Taylor swayed on her feet, but she didn't fall. She snatched up her backpack and ran through the door. Her footfalls echoed on the concrete floor of the hallway.

As the girl took flight, Marge rose from the floor, determined to follow; but her hip froze, and she rolled onto her side on the unforgiving surface of the locker-room floor.

"St. Mary's," she said though her teeth.

Marge had to report the situation. Struggling to sit upright, she grabbed her purse and dug inside, wasting precious minutes in a fruitless search for her phone.

She couldn't find it. Because she'd left the damned thing at home.

Chapter 44

MARGE BREATHED A grateful sigh when she saw an empty parking spot on the town square, directly in front of the Barton Police Department. She pulled in and cut the engine, then turned to inspect her companion in the passenger seat.

Burton Ashlock sat with his head bowed. He made no move to exit the car.

Marge kept her voice brisk. "Time to see your dad, Burton. He's waiting."

Burton lifted his head. Training his eyes on the windshield, he said, "You can tell him."

Marge's forehead wrinkled. "No sir. Come along." She pulled out the handle on her car door, but the boy didn't follow suit.

Instead, he fixed Marge with a look of entreaty. "You tell Dad. Please. I just can't."

A cold wind blew Marge's door open. With an effort, she pulled it shut. "Burton. You have to tell your father about it."

"Why? It wasn't my iPad." His face was pale, his eyes reddening.

She spoke in a tone that was not unkind. "Because you're the one that saw the pictures, Burton. I never did."

He turned away from her. "Mrs. Arnold, I swore. They said I could only look if I wouldn't tell my dad. I swore to God."

"Why on earth did you do such a thing?"

"I didn't believe it. I didn't think that Taylor would be in internet porn. I wanted to prove they were lying."

Marge reached over and took the boy's hand. His fingers were cold, even for a chilly day. Teachers were warned against touching students these days, even to comfort them. But sometimes the rule had to be disregarded.

"Burton, honey. That's a promise you can't keep. And shouldn't keep. The Lord wouldn't want you to stand by that bargain."

He dislodged his hand from hers, as if embarrassed by the contact. But he said, his voice cracking, "Are you sure?"

"I guarantee it." She opened her door and the wind took it again, as if the weather was urging her to hurry. "Now let's get moving."

Once inside, the boy moved fast, leaving Marge behind as she limped up the stairs on her trick hip. Ashlock awaited them at the top of the stairway. Taking Marge's elbow, he led them to the conference room. Marge sank into a chair, with Burton sitting beside her.

Ashlock stood, his face stormy.

"What the dickens is going on?"

Burton seemed to have been struck dumb again, so Marge spoke.

"I asked Burton to text you, Bob. A boy brought a device to school with pictures on it." She nudged Burton. "Tell him, Burton."

He spoke in a whisper. "He had an iPad."

"Who had an iPad?" Ashlock sounded like a cop, not a concerned father. Marge wished he would sit down. He was scaring the boy.

When Burton didn't answer immediately, Ashlock placed his hands flat upon the tabletop and asked again: "Who had an iPad?"

Marge raised a hand. "Bob, I believe that you should—"

He cut her off without an apology. "Marge, please."

Burton spoke. "It was Greg. Greg Branson."

That's the boy, Marge thought. *Now I remember. I'll be forgetting my own name before you know it.*

"What was on the iPad?"

Burton spoke with an effort; his voice cracked again with the vocal transition of puberty. "Pictures of Taylor. In a bed, wearing red underwear. And other pictures of her."

Ashlock's face betrayed his disbelief. "Taylor Johnson? Breeon's Taylor?"

Burton nodded.

"Are you certain, son?"

"I'm positive." He lowered his head. "I saw them with my own eyes. She asked him—Greg—not to tell anybody. Or show anybody."

Ashlock raised his chin, and focused his eyes on the side window, which framed the county courthouse across the street. "So when did the Branson boy tell Taylor he'd seen the pictures?"

"He showed them to her in the locker room, after school. That's why I went along. Because I was worried about what Taylor would do."

Ashlock's face softened. Marge rummaged through her purse again, just on the off chance that her errant phone might be lodged in a corner of the bag. "Bob, I need to use a phone—a landline in your office, if that's all right. I need to report this to Children's Services."

He rose, nodding toward the door. "Let's all head to the office. You can call while I fill out the paperwork."

"For a police report?" Burton asked, his voice fearful.

"For a search warrant. Burton, you'll have to swear out an affidavit. You too, Marge." He checked the time on his wrist-watch. "Breeon should still be at the Prosecutor's Office. I'll call her first."

He opened the door and waved them through.

Chapter 45

Taylor huddled in the corner of the sofa of her living room, hugging her legs. Her forehead rested on her knees. She'd been curled into a fetal position ever since she'd arrived, after running all the way home from Barton Middle School.

She needed to see her mom. But she waited in a state of panic and dread, wondering how she could possibly explain.

When she heard the garage door open, rattling in its tracks, Taylor braced herself. A moment later, her mother's footsteps clattered across the kitchen floor. She was wearing heels. It must have been a court day.

The moment she'd been shrinking away from, out of cowardice and fear, had arrived at last. Taylor lifted her head and met her mother's eyes as Breeon strode into the room.

Taylor was determined not to cry. When she'd broken her left arm on the basketball court in seventh grade, she hadn't shed a tear. But the sight of her mother's face broke her resolve.

A massive sob shook her chest, and her voice came out in a wail. "Mama."

Breeon launched across the rug, landing on the spot beside Taylor, and clutched her to her chest. Taylor could feel her mother's heart beating fast, and the sensation comforted her, like when she was a little girl in her mother's arms.

She tried to speak. "I did something bad," she said; but her throat swelled up, and she couldn't continue.

Breeon rocked her back and forth as they sat on the couch. After a moment, she pressed her cheek on the top of Taylor's head.

"Baby, we're going to get through this. But you have to tell me what happened."

Taylor squeezed her eyes shut, uncertain where to begin. Her misdeeds loomed like monsters overhead; how could she explain?

When she didn't speak, Breeon prompted her. "Detective Ashlock called. He said that his son saw pictures of you on an iPad."

Taylor's eyes burned. The thought of Ashlock seeing the pictures filled her with shame. "Oh God," she whispered.

"Tell me, honey. Who took the pictures?"

"I can't."

The arms that held Taylor tightened. Her mother's voice was close to her ear, and she spoke with unshakeable resolve.

"You have to, Taylor. It can't wait."

"I don't remember."

Breeon released Taylor from the tight embrace. With strong fingers, she lifted Taylor's chin, forcing the girl to meet her gaze.

"Baby, you've been hiding things from me. That stops now."

The tears flowed again, making Taylor's throat hurt. "But I don't remember any pictures. Not of me. He took pictures of Desiree, but I just sat on the other bed. I went to sleep, I think."

Taylor buried her face in Breeon's shoulder, wetting the fabric of her mother's jacket with tears and mucous from her running nose. When she felt Breeon's hand stroke her back, the sensation gave her the strength to speak again.

"Tony wanted me to wear red underwear and audition, but I didn't want to. It felt weird. And he gave me a cherry drink, and I told him I don't drink alcohol. Mom, you know I don't."

Breeon's voice was reassuring. "I know."

"And it made me sleepy. And then Dede drove us back to Denny's later. It was really late, and I didn't feel good. I told Desiree I didn't want to model for them anymore."

She peeked up at her mother's face. Breeon's expression scared her, it was so fierce. But when she spoke, her mother's voice was calm and low.

"Taylor, the police need to find Desiree. She's been missing for five days."

"It was a hotel. I don't know where; I wouldn't lie about that. If I knew where she was, I'd have told. Des is my friend."

"I know that. She is." Breeon settled back on the couch, circling Taylor with her left arm, stroking her hair.

Breeon said, "That's what I don't understand. You knew Des was missing, that she was in trouble with bad people. And you didn't tell everything you knew. Not to Detective Ashlock. Not even to me."

There it was, Taylor thought. The monster in the closet.

Taylor had wrestled with guilt and fear in the past week. At night, she would lie awake in bed, her eyes wide in the darkness, her chest tight with panic. During the day, she lived in dread of her cell phone's ring. And the worst part was keeping the secret. That, and telling the lies.

Taylor drew a shaky breath. She avoided her mother's eye.

"I wanted to tell you. But I couldn't."

Bree's voice grew sharp. "Don't play with me, Taylor."

"I couldn't," she insisted. "You don't understand."

Breeon shifted on the sofa, putting distance between them. "Then explain it to me. Tell me, so that I can understand."

It felt like a rock had lodged in Taylor's throat. She tried to swallow it down, but it remained.

"He wanted me to come back, but I said no. I told him my mom wouldn't let me."

A ghost of a smile crossed Breeon's face. She lifted her brow, a sign that Taylor should continue.

"And Des wanted me to go back, with her. On Sunday. But I said no way. That it creeped me out when we went the first time."

Breeon broke in. "Baby, that doesn't explain why you misled Ashlock. And me."

Frustration made Taylor cover her face, rubbing her eyes so hard it hurt. "He wouldn't give up."

"What?"

"Tony. He had my phone number. He kept bugging me."

"Taylor, what are you trying to say? What did he do?"

The dam burst. "He showed me the pictures. The ones of me. He texted them to me over the phone. He said if I didn't come back with Des, he'd do something I wouldn't like."

She saw awareness dawning in her mother's face. "I see."

Taylor's voice dropped to a whisper, even though she and her mom were alone at home, in their own living room.

"I still wouldn't go back. So, he told me that if I told anybody about him—my folks, or friends, or teachers, or cops—he'd send the pictures to everybody I knew. Post them on my Facebook page. Send them to you."

Her voice dropped so low, it was barely audible. "Send them to Dad."

A mighty sigh escaped Breeon's chest. "The man blackmailed you."

Taylor looked up at her mother, confused. "Isn't blackmail where somebody makes you give them money?"

"Sometimes. But there are things more valuable than money. A blackmailer can control people in other ways."

Taylor hung her head. "I didn't know what to do. I was scared. Ashamed. And I couldn't ask you about it. Because if I did, Tony would post the pictures."

Breeon seized her hand, and they sat quietly for a moment. A thought occurred to Taylor. She looked up.

"Mom, one thing I don't get. How did the pictures show up on Greg Branson's dad's iPad? Because I did what Tony told me to do. I kept quiet about him. He said if I kept my mouth shut, there wouldn't be any trouble."

"Some people can't be trusted, baby. The man is dangerous. A criminal. A predator. There are websites that buy and show bad pictures and videos; but they can't just be accessed by a simple internet search; that's why it can be hard for the police to find them. There are some dark webs on the internet that can only be accessed through peer-to-peer file sharing. Bad people set them up; and other sick people will pay to look. Your images ended up on one of those, and Greg ran across it on his dad's iPad."

"So Greg looked me up on a bad website?"

"Oh no, honey. Not Greg. His dad, most likely."

Breeon stood, extending her hand to Taylor. Taylor took it, and her mother pulled her to her feet.

"We need to get in the car, Tay-Tay. We have an appointment, and it's almost time."

Taylor tensed. She didn't recall anything about an appointment scheduled on their calendar.

"With who?"

Breeon stood erect, and braced Taylor with an arm around her shoulder.

"With Detective Ashlock. And an FBI agent."

Chapter 46

Marge Arnold limped up to the reception desk at the Prosecutor's Office. Waving at the receptionist, she said, "I'm heading on back to see Elsie, Stacie."

Stacie looked up from the computer screen. "She's not here."

Marge's eyes closed, and her hand grasped her hip. With a weary effort, she focused on Stacie with a smile.

"Which courtroom will I find her in? It's important. She's not left for the day, has she?"

Stacie gave Marge a look of surprise. "Nope. She's sick. I figured you'd know."

Marge's brow wrinkled. "Sick? Sick with what?"

"She didn't say. She ran out of here in the early afternoon, said she was coming down with something." Stacie peered at her reflection in the brass county seal that hung over her desk, taking a moment to toy with her bangs.

When she turned back to face Marge at the counter, Stacie blew out her breath with a huff. "She complained about it all morning long. All I know is, I'm glad she got out of here. Whatever she's got, I don't want to catch it. It's almost the weekend."

Marge leaned on the counter, frowning. "Elsie wouldn't go home sick unless she's in a bad way. We raised her better than that."

Stacie, who regarded sick days as an unofficial extension of paid vacation time, just shrugged.

Stacie returned her focus to the computer screen, effectively ending the conversation. But Marge lingered.

"Is there a bug going around the office?" she asked.

After a beat, Stacie looked up, her brow lifting in a clear show of annoyance.

"A bug? Don't think so. Not that I know of."

Stacie returned to the keyboard, hitting the keys with a vengeance. Marge watched her, while a finger of worry nagged at the back of her head.

"And she didn't say anything about what she was coming down with?"

Stacie's fingers froze, resting on the keyboard. Without glancing over, she said, "Why don't you call her and ask her?"

Marge nodded, slipping around the counter that separated the public from the receptionist's desk. "That's a good idea. May I use your office phone? I dial 9 to get out, right?"

Stacie stared with righteous indignation as Marge lifted the landline receiver from its cradle and dialed Elsie's number. Marge gave her a reassuring wink.

"This will just take a sec."

As the phone rang, she silently urged Elsie to pick up; but the call went to voice mail. Marge smiled into the receiver, taking care to speak in an upbeat tone as she left her message.

"Honey, it's Mom. I came over to your office to see you, and Stacie says you went home sick. I'm awful sorry to hear you're under the weather. I can bring some 7UP and soup over, if that would help—"

She would have said more, but the buzz sounded in her ear, an electronic hum that let her know she'd said her piece. Marge returned the receiver with a worried sigh.

"She's not picking up. I sure wish I knew what was wrong. You reckon she's sleeping?"

Stacie didn't answer immediately. She spun her chair to check the wall clock, which was about to hit 5:00 P.M. With a meaning look in Marge's direction, she lifted her purse from the spot beneath her desk and pulled out her keys.

"Mrs. Arnold, I'm gonna have to lock up."

Marge nodded absently. "You do that. Honey, is there any chance that Breeon is around? We need to visit."

The second hand was barely past the five o'clock mark as Stacie thrust her arms into the sleeves of her coat. "Well, she's not here either."

Marge regarded Stacie with a knowing look. "Bree's out, too?"

"Yeah. About thirty minutes ago. Went tearing out of here. Didn't say where she was going, or when she'd be back. In case you're wondering."

Marge was certain she knew the news that sent Breeon on a tear, but she kept the information to herself. Moving for the door with renewed energy, she shouldered through, letting it bang against the wall.

Something was the matter with her daughter. She could feel it, deep inside her gut, just like she sensed Elsie's needs and moods in infancy and childhood and adolescence.

Marge intended to get to the bottom of it. And not over the phone. She wanted to see Elsie in the flesh.

She would hunt her daughter down at her apartment.

The wind made her shudder as she limped out to her car, still parked on the street in front of the Barton Police Department. Maybe her preoccupation made her less careful than usual; or maybe it was the sore muscles that made it difficult to twist around and see over her shoulder. As she backed her sedan into the road, all she could think of was Elsie; and her daughter was the last thought on her mind when she heard brakes screech on the town square, the thump of a mighty crash and shattered glass, right before everything went black.

Chapter 47

A KNOCK AT the door of 217 went unanswered.

The sound roused Dede. She looked over at Tony, snoring on the opposite bed, his mouth agape.

Uncertainty marked Dede's face. "Tony?"

He didn't stir. The knock sounded again, louder this time. She fumbled for the phone, to check the time. Surely Tony wouldn't have slept through his client's business appointment. But no: a glance at the phone confirmed that they weren't due to appear for another couple of hours, after the bars closed. Stealing another glance at Tony's prone figure under the covers, Dede rose with a whispered curse and crept to the door.

She unlocked the dead bolt, but left the security chain attached in its metal track. The chain let the door open only a couple of inches. She peered through the crack.

"Damn, Dede. Let me in. It's cold out here."

Mandy stood on the other side of the door, shivering. She rubbed her hands up and down her bare arms.

Dede released the chain lock and let Mandy inside. "Keep your voice down. He's sleeping."

Mandy crossed to Tony's bed, teetering on ill-fitting stiletto shoes. Looking down, she snorted with a brief laugh.

"He's out. You could set off a bomb in here and it wouldn't bother him."

"Don't be so sure. He's not in a very good mood when he wakes up."

Mandy crossed over to the desk. She picked up a red plastic cup and looked inside.

"Is this clean?"

"I dunno. Maybe."

Mandy's face wore a skeptical expression, but she poured a measure of vodka into the cup and added fruit punch. After taking a long sip, she strutted to Dede's bed and extended her hand, palm up.

"Gimme."

Dede punched a pillow and propped it against the headboard. Leaning back, she gave Mandy a flat stare.

"It's mighty early. Not last call at the bar for a couple hours. I'm surprised to see you back here already. How'd you do tonight?"

"Seven dates. In six hours. I want my medicine. I earned it."

"Where's the money?"

"In my cooter."

Dede nodded with approval. "That's the safest place."

Mandy winked over the rim of the red cup. "Not like I can stuff it in my big old titties." She arched her back, displaying her flat chest.

Dede opened the drawer of the bedside table that separated the hotel beds. Fishing through a collection of pill bottles, she chose one and shook out two tablets.

"This'll relax you."

"Good." Mandy popped the pills and swallowed them with a gulp from the cup. "I'm going to hop in the shower. I can smell myself."

Mandy kicked off her shoes and picked up a damp towel from the floor. In a voice of warning, Dede said, "Not in here. You might wake him up. He's been kind of strung out, making important business connections, plus handling the new girls."

"Yeah, well. Too bad."

"I ain't kidding. He'll eat you alive."

Mandy paused, seeming to rethink the warning. She stepped away from Tony's bed and inclined her head at the door that connected to the next room.

"You want me to go in there? With the little pageant princess?"

"Yeah." Dede rolled off the bed; opening the connecting door, she took a look inside. "It's okay, just don't raise a ruckus. They're both out."

"Both? Who's in there with the new girl?"

Dede shook her head, with a look of misgiving. "Some old broad. I told him we shouldn't fool with her, but he's got a lot of trade coming in. And she was eager, at first anyway. But she got kind of feisty. Tony had to use the cuffs on her. She's so damn big, he just cuffed one of her wrists to the bed."

"I thought he still had the princess in cuffs."

Dede shook her head. "She's settled down. But he's got her tied up."

A crust of mucous circled one of Dede's eyelids, and she rubbed at it. "He sent me to Walmart for more rope. I got the yellow kind. Hope it doesn't mark her up too bad."

Mandy peered into the dark room. "Old Tony's got his hands full."

"And he's out of duct tape. I'm supposed to get some tomorrow."

Mandy glanced over her shoulder. "Why wait? The place by the gas station is open twenty-four hours."

"He thought it would be funny, buying duct tape in the dark of the night. Could draw some attention. Besides, the big old broad is out like a light. Shouldn't wake up for a long time. We can stuff a sock in her mouth if she makes any noise. That's what he said."

Mandy pushed the door open. "Where am I supposed to sleep?"

"On the floor."

Mandy turned, her voice indignant as she said, "I been working all night long. And I'm supposed to sleep on the fucking floor? Like a dog?"

Dede jumped off the bed. "You keep your voice down."

"What am I supposed to use as covers? It's cold."

Dede waved a hand in the direction of the bed near the bathroom. "Take her bedspread. Hell, take the blanket, too. She's not going to notice. And Tony will wake up here before long, for the late-night business. Then you can come back in here."

As Mandy walked into Room 218, Dede closed the door shut behind her, leaving Mandy in darkness. She felt her way across the room, dragging her fingers along the top of the dresser.

When she reached the bathroom, she groped for the light switch on the wall and flipped it on. A few bottles of hotel toiletries were scattered beside the sink. The shampoo bottle was empty.

"Shit," she said, not bothering to whisper. Even a cheap motel ought to hand out fresh shampoo every day. Tony probably wasn't giving the hotel maid access to the room. Pretty hard to explain the restraints on the new girls.

She jerked the plastic shower curtain aside and saw a small bar of soap resting on the drain of the tub. She picked it up and placed it in the soap dish, then turned on the shower full blast. Sticking her hand under the spray, she shivered.

"What kind of shithole doesn't have hot water at this time of night?" she groused. She adjusted the faucet; the water warmed up a shade. She would give it a couple of minutes.

As she waited, she leaned against the doorway of the bathroom, idly watching the occupants of the two beds. The handcuffed woman snored, her head turned away on the pillow.

Mandy intended to appropriate that pillow. And the bedding. Walking barefoot to the near side of the bed, she jerked the bedspread off the woman's prone body. As Dede had predicted, the woman didn't stir. And Dede was right; once her underwear-clad figure was revealed, Mandy could tell she wasn't the young brand of hooker that Tony preferred.

She walked to the head of the bed, grabbed the pillow, and pulled it away from the woman's head. The movement made the sleeping head rotate slightly, exposing the hooker's face in the light shining through the bathroom door.

Mandy suppressed a screech. It couldn't be.

Her hand trembled as she grasped the woman's chin in her fingers, turning her face to the light. No duct tape covered her mouth. Even with her eyes closed, Mandy knew that face.

She stepped away, bumping into the wall. As her heart began to race, Mandy's chest rose and fell. She shot a frightened glance at the closed door that separated her from Tony; then looked back at the unconscious woman.

Her wrist was cuffed to the bed. Mandy tiptoed up to the mattress and ran her finger along the chain, where it connected to the frame. Grasping the cuff that encircled the bed frame, she gave it a jerk. It was secure.

She backed away, chewing on her knuckle. The shower sent a cloud of steam into the room. Mandy walked back to the bathroom and faced the mirror. It had fogged. "Oh my God," she said. She turned around and looked again at the unconscious figure. She said, "What the fuck do you think you're up to, Elsie?"

There was, of course, no answer. In a whisper, Mandy added, "When he finds out you set him up, he'll kill us both."

She leaned into the tub, gave the faucet a twist, and the shower dripped to a halt. Standing with her hand on the knob, her mouth worked, as if Mandy was engaging in an internal debate. She gave her head a brisk shake. "Just a pack of Parliaments," she said. "That's all she ever done for me." Still, a look of regret etched across her face. She lifted her shoulders in a helpless gesture.

With a sigh, she checked the closet outside the bathroom. A woman's winter jacket hung inside, dangling over a pair of shoes. She slipped the jacket over her tank top. The sleeves hung past her fingertips; and when she donned the shoes, she looked like a kid trying on her mother's footwear.

She wobbled toward the door of Room 218, her feet slipping out of the high heels of the too-large shoes. She unlocked the door with care, making sure that the battered chain didn't make a sound. As she eased through the door, she glanced over her shoulder and gave the sleeping woman a final look.

Shaking her head, Mandy disappeared into the night.

Chapter 48

Elsie struggled to wake up, but consciousness remained just out of reach. Her head was swimming toward awareness but remained in a riptide of darkness.

Something was wrong. She knew it on a basic level. Everything was out of whack. The scent in her nostrils was unfamiliar. The sheet that covered her felt slick rather than smooth. Even the quiet held whispers of darkness, sounds of breathing and stealthy movement.

She opened one eye. Dim light filtered under a crooked curtain hanging over a window; but it wasn't daylight. The light flashed on and off, from a neon sign nearby. A motel sign.

She was in bed, at the EconoMo.

And she wasn't alone.

Elsie had a roommate. She rolled her head to the side to scope it out. Though her vision blurred, she could make out a girl in the next bed, with a mop of frizzy ringlets and a strip of silver duct tape over her mouth.

Elsie ran her dry tongue over her lips, registering with belated surprise that her own mouth was not similarly covered. With a herculean effort, she slid to escape the bed, intending to remove the tape from the girl's mouth.

But she couldn't get either of her feet onto the floor. Her right arm would not cooperate. Elsie turned her head to determine the problem. What she saw sent dread washing over her in a wave. She was handcuffed to the bed.

The sight helped to clear her foggy head. She rolled onto her side and inspected the cuff. It looked like the real thing; like the handcuffs that officers carried on their belts at the Barton Police Department. She tugged at it, a reflex reaction; but it remained secure.

Her head fell back onto the mattress. With her eyes focused on the ceiling, she thought, *What have I gotten myself into?*

Her head clouded again, and her body ached to return to sleep. But the shifting noises on the next bed roused her.

Groaning, Elsie rolled onto her side; she stretched across the bed as far as the restraint would permit and spoke to her companion.

"Are you Desiree? The girl from Barton, Taylor's friend?"

The eyes widened under the mass of hair, and the girl nodded emphatically.

Elsie's heart was pounding, her mouth as dry as burnt toast. She spoke in a ragged whisper.

"They're looking for you, honey. I'm Elsie, I work at the courthouse in Barton."

Desiree's eyes were wild. She tried to speak, but the duct tape garbled the words.

Elsie said, "My mom is your English teacher. Mrs. Arnold."

Clearly, the revelation soothed the girl. Elsie saw the tension in her shoulders relax; and she bowed her head, breathing deeply.

The girl's slow breathing caused Elsie to follow suit, and the oxygen helped keep the fog in her head at bay. Elsie scoured the room in the flashing light, taking in the few fixtures of the hotel room, and noting the door in the wall that connected them with the adjoining room.

She whispered, her voice ragged. "Are they next door? Tony and the woman?"

Desiree looked up, nodding again. Elsie saw that Desiree was wearing a lace push-up bra on her girlish chest; but she couldn't tell whether she wore other clothing, because her lower body was covered by the bedsheet. Her arms were behind her, and she resumed the shifting movements.

Elsie tugged at her handcuffed wrist. "Are you cuffed, too?"

Desiree shook her head. Shooting a frightened glance at the door to Tony's room, she scooted sideways on the bed, revealing her restraints.

Her hands were bound with yellow nylon rope; her wrists raw and bloody. But the rope had loosened. One of the knots was undone. As Elsie watched with wonder, Desiree's bloody fingertips plucked at the rope, moving relentlessly over the hairy nylon. Elsie thought, that's got to hurt like hell.

She watched the girl's bloody hands move; her wrists were slick with gore that had stained the bedsheets as well as the rope. With a muffled howl, the girl's arm muscles tensed, and she tried to pull her hand free.

The rope gave, but not enough to slip her hand through. Elsie saw the girl's head bow; Desiree breathed deeply for ten counts or more. Then her arms tensed again; she growled behind the tape; and pulled.

This time, the wet hand slipped through the rope. Desiree

collapsed on the bed, her chest rising and falling as she breathed through her nose.

When she lifted her head, Elsie said, "The tape." And Desiree ripped it from her mouth, leaving a bloody streak across her cheek.

The girl groaned, and Elsie extended a hand in comfort, but she couldn't reach. So, she said, with awe, "You did it. How'd you do that?"

Desiree's voice was so low that Elsie barely caught the answer. "Mom taught me how. The Houdini Act." She shook the nylon rope that still hung off her left wrist. "But that was a lot harder than the pageant."

She glanced over at Elsie's bed, where her arm was attached to the bed frame by the metal cuff. "They kept me in handcuffs till you came along. I can do handcuffs. But I gotta have my pin. I don't have one. We used to hide it in my costume."

Elsie had no clue what Desiree referred to; but it didn't matter. "Can you get your feet free?"

Desiree kicked the sheet off; her ankles were bound together with the yellow rope as well. Elsie watched, holding her breath, as Desiree tried to pick at the knot with her raw fingers. The girl paused, clenching her fists together with a moan. "My hands hurt too bad."

Elsie swiveled her head to survey the room. "Does he keep a knife? He has to have something he used to cut the rope and tape."

Desiree shook her head. "It's not in here. He keeps it on his belt, in a holder thing."

She wriggled off the bed and hopped to the desk. The landline phone was missing, its space deserted; but on the dusty surface of the desk, a small pad of paper sat beside an ink pen. Desiree picked up the pen, then crouched on the floor, and thrust it into the yellow knot at her ankles. The blood on her hands made the tool slippery, but Elsie watched the girl work patiently at the bindings, stopping to wrap the bedsheet around her hand to quell the bleeding.

Elsie's fists clenched and unclenched in sympathy. Desiree studied the tool, and proceeded to pick at the knot with the pointed end. Just as the tip of the pen wormed inside the rope and looked like it would pull the biggest knot free, the plastic case shattered, and scuttled across the floor.

"Shit," Elsie hissed, trying in vain to reach it with her foot. "Desiree. I think it rolled under my bed."

But Desiree wasn't listening. Her bloody hand groped the desktop and picked up another item that lay on its surface: a pink plastic headband covered in sparkly hearts.

"Desiree," Elsie whispered, but the girl ignored her. She took the headband in both hands and broke it in two.

Elsie watched, her unease growing; it looked like the girls' eyes shone with unshed tears. But she wiped them away with the back of her raw wrist and poised one of the pink plastic shards over the knots. It had a pointed edge. After long minutes of effort, the pink spear loosened the knot sufficiently for Desiree to pull the ropes loose.

She shed the yellow rope, kicking it away from her ankles. With a woebegone face, she set the pink plastic on the desktop and looked up at Elsie.

"I always thought it was lucky. The headband."

"It is. Lucky you had the sense to use it like that." Elsie held her breath, straining to hear whether any sound came from the next room. "Sounds quiet next door," she whispered.

Desiree crawled to the adjoining door and pressed her ear against it. "I can't hear anything."

Elsie pulled to a sitting position against the backboard, her heart beating with urgency. "You've got to get out of here."

Desiree's face twisted with panic. "I don't have my clothes."

Elsie's eyes darted away from the girl, who was dressed in scanty underwear. "It doesn't matter. We're on the second floor; make a run for the stairway. This motel is on the highway. There's a gas station right by us, and a fast food place. Taco Bell. I think."

Desiree hesitated, her face a mask of distress. "I'm almost naked."

"Take the sheet. Or get a towel."

Elsie watched her pull the flat sheet from the bed and drape it over her shoulders. "Isn't it stealing?" Desiree asked.

Elsie waved off the question with her free hand.

"The defense of necessity," she said. To Desiree's confused face, she added, "I'm a lawyer."

Desiree tiptoed to the window and peeked through the curtain. "I don't see anyone," she said.

"Good. Run for it. There's an Amber Alert out for you, Desiree. When you get inside—the gas station, or a restaurant, yell. Say 'I'm Desiree Wickham from Barton, Missouri. There's an Amber Alert for me.'"

Desiree nodded, clutching the sheet to her with her bloody hands. The yellow rope still dangled from one wrist. "And I won't be in trouble?"

"God, no."

Desiree put a hand on the doorknob and flipped the dead bolt. At the metal click, Elsie winced, as if the sound could be heard for miles.

As she pulled the chain lock free, the girl paused. "Tony is going to make you do things with some guys from the casino. I heard him say so, when you were too out of it to understand. He told them to come back here after last call, whatever that is."

Last call: Elsie knew what it was. The alcohol supply was cut off at 1:30 A.M. She gave a frantic glance around the room to check the time; but the numbers on the clock were black. She lifted her chin and spoke in a confident whisper. "The cavalry's coming," Elsie said, hoping it was true.

Desiree darted over to the desk and picked up the broken pieces of the pink headband. Before she left, she dropped them onto the sheet, near Elsie's left hand. "It's lucky."

"Go," Elsie urged.

Desiree pulled the door open and slipped outside. The door closed with a thunk, leaving Elsie alone.

Chapter 49

SHE WANTED TO call out for help. But she was afraid.

Elsie knew she could make her voice heard. She had powerful volume; a voice that was made to call the hogs, as her mother always said.

But as she stared at the outline of the door that adjoined the next room, Room 217, she knew that the people closest to her might be Tony and his assistant, Dede. If she roused them, they'd shut her up. And she'd be in an even worse position.

Wait, she thought. At some point, footsteps would sound outside. They might belong to other lodgers at the hotel; or an employee; or even law enforcement, if Desiree made it to the gas station or Taco Bell. She could remain silent until she heard noises outside. Then she would shout like hell.

She could hear her pulse in her ears, pounding like a cattle stampede. The fear dissipated the remaining clouds in her brain and sharpened her senses as she lay panting on the bed, praying for assistance to arrive.

Tension wound her nerves so tight that she almost shrieked when a black shape tickled her cuffed hand. She swallowed the cry, choking it back as she watched the creature scamper across the sheet.

Cockroach.

She hated cockroaches.

Elsie used her foot to kick it off the bed. She failed to deal the vermin a fatal blow; from the flashing pool of light that shone beneath the crooked window curtain, she saw a shadow running beneath the plywood desk.

The bedsheet was jumbled at her feet. She pulled the sheet to her neck with her free hand, shivering in the frigid room. Her bedspread was missing; she couldn't remember why.

As she waited, lying in the cold bed, she tried to piece together the prior evening. She remembered parking her car outside the motel, leaving a message for her mother. She was certain she told her mother to call Ashlock if she hadn't returned by midnight; and from the dark night outside the room, she knew that midnight had surely come and gone.

So, where the hell was he?

Tony had drugged her; that incident burned in her recollection. She grimaced as she remembered his hand around her throat, his tongue in her mouth.

But after that: nothing. She didn't even recall removing her clothes; but they were missing. She wore nothing but her bra and panties.

Remembering Desiree's revelation, Elsie thought: Thank god, she still wore her panties. When she'd conceived this risky plan, Elsie never really believed she'd be caught in the trap. The notion that she might be in danger of gang rape was not a consequence she'd entertained.

Tears gathered in the corners of her eyes; when she blinked, they ran down the side of her face and pooled into her ears. She had been right—right about everything. But no one had listened to her.

This was the price she paid for being right.

She squeezed her eyes shut, and the thought pounded again: where was Ashlock?

Then she heard it. A muffled noise at first, coming from a distance. The sound of car doors slamming shut. Men's voices sounded in the night—but whose?

She raised up on one elbow, clutching the sheet, waiting for the moment it would be revealed. Like the old tale, where the door in the arena would open to either the lady or the tiger.

Eyes straining in the dim light, she held her breath as she listened. In the lot below, gravel crunched underneath shoes. It was the sound of multiple feet: but whose?

Come on, Ashlock, she prayed.

Then she heard a laugh. A drunken bellow of a laugh. Her empty stomach did a flop.

Police officers wouldn't be laughing.

The shoes marched up the steps, coming her way. She tensed on the bed, her muscles taut as a fiddle string. If it wasn't Tony, she could still shout for help. If it wasn't Tony.

When the voices—hushed now—drew close to her motel room, she drew a mighty breath, ready to cry out.

Then the door opened. The door to the room next to Elsie. Room 217.

When she heard it slam shut, she lay back on the mattress, twisting the sheet over her chest with sweating hands. Inside the adjoining room, the voices were no longer muted. She heard Tony's voice, ordering Dede to wake up and make a round of drinks.

And more laughter sounded; though what the joke was, she couldn't say. Dede was talking, and her voice carried an injured bleat. So maybe the joke was on her.

Elsie twisted her head, inspecting Desiree's bed. The bedspread was tumbled atop the bloodstained fitted sheet. Its elastic corners were pulled away from the mattress.

The noise level lowered next door; there was a discussion that held the tenor of negotiation. It had the rhythm of men striking a bargain.

When the knob turned on the adjoining door, the hardware creaked. Elsie slitted her eyes, looking through her lashes, though that side of the room remained in darkness. The door opened and the sudden burst of light shining in from Room 217 blinded her. She steeled herself to keep her face still.

Tony's figure was silhouetted in the light of the adjoining room. He said, "I'm going to rouse these sleeping beauties. We'll keep our little princess in 218, so her and Denny can have some privacy. I'll bring out the plus-size model in here for y'all. Her and Dede can put on a big old party for you."

He shut the door behind him, then flipped on the table lamp.

Through her lashes, she saw Tony's face as it registered: Desiree was gone. His eyes bulged, his mouth twisted into a fierce snarl, baring his teeth. The tendons of his neck rose under the tattooed snake on his neck.

He swung an arm and flung the red cup he held. When it hit the wall over Desiree's bed, Elsie flinched.

He must have seen her reaction. Leaping into the space between the beds, he grabbed Elsie by her hair, jerking her head up off the mattress. Her eyes flew open.

Tony's face was inches away from hers. "Where'd she go?"

Chapter 50

ELSIE TRIED TO roll away from him, but he held her fast. Giving her hair a vicious twist, he lowered his voice to a growl.

"Where the fuck is she?"

His face bent close to hers. She could smell his breath, such a vile odor of stale booze that she tried in vain to turn her head.

When she didn't answer, he released her, flinging her head back onto the mattress. He turned to the empty bed, throwing the bedspread to the floor, as if Desiree might be found beneath it.

The adjoining door opened. A man dressed in camouflage with a cap over his graying hair stood inside the doorway and stared at Tony. He spoke in an impatient voice.

"Where's the little girl you promised me? The new one?"

Tony ran to the bathroom door and peered inside. The camouflaged man strode into the room behind him, saying, "Goddamn it, you're not going to screw me over a second time. You've lost a paying customer, man."

And Elsie's brain fired at the familiar face.

She jerked her arm, screaming. "Help me! I'm a prisoner!"

The camouflaged man turned to face Elsie, taking a step back. When their eyes met, confusion clouded his face. Tony returned to her bedside and slapped her so hard that her head snapped to the side.

The blow made her see stars. She opened her mouth and screamed.

As her vision cleared, she saw the face beneath the bill of the camouflaged customer's cap again, and knew that she was not mistaken. It was someone she knew.

He bolted from the door, back into the other room. She heard another man's voice; he said, "What's going on here, Denny? We didn't pay for this kind of shit."

Tony turned and tore back into Room 217. "I can straighten this all out, make this right. I got another girl, a young one. I'll call her right now."

Elsie shrieked again, her voice cracking from the strain. "Help me. Call the police. Help me."

A low voice sounded through the open doorway. "I'm out of here, boys."

It was a voice she'd heard before.

She raised up on her elbow again, struggling to see through the doorway. The man in camouflage crossed in front of the opening; she caught a final glimpse of him. Her breath hitched in her chest.

The man looked like Dennis Thompson.

And he sounded like Dennis Thompson.

Madeleine's husband, Dennis Thompson.

Her head reeled as she heard a door slam, booted feet echoing as he departed. Why didn't he come to her aid? She recognized him; surely, he knew her by sight. In frustration, she howled aloud, her voice drowning out the voices in the next room.

The door opened and shut again; she heard more footfalls running away. In a final effort, she screamed: "911! I'm Elsie Arnold!"

When she paused to gasp for breath, there was no sound of rescue. She was alone, trapped in the bed by the handcuffs. Tony advanced on her with blood in his eye. As he pushed his shirt sleeve to his elbow, he doubled his right fist. "Girl, I'm gonna wear you out."

Dede followed behind, with a haunted look. "Tony. We got to get out of here."

He ignored her. Grasping Elsie's neck with his left hand, he raised his right fist, pausing to smile at her.

She winced as she waited for the blow to fall; but Dede clutched his shoulder, saying, "Tony, we don't have time for this."

He released Elsie, wheeling around and punching Dede in the stomach. She made a guttural sound as she stumbled backward, doubling over.

Elsie scrambled under the sheet, moving as far from Tony as the handcuffs permitted; and something scratched her bare leg. She felt for the offending object with her hand, and found the plastic shard, the remains of Desiree's headband. The lucky headband.

She gave it a glance. The broken edge was sharp. Could it hurt him? Deter him? She'd once fended off an attack with a sharpened pencil.

But she hadn't been handcuffed to a bed on that occasion.

While Dede leaned against the plywood dresser for support, gasping for breath, Tony knelt and picked up a silver item from the floor: Desiree's discarded duct tape.

He slapped it over Elsie's mouth, bearing down so hard with the heel of his hand that her teeth cut into flesh behind her lips.

Despite the pain, she prayed he'd forget the fact that her right hand was still free.

She kept the free hand hidden under the sheet, her fingers clasped around the pink plastic shard.

Tony stared down at her, opening his mouth to speak; but a pounding noise sounded from the other side of the wall, behind Elsie's head.

Tony's chin jerked up, his eyes flashing. "What?"

A voice shouted through the sheetrock: "Keep it down. We can't sleep."

Tony darted to the wall, and began pounding on the sheetrock over Elsie's head. "Fuck you," he said, battering the wall until his fist made a gaping hole.

"That's it," Dede said, pushing away from the dresser. She coughed, gesturing at Tony to stop. "We gotta go now."

The voice from the next room shouted in protest; and Tony raised his voice to a shout.

"Motherfucker. You want me to come over there?"

At the muffled response, he shouted again. "I'll kick in the door and beat your ass."

Dede groaned. "Please, Tony."

He turned away from the battered wall and stared down at Elsie. "What about her?"

"Let's just go."

He bent over the bed, ripping off the sheet with a sudden movement, and revealing the pointed pink shard gripped in her free hand. Laughing, he jerked it from her grip and held it up, saying, "Look there, Dede. Bitch was going to shank me with a little piece of plastic."

Then his hand whipped down and raked it across Elsie's face.

Crying out behind her taped mouth, she reared back, bending both legs at the knee; then kicked out, connecting with his chest and knocking him to the floor.

He recovered swiftly, jumping atop her and sinking his teeth into her shoulder. She tore at his hair with her free hand, but he hung on.

Dede came up behind him. She grabbed his arm, pleading. "We got to go; we'll leave her here, she don't matter. You get the money, I'll get the drugs and computer and let's go."

He released Elsie's shoulder. Her eyes widened with shock when she saw his teeth stained with her blood. As he rolled off her, he said to Dede, "But what about the fat bitch?"

"Leave her."

"She'll talk."

"Tony, what are you always telling me? It don't matter if she talks. Nobody listens to a whore."

Over the sounds they made in the next room, of drawers opening and slamming shut; whispered curses and orders; the door closing behind them as their footfalls descended down the concrete steps; Elsie could hear the conversation she'd had with the public defender in the coffee shop: no one listens to a prostitute. She ripped the duct tape from her mouth, wincing.

When silence fell, she didn't recognize it. Her ears buzzed like a beehive; and her heart still pounded so violently that she could feel every beat of her pulse. Once she decided that they were truly gone and unlikely to return, she tried to gauge the time. How long had it been since Desiree departed?

She scooted backward and kicked the wall, shouting for help from the occupants on the other side of the battered sheetrock, but got no response. Why hadn't the police arrived? Was she going to have to rely on the hotel maid for her salvation?

The bite on her shoulder burned, and the cut on her face smarted. She wiped the blood on her face away with her free hand then used the dirty sheet to staunch the flow.

It seemed like a long vigil as she watched the glow of the lights under the curtain and listened to the sounds of the nearby highway; but the sun had not yet risen when a siren blared in the distance.

She shut her eyes, mouthing a prayer. The siren came closer, and did not pass her by. The red lights flashed against the crooked curtain at the window.

She screamed again, keeping up the wail until her throat spasmed in protest. Again, feet ran up the stairs. An argument sounded outside the door; but she didn't hear the details over the sound of her own shrieking.

A kick made the door to her room shake. It took three tries to break the lock. Then they all burst inside: two men and one woman, wearing Missouri State Highway Patrol uniforms. She had always admired those uniforms.

And in jeans and a rumpled flannel shirt, she beheld a welcome sight: Ashlock.

"Ash," she croaked, trying to smile.

But he didn't speak. He stared at her as if he didn't know her, his face stony with shock.

Chapter 51

ELSIE SHIVERED IN the plastic chair as she sat in an administrative office at St. Mary's Hospital in Albany, shuffling her bare feet on the cold tile of the office floor. After Ashlock had freed her from the cuff that chained her to the hotel bed, she had hunted in vain for her clothing. She succeeded only in finding the tawdry nylon dress, lying on the floor of the closet. The jacket and shoes she'd worn to her meeting at the EconoMo were missing.

A trooper plugged in the recording device that sat on the desk, then studied the dials on the box. She looked up at Elsie. "Are you cold?"

"No, I'm fine," Elsie said. It was a lie, but she was so grateful to be in the safe haven of the local hospital, it seemed selfish to ask for more. "Have you seen Bob Ashlock?"

"Last I saw of him, he was talking to the girl—Desiree—and her mother in the hospital ER." The trooper shot a worried glance of Elsie's face. "You got in and out of the ER pretty fast. Have they taken care of you?"

"Yes. I'm fine."

"Did they go over everything? Conduct a rape screen?"

Elsie gave her head a decided shake. "No, ma'am. I don't need a rape screen. Thank God."

The officer hesitated, pulling a face. "You told us you were unconscious for a while. Something could have happened."

"Nothing did," Elsie said with a stubborn set of her jaw. "I would know."

"We'll need a blood draw. For toxicology reports."

"They took one. And they stitched up the bite on my shoulder. Photographed it, too."

"Did they document that scratch on your face? Photos?"

"Yep."

"It looks pretty bad."

Elsie's hand raised up instinctively, to cover it. Resolutely, she dropped the hand back in her lap. She wasn't supposed to touch it. With a show of bravado, she said, "It's not gaping. No stitches. They cleaned it up in the ER. They gave me instructions, how to care for it when I get home. Put antibiotic ointment on it."

The trooper whispered, "They won't tell you this: but my mama always used hydrogen peroxide. It stops an infection in its tracks."

Elsie nodded. Hydrogen peroxide was what Marge Arnold would recommend. Which reminded her: Why had her mother failed to sound the alarm? Elsie had been hustled out of the hotel room so fast by the troopers that she hadn't had a chance to ask Ashlock for an explanation.

To demand an explanation, to be precise. She had a bone to pick with that man.

The trooper pulled a chair from the table and sat. "Are you ready to give a statement?"

Elsie took a breath. "Ready."

"I'll ask questions, you just answer to the best of your recollection. Okay?"

"Sure." Elsie pulled her shoulders erect, tucking her bare feet beneath the chair. "I know how this works. I'm a prosecutor."

The trooper gave her a small grin. "Right."

She pushed the button; but before they could begin, there was a sharp knock on the closed door. The trooper gave an impatient look as she stopped the device. Reaching over, she pulled the door open.

Ashlock stood in the entryway. His eyes were shadowed, and he looked in need of a shower and shave. But it was his expression that took Elsie by surprise. He looked like he wanted to take a swing at someone.

"Am I interrupting?"

"Yeah," the trooper said. "She's about to give a statement."

He took a half step back. "Okay. I'll wait."

Elsie shot him an inquiring glance, and he shook his head, cursing softly.

He said, "No. It can't wait. Give us a minute, trooper."

The young woman exhaled softly, but stepped outside. Ashlock pulled the door shut. And turned the lock.

Elsie wasn't certain just what she expected. An embrace, maybe. An apology. Not the angry silence that confronted her.

She broke it. "You took your sweet time."

"Goddamn it. God damn. What were you thinking?"

A wave of heat rolled through her, and she stood, not caring about the frigid temperature that met the soles of her feet.

"I was thinking I'd help that little girl out. Seems like I was the only person who was on it."

"You were not. We've all been on it. Even the Feds. They tried to solicit Marvel through the Backlist ad, using an undercover identity; but he wouldn't bite. Like he could sniff out the trap. So then we were looking at it from the online P2P network, going backward to find him." He sighed, shaking his head. "You sure as hell got to him faster. But do you understand the danger you were in?"

"Fuck yeah," she said, as she pulled the neck of her flimsy dress to display her bandaged shoulder. A ring of bruised skin circled the wrist that had been cuffed to the bed. "I figured that out pretty fast."

"And you ran off without bothering to tell me."

"I told my mother." Remembering her instructions to Marge, she flushed with indignation. "I told my fucking mother to call you if I wasn't back by midnight. So either Marge blew me off, or you did. Either way, I am really pissed at somebody."

His eyes were bloodshot. He didn't blink. "Your mother is in the hospital."

The shock took the wind out of her. She dropped into the chair. "Mom? The hospital?"

"Barton Memorial. She was in a collision. I worked it."

Tears burned in Elsie's eyes. "Is she okay?"

"She'll be all right. She suffered a concussion, broken collar bone."

Her head dropped, and she tried to speak, but only a sob came from her throat. The trauma of the past twenty-four hours swamped her, and she was seized by an urgent need to see her mother.

Ashlock's angry voice assaulted her ear. "You left word about this fool scheme with your mother. Not me."

She nodded. It had made sense at the time. In retrospect, not so much.

The doorknob rattled; when it wouldn't open, a rap sounded. The trooper's voice came from the other side. "We need to get moving on Miss Arnold's statement. The captain wants it."

Ashlock ran a hand over his face, and then turned to unlock the door. "Why haven't they completed your exam? You haven't had a rape screen. I checked with the nurse."

"I don't need a rape screen."

His head jerked to face her, and his face reddened. "You need to go through with the goddamn procedure."

The knowledge that everyone would hear their shouting match did not deter Elsie from raising her voice to meet his.

"Don't tell me what to do."

"Jesus," he said, and shouldered his way from the room.

The trooper looked askance at his retreating figure. "I was going to tell him. Oklahoma has pulled over a vehicle bearing the license plate that you provided. The occupants match the description we've got. That's why the captain wants us to get this out."

A chill ran through her. "Are they in custody? Tony and Dede?"

"They're holding them. So, let's make sure you give a thorough description, okay?"

"Okay. Let's do this."

The trooper's hand poised on the button of the voice recorder. "And the men who came into the hotel, the prospective customers. Did you get a chance to observe them?"

"One of them." Elsie's voice was grim. "He shouldn't be hard to find. Just walk into the John Deere dealership in McCown County."

Chapter 52

Elsie tore through the door of the red brick house, the sturdy Georgian structure in Barton where she was born and raised. As she paused on the hardwood floor of the entryway, she cried out at the top of her lungs: "Mom!"

Her father's voice sounded from the second floor. "Elsie!" She heard his footfalls echo overhead. She dropped her bag at the bottom of the stairwell and made a run up the stairs, slipping only once or twice from the thin flip-flops the hospital in Albany had provided to cover her bare feet.

George Arnold stood at the head of the stairs. He seized Elsie in a bear hug when she reached the top, lifting her up off her feet. She was so relieved to see him at last that she hardly noticed the pain when his hand clutched the bite on her shoulder.

Through the open doorway, her mother said, "George, set that girl down so she can come to her mama."

Elsie's feet hit the floor and she hurried through the open door of her parent's bedroom. When she saw her mother, she paused. It took a moment to absorb the shock: the sight of her capable mother in bed, sporting a cervical collar and two black eyes.

Recovering, she approached the four-poster bed with a cautious step, encircling her mother in a loose embrace, as if she feared she might break.

"Give me a proper hug, baby," Marge said, sighing out with relief, squeezing her tight.

When they parted, Marge reached out and gently lifted Elsie's chin with her finger, turning her face to the side as she inspected the angry cut that slashed across her cheek. Marge's mouth worked involuntarily, her lips pinched together; and her eyes grew wet and blinked.

Dropping her hand, Marge said, "That scratch looks bad. It needs hydrogen peroxide." She tossed the bed clothes aside and scooted off the mattress.

George stopped her. "Where are you going? You've got a concussion. And a broken collar bone. I'm supposed to see to it that you stay in bed."

"I'm going to the bathroom. I've got a bottle of hydrogen peroxide in the medicine cabinet, by the Q-tips."

Elsie held out a restraining hand. "Mother, I'm fine. Really."

"You look like you've been in a knife fight," Marge snapped.

"You look like you've been in a fistfight," Elsie retorted. "Lie back down, Mom. Please."

Her mother tried to scoff; but the noise turned into a sob that caught in her throat. George turned on his heel. "I'll get it," he said, and left the room.

Elsie studied Marge as she pulled the quilt to her chest. "Mom, are you okay?"

Marge closed her eyes briefly. "My head hurts. And this old

bone aches. That airbag punched me in the face, gave me these black eyes. But mostly, I'm ashamed of myself."

George returned, bearing a black plastic bottle and a cotton swab. "Don't you go there again, Marge. Don't get started. Nobody thinks any of this is your fault."

Elsie's glance shifted from Marge to George, and back again. "What?"

"I failed you. My only child. When you needed my help. Stupid damn phone."

"We're getting a new phone for your mother tomorrow. An iPhone," George said as he set the bottle on the bedside table. "And she's going to let you show her how to work it."

Elsie didn't groan at the prospect of tutoring her mother on the device—a sign of the toll the past day had taken. Marge unscrewed the cap on the black bottle and dipped the swab inside. As she applied the wet cotton to Elsie's face with a shaking hand, Marge grimaced and said, "And having a wreck, in the midst of everything. I'm an old fool."

"Mom, stop it."

The hand holding the swab jerked back. "Am I hurting you, sweetheart?"

"No—not that. I don't want you to beat yourself up. None of this is your fault, for God's sake."

Marge's countenance crumpled as the tears came in earnest. "Just look what he did to your sweet face."

Seeing her mother cry broke something deep within Elsie's chest; and she shuddered in a vain attempt to mask her own reaction.

George said, "It's a good thing that SOB and his girlfriend are locked up in Oklahoma tonight. There's a lot of folks around here that would like to skip the trial. Put an end to them both with a shotgun."

Elsie shook her head. "Oh Lord."

Marge interrupted. "George, please. Don't upset her. This day has burdens enough." She set the damp swab onto a coaster, careful not to let the wet tip touch the tabletop. "Elsie, has Bob Ashlock brought you up to speed? On everything?"

Elsie shook her head. "I haven't talked to him, except for a minute back at the hospital."

An alarm made a dinging sound. George pulled his phone from his pocket. "Time for your medication, Marge." He picked up an empty tumbler sitting beside a pill bottle. "I'll get you some ice water."

As he left the room, Marge wrestled a wad of tissues from a Kleenex box that sat nearby. In a ragged voice, she said, "I'll never forgive myself. Never."

"Mom. It's on me. I never should have placed you in that position. If I was going to take the risk, it was unfair to put the burden on you. I should never have sent you that text."

Marge swiped her nose a final time with the tissues, and then studied Elsie, frowning. "Why not?"

Elsie met her mother's eye and held it. "I'm a grown woman. A trial lawyer. Not a child."

Marge laughed softly, shaking her head. "No matter how old you are, or how old I get, I'll always be your mother. You can always call on me; and I'll hear you, now that I'm getting rid of that phone. We're your family. This is your home. Always."

Elsie wanted to argue, but something in Marge's face made her hold her tongue. After a quiet moment, Marge said, "Don't worry about Bob not being in touch. He's a busy man. Working with the FBI and the highway patrol, for goodness' sakes."

"I expect that's right."

"Is he coming for Thanksgiving?"

Elsie rubbed her forehead. "I keep forgetting to mention it."

"Well, then, I'll call him myself. I'm the hostess; I should be making the invite, anyway. I'll do it this week." Settling her head on the pillow, Marge smiled, as if the matter was finally settled.

"Mother. You can't put Thanksgiving on this year. It's out of the question."

"I'd like to see someone try to stop me."

The sound of her father's feet marching up the stairs made them both pause. He entered the room, passing off a fresh water glass to Marge. As she swallowed her pill, George said, "Who do you think will be working on the extradition? Isn't that what they'll need to get those people back into Missouri to face charges?"

The question made Elsie's head throb. She rubbed her forehead again, at a spot over her right eye. "It depends on who's handling the case. Whether it will be state or federal. They're all working together right now. If the Feds decide to take it, there will have to be a grand jury hearing, to see if they'll hand down an indictment in Federal Court."

Her mother interrupted. "Then Madeleine Thompson won't need to worry about it. Poor woman."

Elsie gave her mother a curious glance. Marge was not fond of Madeleine. And she didn't suppose that the information about Dennis Thompson's involvement in the trafficking case had been made public. "No, Madeleine won't be involved. I'm certain of that."

Elsie stopped before she let confidential information slip. There were things that she shouldn't divulge at this juncture, not even to her parents.

Marge settled back on her pillow. "Poor Madeleine. Poor thing," she said in a murmur, closing her eyes.

Confused, Elsie turned to her father. "'Poor thing'—from Mom? She can't stand Madeleine."

Marge's chin dropped and she snored lightly. George bent down and whispered in Elsie's ear. "Your mama got a phone call right before you got here, from the prayer chain at church. A woman whose husband works at the John Deere."

"Ah." Elsie nodded. The word must be out.

"Madeleine is a widow."

"What?" Elsie jumped off the bed, causing Marge's body to rock; but she didn't awaken. George gave her a warning look.

"You need to brace yourself; this will come as a shock."

"Tell me."

"Dennis Thompson was found dead in his office this morning. His secretary heard a gunshot. She ran back there, saw the body. Self-inflicted gunshot wound."

Elsie felt the room spin. She clutched the bedpost, afraid she might fall.

Her father's voice continued. "They say Madeleine didn't even know he was in town. He was supposed to be on a hunting trip with some of his buddies. She says he's been off hunting most every weekend this fall."

Chapter 53

DESPITE MARGE ARNOLD's urging, Elsie skipped the Dennis Thompson funeral.

She opted to cover the office, instead; even answering the phones, so the clerical staff could attend. Elsie had no interest in Dennis Thompson's last rites. Truth be told, she was glad he was dead.

And though she dreaded an ugly confrontation with Madeleine, she'd avoided it so far. Madeleine was on leave. An indefinite leave of absence. The McCown County Commission had appointed Chuck Harris as acting prosecutor in her absence. So there was that.

The two weeks that had passed since Elsie walked into the EconoMo Motel flew by in a blur of activity, which led to a landmark day: Elsie had been summoned to Federal Court, to appear before the grand jury.

Walking into the federal courthouse for the first time felt very strange indeed.

The security personnel, two stern-faced men wearing navy

blazers and striped neckties, bore no resemblance to the affable deputies who guarded the entry of the old stone courthouse in McCown County. Elsie had to stand patiently and wait without comment as they examined her driver's license and the contents of her briefcase, searching for what, she didn't know. Weapons, maybe. Or explosives. Or contraband.

The elder of the two security guards spoke to her. "You'll need to hand over your phone, ma'am."

Startled, she pulled it from her bag. "Will I get it right back?" she asked.

"When you leave the courthouse." He gave her a reassuring smile, which made him seem far less forbidding. "I'll give you this wooden token. You'll exchange it for the phone when you leave."

She looked at the token she held in her palm. It was numbered: 13. She frowned. "We don't do anything like this at the courthouse in McCown County. I never heard of people giving up their cell phones."

"Only lawyers can take their phones into Federal Court," the man said.

Elsie felt the heat rush into her face. "I'm a lawyer."

The guard didn't dispute her claim. He remained polite and businesslike. "May I see your Bar Association membership card?"

As she dug the plastic card from the bowels of her battered wallet, Elsie pondered the changes she might make to pass as a barrister in this town. Maybe she should cut off her hair; she was past thirty, after all. Or maybe it was finally time to invest in a new suit.

With her cell phone safely tucked back inside her briefcase, she walked in a circle around the small lobby area. Elsie wasn't familiar with the layout of the building. She had to study a map near the elevator to figure out where she needed to go.

When she stepped off the elevator, en route to the U.S. Attorney's Office, she spied Desiree Wickham and her mother in the hallway. They were groomed for the cameras, it appeared. Desiree's curly hair had been fashioned into loose corkscrew curls; and Kim wore a full face of pancake makeup, with bright red lipstick on her mouth.

When Kim Wickham saw Elsie, she let out a screech. Running over, she clutched Elsie in a tight embrace.

Calling over her shoulder, she said, "Des! Get over here! It's our hero."

But Desiree hung back, looking shy. Elsie broke free from Kim's hold and walked up to Desiree, taking the girl's hands in hers and clasping them.

"You look wonderful, Desiree. How are you feeling?"

Desiree met her eyes and managed a wobbly smile. "Better. Good."

Kim joined them, placing her arm around Desiree's shoulder. "Good? We're great. I don't know if you heard, but Lifetime has been in touch with us. They want to buy Des's story. For a made-for-TV movie. For television."

Kim punctuated the announcement by planting a kiss on her daughter's cheek; then paused to wipe the red lip print away with the pad of her thumb.

Elsie caught Desiree's eye. "Wow. National television."

With a look of resignation on her face, Desiree shrugged her shoulders in response. "Mom thinks it'll be good for my career."

Studying the girl, Elsie considered the price of fame. *Be careful what you wish for,* she thought.

She glanced around the hallway, trying to gauge the activity around them. "Have you testified yet, Desiree?"

Desiree shook her head. "I'm real nervous."

Elsie squeezed her hand. "Oh hon. You have the heart of a lion. Testifying before a grand jury is gonna be a walk in the park for a fierce woman like you."

Desiree's eyes shone with a glassy sheen of tears. She threw her arms around Elsie's neck with a muffled sob.

A young man with a neck like a pencil appeared behind Desiree's shoulder: the assistant U.S. attorney, Steven Bennett.

"Hey, ladies. Miss Wickham, Ms. Arnold, right? We'd best separate you all. Don't want it to look like you're colluding over your testimony."

Elsie stepped back thinking, *As if I don't know better than to compare notes with another witness.* She was tempted to snap at the man. But she held her tongue. She gave Desiree an encouraging grin and shot her a wink.

"Go get 'em, baby."

Desiree nodded. As she walked away, escorted by the U.S. attorney, she gave Elsie a backward look.

Elsie found a bench in the hallway and dropped onto it, looking around. The federal structure was fancier than Barton's old courthouse; it had a glass atrium overhead, and under foot, a carpet emblazoned with the seal of UNITED STATES COURTS WESTERN DISTRICT OF MISSOURI. But she wished that the federal courthouse in Springfield had a friendly coffee shop, like the one in the basement of the county courthouse in Barton. She could use a jolt of caffeine. And an encouraging word. As she gazed up and down the hallway, hoping to see a familiar face, her phone hummed.

She pulled it out of her bag: Marge Arnold.

"Hey, Mom. What?"

Marge's voice soared out of the phone. "Springfield is only

thirty miles down the highway. I can be there in forty-five minutes, tops."

Elsie smiled into the phone. Lowering her voice to a whisper, she said, "Mother. You're a sweetheart, honest to God. But I told you before, I don't need you to babysit me at the courthouse. I'm a trial lawyer."

"Not today, you're not. Today, you're a witness at a grand jury hearing. And a victim of crime. I'm ashamed to think you're sitting up there alone, when you should have the support of your family."

Elsie shook her head. They'd gone around and around on the topic the night before, over supper.

"Your dad wants to be there, too. But he says we should leave it up to you."

Despite her denials, Elsie took comfort in her mother's voice. And the mention of her dad made her eyes sting with a sudden wash of tears.

"Mom, you should be at home, staying off your feet. You're still recovering. I still can't believe you wrestled that Thanksgiving turkey onto the table. We shouldn't have let you do it."

"I'm not ready for the nursing home yet. And you were real good help this year."

The thought of her feisty mother in a nursing home made Elsie laugh, in spite of the somber surroundings. "You're the best, Mom. You and Dad. But he's right; it's my call. And I've got this."

She could hear Marge's disapproval radiating through the iPhone. "All right, then. Is Bob Ashlock there?"

"I think so. He's surely around somewhere. I texted him yesterday." Elsie did a one-eighty, her eyes searching the hall for a sign of him. They hadn't talked in days. And she hadn't seen him in well over a week. Recently, communications with Ashlock were sparse, and had been conveyed by text.

The silence between them had grown increasingly troubling as the days slipped past. At first, she was able to rationalize his absence. He had traveled to the Bootheel for the four-day Thanksgiving weekend; of course, he was out of pocket. And since then, they had both been busy. Elsie, Chuck, and Breeon ran the McCown County Prosecutor's Office in Madeleine's absence; and Ashlock was part of the federal child pornography case, as well as the abduction and trafficking cases. Although she tried to reassure herself that nothing was wrong aside from overwork, it nagged at her. What was up with Ashlock?

Her thoughts were interrupted when a young man approached her, walking her way with a determined step. Looked like she was about to be tapped.

"Mom, I've got to go."

"Okay, baby. I love you."

Love you, too, Elsie thought, as she tucked the phone away.

The young man appeared at her elbow. "Ms. Arnold?"

She looked up. He was just a kid, too young to have completed law school and passed the bar exam, though he dressed the part. Elsie gave him a suspicious eye.

"Yeah?"

"Ms. Arnold, I'm Conor Wadle, an intern in the U.S. attorney's office. Mr. Bennett asked me to find you."

She stood, dropping the phone into her bag. "I'll follow you to the courtroom. I don't know my way around this building."

He smiled. "You won't be in court, ma'am. The grand jury meets in a conference room. There's no indictment yet."

A blush crept up her neck. She felt like a fool; why hadn't it occurred to her that the testimony would be outside of the courtroom? She knew that grand jury proceedings were secret, and that court proceedings were a matter of public record.

In a voice that was deceptively casual, she said, "Of course. At the county level, we don't use grand juries too often. We have a preliminary hearing before the associate circuit judge."

"I know." He gestured down the hallway, and she fell into step with him.

"So where do you go to school?'

"Wash U. I'm a junior."

"Oh, Wash U. St Louis. Fancy."

"Yeah, the campus is nice." He moved a half step ahead of her. She had to walk fast to keep up, a difficult trick in her high heels.

It made no sense that she wanted to prove herself to the college kid, but she chattered on, nonetheless. "Seems like the U.S. attorney handles a lot of drug cases around here. White-collar crime, too. I'm a trial attorney. Mostly violent offenses."

"I know."

That surprised her. "How's that?"

"I interned at the Southern District Court of Appeals last summer. I read two of your trial transcripts." He winked at her. "You're funny. Cracked me up more than once."

Elsie decided to take the comment as a compliment. Finding that the boy was growing on her, she said, "You sure are getting some plum internships for an undergraduate student."

"Yeah. My dad is a federal judge." He said it without vanity, just a statement of fact. They turned a corner and reached a pair of closed doors in the hallway marked PRIVATE. He pointed with his index finger.

"That's where the grand jury sits. There's a small office connected to it. Kind of a waiting room. That's where Mr. Bennett wants for you to sit and wait."

"Okay." He opened a door and she followed him inside. An FBI agent was seated in the waiting room; Ashlock sat next to him. At the sight of Ashlock, Elsie caught her breath.

The intern held the door open, regarding Elsie with a curious eye. "Are you okay?'

She exhaled. "Sure."

"Take a seat, then. They'll call you when they're ready."

Elsie stepped into the room, the door shutting behind her.

"Hey, stranger," she said.

Ashlock stood. "Would you like my seat?"

"No. I'd like a minute of your time, though. Whenever you can spare it."

He turned to the FBI agent. "Karl, this is Elsie Arnold. She's with the McCown County Prosecutor's Office."

The man extended his hand for a shake. "I read your statement."

"Nice to meet you, Karl. So, Ashlock. What you doing after the hearing?"

Their eyes locked. She could see the wheels turning in his head, as he contemplated his reply. Waiting, she felt beads of sweat form on her upper lip.

Just as he started to speak, the door adjoining the grand jury cracked open, and the U.S. attorney stuck his head into the room.

"Detective Ashlock? We're ready for you."

Ashlock stepped to the doorway, turning his head to give Elsie a departing look. She couldn't read his face.

Chapter 54

At last, it was Elsie's turn. During her wait, as she paced the carpet of the small room, she developed a new respect for the angst suffered by witnesses in the courtroom process.

Steven Bennett, the U.S. attorney handling the hearing, held the door open for her to enter, and she nodded at him as she passed. But once she arrived inside the grand jury room, she paused, baffled.

The room didn't resemble any courtroom she'd ever seen. It was set up like a college classroom, with a conference table at one end, and roughly two dozen men and women seated at a distance, facing her.

She looked for a judge, but observed no one wearing a black robe.

"Ms. Arnold," said the attorney, his arm indicating a seat at the conference table.

She turned to him and whispered, "Who is going to swear me in? There's no judge."

A court reporter sat before the table, with his court reporting device. "Leonard," Bennett said, "please swear the witness."

The court reporter instructed Elsie to raise her hand; she followed his orders, repeating the familiar oath. As she sat at the table, she felt heat rise in her face. She was glad she didn't wear eyeglasses; she might steam them up. It was the product of nerves and the discomfort she felt as a fish out of water.

Steven Bennett stood beside her and spoke. "Please state your name."

"Elsie Arnold."

"What is your occupation?"

"Assistant prosecuting attorney of McCown County, Missouri."

"And where do you live?"

"1100 East Kimbrough Street. In Barton, Missouri."

"And Barton is?"

"The county seat of McCown County, Missouri."

"Thank you. Ms. Arnold, I'd like to direct your attention to November 18 of this year. Where did you go on that date?"

Elsie broke eye contact with the U.S. attorney and scanned the grand jury members. They were attentive; several jotted notes on pads of paper. Most of the jurors were older than Elsie by a decade or more; but she was chagrined to note they were more fashionably attired than she. A woman in the front row wore a silk scarf in autumnal hues draped artfully around her neck and a smart pair of brown shoes polished to a high shine. Elsie glanced down at her own feet. The toes of her best shoes bore scuff marks. She wished she'd thought to polish them before court. And the sole of the left shoe was coming loose, separating from the leather at the toe.

Lifting her gaze, she locked eyes with the attorney. "I drove to the EconoMo Motel on I-44, in Bodine County, Missouri. It's on the outskirts of Albany."

"And for what reason did you go to that location on that date?"

"I went to meet a man who called himself Tony, who claimed he was an agent for a business called Marvel Modeling. I had an appointment for an interview."

The attorney's lips twitched. "Do you moonlight as a model, Ms. Arnold?"

Someone in the room chuckled. Elsie resisted the urge to hunt him down and give him the stink eye.

"I do not."

She straightened in her seat, raising her chin. The attorney gave her a quizzical look, as if he expected her to continue. When she maintained her silence, he said, "Why did you have the appointment with Marvel Modeling?"

"I had reason to suspect that young women in my community were being lured by a false modeling enterprise. A young girl, a student at Barton Middle School, was missing. I wanted to see whether there was a connection with Marvel Modeling."

"How did you happen to make the connection with Tony?"

Elsie paused before she answered, instinctively wary of a question that called for hearsay information. In state court proceedings, hearsay evidence—where a person testifies about what they heard another person say—was inadmissible.

But this was a grand jury hearing. The rules were different. No defense attorney was present to jump up and object.

She spoke. "I'd seen a modeling page on Taylor Johnson's computer search. And in a conversation with Desiree Wickham's mother, Kim, she made a reference to Tony at Marvel Modeling. She said that Desiree found the agency from an ad on Backlist.com."

"So, you hunted Tony down on your own."

"I did."

"And made an appointment to meet with him."

"I did."

"Did you tell him you were a prosecutor?"

"I did not."

The fashionable woman on the front row raised her brow. Elsie focused on her as she said, "I told him I was interested in modeling."

Steven Bennett stepped away from the table where Elsie sat and paced in front of the assembled grand jurors.

"Are you a police officer, Ms. Arnold?"

"No."

"A law enforcement official?"

"No."

"An investigator of any sort?"

When she didn't answer, the attorney swung around, a look of impatience on his face. "Did you hear my question?"

"Yes."

"And?"

"And I'm considering my response." Elsie shifted in her seat, leaning forward so that she could see the faces of all of the grand jurors.

"I'm an assistant prosecuting attorney in a small county. I prosecute crime; as a felony prosecutor, I largely prosecute violent and sexual crime, and try these cases before juries."

"How is that—"

She cut him off. "In my job as a trial attorney, I don't have all the resources that are at your disposal in the U.S. Attorney's Office. You have the FBI at your beck and call. I'm putting together the cases on my own. And yes; at times, that means my job bleeds over into an investigative role of sorts."

"So, what happened to you at the EconoMo is a regular occurrence."

To Elsie's horror, a sudden rush of hot tears choked her throat and came dangerously close to running down her face.

She ducked her head, and cleared her throat to hide her discomfiture. When he said, "Ms. Arnold?" she raised an index finger and shook her head.

It took a moment to pull herself together. She rubbed her eyes, to make sure no moisture seeped out. When she raised her head, her face was calm and resolute.

"Beg pardon. No. What happened at the motel in Bodine County is not a common occurrence. Not in my experience."

The attorney had the grace to look regretful.

"What happened at the motel, Ms. Arnold?" His voice held a respectful note, for the first time in their acquaintance.

She took a breath. "I was invited into Room 217 by a woman who identified herself as Dede."

The attorney poised on the edge of the conference table, his eyes steady as they studied her. "Go on," he said.

And she did. She told the whole ugly story, from start to finish.

Chapter 55

SHE STILL HADN'T had an opportunity to talk to Ashlock. Elsie was determined to grab him outside the courtroom, but she didn't see him in the crowd milling in the hallway.

She shoved her way to the elevator bank; but just as she pushed the button, she saw a familiar figure on the stairway, heading down at a fast clip.

"Ash," she said, but he didn't pause, didn't look around.

Elsie's jaw tightened; and she made a beeline for the stairs. When a man wearing a business suit blocked her way, she shouldered him out of her path, not pausing to offer an apology. She called Ashlock's name again, but he had disappeared down the stairwell.

She grasped the banister, moving as fast as her feet permitted. She regretted her choice of footwear, wishing she hadn't opted to wear the aging pair of spiked heels. She'd thought they would give her confidence when she walked into court. Hadn't considered how they might interfere with a chase.

Her shoes echoed on the concrete steps. When she reached

the ground floor, she ran for the exit. As she stormed the doorway, the loose sole on the toe of her left shoe caught on the metal threshold strip. Like Cinderella's glass slipper, the shoe remained in place on the strip, throwing her off balance. She stumbled and fell to her knees on the concrete just outside the courthouse door.

"Fuck!"

Ashlock must have heard her, at last. He paused on the sidewalk and turned around with a bemused expression.

Elsie crouched on her hands and knees, trying to swallow back the string of curse words in her chest. A man bearing a briefcase paused nearby.

"You okay, ma'am?"

She shook her head. She wasn't okay, far from it. When he offered a hand, she grasped it, managing to get to her feet. Her pantyhose were shredded, and the skin was scraped off both knees. Examining the injury, she saw blood begin to seep out and run down the front of her legs.

Ashlock appeared at her side. To the man with the briefcase, he said, "I'll take care of this."

Elsie was so glad to hear his voice, tears welled up; but she blinked them back. With a phony show of bravado, she laughed.

"So, this is what I have to do to get your attention these days."

Instead of offering a reply, he squatted on his haunches in front of her bloody knees. Looking down at the top of his head, she saw that he had more gray hair then she'd realized. It looked good on him.

Elsie cleared her throat; it felt like something was lodged inside her trachea. "I don't suppose you're carrying a handkerchief. I could use one."

He shook his head. "Sorry. I'm not a hankie-carrying guy. You have any Kleenex?"

"No. Not since ragweed season ended."

He stood, sighing. When he didn't offer any further comment, Elsie added, "I wish I'd let my mom come along today. She's always prepared for every possible disaster. Never goes anywhere without a packet of tissues."

Ashlock's eyes shifted. Looking past her, he said, "About Marge. I need you to pass on a message for me. Let her know I'm sorry I wasn't able to make it for Thanksgiving dinner."

"Okay." Elsie tried to make him meet her eye, but he wouldn't look her in the face.

"Tell her I appreciate the invitation."

"Sure. I'll do that." When he didn't speak again, she said in a voice that couldn't quite disguise the hurt, "She knew not to boil an extra potato. Because she got your text on Thanksgiving morning. Did you have a nice time in the Bootheel?"

He nodded, without further comment.

She could feel the blood trickle down her skin, but she chose to ignore it. "You want to get a cup of coffee somewhere?"

He scanned the street. "There's got to be a pharmacy around here. I saw a Walgreens when I drove in. You can get some Band-Aids, something like that."

She nodded as she digested his choice of words. Elsie could get the Band-Aids. As opposed to Ashlock getting Band-Aids on her behalf.

Elsie squared her shoulders. "Let's talk."

Finally, he met her gaze. "Okay."

"Where do you want to go?"

He pointed at a bench nearby. "We can sit down over there."

Elsie led the way, ignoring the pain in her knees as she attempted to walk tall, pretending that the ensuing conversation wouldn't devastate her.

As she sat, she thrust her legs before her, reluctant to flex her shredded knees. When Ashlock joined her, he looked at her scraped skin with concern on his face.

Elsie didn't want to see it. She shucked off her suit jacket and threw it over her kneecaps, not caring that the stains would be impossible to remove.

Keeping her voice deliberately casual, she said, "So how was your Thanksgiving weekend? Did your ex-wife put on a good feed?"

"It was nice. Family time." He reached over and took her hand. His grip was cold. "Elsie. We've been down this road before."

Before he could continue, she interrupted. "What road is that?"

He looked at her, regret in his eyes. "Elsie, hear me out. You know I really like you."

In spite of herself, she laughed. "Those three magic words. What every woman longs to hear. *I like you.*"

A muscle twitched in his jaw. "This isn't easy for me."

A ball of fury started to form in her chest; she welcomed it. It would replace the longing and self-doubt she'd suffered in recent days.

The anger kept her voice steady as she said, "That's so pitiful. I'm really feeling sorry for you now."

He gave her a warning look, but she waved it off. "Just do it. I'm ready. Kick me to the curb. But don't tell me it's gonna hurt you more than it hurts me."

He took a deep breath and held it for a long moment. Then he exhaled, and said, "My primary responsibility—"

Elsie groaned. "Oh God. Here it comes. I wish I had a drink."

At that, he snapped. "That's the problem. You still want to be a kid. And I have kids, three of them. They are number one, the most important thing in my life."

She slumped on the bench. Bending over, she lifted her suit jacket and used one of the sleeves to swipe at her legs, bloodying her hand in the process.

He went on, his voice growing heated. "When you're a father, you can't let an irresponsible relationship stand in the way of parenting. I have a son at home, two little girls down in Kennett, and an obligation to enforce law in my community."

"Our community," she muttered.

"Okay, fine. But I can't be worrying about what kind of trouble you've gotten yourself into. And Elsie, you're always in some kind of mess."

Her face twisted. "True that." She tossed the ruined jacket onto the ground. "Let's part as friends."

His face registered surprise. "Good. I'd like that."

"Will you give me a hug? As an old friend?"

Ashlock nodded. "Sure."

They embraced, facing each other on the bench. When he tried to break away, she squeezed him tightly, her hands gripping his suit coat.

He finally pulled away, running a hand down her cheek. "Get to a pharmacy before you head back home. So you can get those knees bandaged."

"I'll do that." It wasn't a false promise. She had planned to visit a pharmacy while she was in Springfield, even before she required Band-Aids.

She watched as he walked off, the lump in her throat returning. She glowered at Ashlock's retreating figure. There was only one thing on earth that gave her satisfaction. It was the sight of her bloody handprint on the back of his gray suit jacket.

Chapter 56

ELSIE NEVER FOUND the Walgreens Ashlock had spotted near the federal courthouse. She cruised from the downtown area to the city limits of Springfield. It was a big town, over 100,000 population. She could find what she was looking for and do what she needed to do. No one knew her in Springfield. No nosy parkers would comment on her errand.

A McDonald's sat at the intersection, and her car pulled in on autopilot. It had two drive-thru lanes. *I'm in the big city now,* she thought.

The voice in the speaker box asked what she wanted.

"Large Diet Coke," Elsie said. "And a large coffee. Black."

As she drove away, she sucked down the soda like a woman stranded in the desert, though the temperature outside was frigid, more like January than early December. A Walmart Supercenter appeared, and she pulled in and parked near the entrance.

Once inside, she didn't dawdle. After briefly pausing to wipe her bloodstained legs with the sanitary wipes near the shopping carts, she went to the women's personal aisle in the health and beauty section. Elsie eyeballed the items she sought. She didn't know there would be so many choices. She snatched the First Response pregnancy test from the shelf. The box claimed that it was over ninety-nine percent accurate.

The woman at the checkout didn't comment on her purchase. Didn't greet her, didn't even look up. Just rang up the purchase and put it in the bag. Elsie was grateful. She was glad she'd thought to buy it in Springfield rather than in McCown County. Had she bought a pregnancy test in Barton, the word would be on the street within minutes.

Bag in hand, she headed for the door; but she paused before she made her exit. An old man wearing a Walmart nametag stood beside the shopping carts.

Elsie said, "Where are the restrooms, sir?"

He pointed. "On the east side. Beyond the snack bar."

She walked in the direction he had indicated, her feet moving of their own volition toward the public toilets at Walmart, where she might have her personal moment of truth.

The women's restroom was empty. She had her choice of stalls, so she chose number three: her lucky number. Her fingers were clumsy as she opened the box. She took a moment to look over the instructions, but it was a no-brainer. Pee on the stick. Wait three minutes. One pink line or two.

Peeing wouldn't be a problem. McDonald's had seen to that. Elsie held the white plastic fortune-teller in her hand, and then she did the deed. She didn't look. Instead, she counted silently.

One Mississippi, two Mississippi. She kept her eyes closed, all the way to two-forty.

When she opened her eyes, there it was. The second line, a faint pink mark.

She checked the box again. As if the pharmaceutical company had read her mind, she saw the answer to her unspoken question.

"Yes, a faint line still counts as a positive."

The box contained a second test stick. She unwrapped it, repeated the process. Didn't bother to close her eyes the second time. Instead, she watched with dread as the pink line appeared.

She checked the expiration date on the box, but it was fresh as new paint. Grasping at straws, she wondered whether it might be a defective, giving her a false positive.

But she couldn't convince herself. She could buy another test, maybe the Clearblue one. But—ninety-nine percent accuracy, two results staring her in the face.

"Save your twenty bucks, Elsie," she whispered.

With her free hand, she rustled inside her purse, pulling out the packet of birth control pills. She'd missed three; two during the turmoil at the EconoMo, one earlier in the cycle, from pure carelessness. When her period didn't start on schedule, her online research had been encouraging: ninety-five percent of women who missed a few pills would not become pregnant. Only five percent ended up with an unintended pregnancy.

Five percent, she thought, as she dropped the packet of pills back into her bag. *I'm one of that five percent.*

Business was picking up in the women's restroom. Someone rattled her stall door, then had the nerve to knock.

"Occupied," Elsie said, her voice sharp.

But she couldn't stay on the toilet forever. She dropped the second test back into the box, beside its mate. Wadded the box inside the Walmart bag and left the stall.

After she dropped the plastic bag inside the trash can, she

looked up, catching her reflection in the mirror over the sink. Her expression was guilty, like she'd stolen something.

She washed her hands with unnecessary vigor, soaping up and then rinsing twice, drying off with four paper towels.

She forgot to buy any bandages for her knees. On her way out of the store, the old man by the carts told her to have a nice day. That's when the tears started to roll.

She took off for her car at a run. Locking herself inside, she rested her head on the steering wheel.

In a whisper, she said, "What the fuck am I going to do?"

She heard a knock at her window. With a start, she looked up. The old-timer had followed her outside. She rolled down the window.

He said, "Are you all right, ma'am?"

The unexpected kindness crippled her. She attempted a wobbly smile.

"I'm fine, thanks."

"You don't look like you're doing fine." He bent down to the open window. "Would you like to come back inside? Sit for a spell? I'll get you a cup of coffee."

Elsie shook her head. "That's so nice of you. But I've got coffee. I'm heading out."

He didn't step away, though she wanted him to leave her. The old man studied her face. He said, "Don't worry."

Elsie nodded in agreement, just to get rid of him.

"Not a single sparrow falls to the ground without God knowing it. And you're more valuable to God than a whole flock of sparrows."

With that, he turned and walked away. Elsie watched his

stooped figure as he returned to the store and took his place inside the glass doors, beside the shopping carts.

Sitting up straight in the driver's seat, she put the car in Reverse. As she drove through the parking lot she pulled the brown lid off the McDonald's coffee cup. She dumped the liquid out the driver's window, where it splattered onto the pavement.

The Diet Coke was harder. She held the Styrofoam cup for a long minute, taking a thirsty goodbye sip before she emptied the cup and headed out on the highway for the return trip to Barton.

She was going home.

THE END

Don't miss the other thrilling Ozarks Mystery novels . . .

THE CODE OF THE HILLS
A KILLING AT THE CREEK
and
THE WAGES OF SIN

Available now in print and e-book!

About the Author

NANCY ALLEN practiced law for fifteen years as an Assistant Missouri Attorney General and Assistant Prosecutor in her native Ozarks. She tried over thirty jury trials, including murder and sexual offenses, and is now a law instructor at Missouri State University. A WOLF IN THE WOODS is her fourth novel.

Printed in the USA
CPSIA information can be obtained
at www.ICGtesting.com
LVHW032251020924
789950LV00038B/2003